영호와 차도리

제1권: 영혼의 세계로 가는 문

한·영 대역판

글·그림·번역
주보경

차례 • CONTENTS

머릿말-INTRODUCTION

1. 작가의 말 7
Author's Note
2. 책을 쓰게 된 동기 13
Why I Wrote This Book
3. "제목이 그게 뭐야?" 17
"Isn't the Title a Bit Off?"
4. '주보경'이 왜 영어로 'B.K. Chu'지? 21
Why Is "Bo Kyung Chu" "B.K. Chu" in English?
5. 한영 버전, 어떻게 읽을까요? 25
How to Read the Bilingual Edition
6. 부록 31
Back Material
7. AI—인공지능 33
AI—Artificial Intelligence
8. Santa Claus, Father Christmas: 차이가 뭘까요? 43
What's the Difference?
9. 이 책에서만 특별하게 쓰이는 단어들 47
Special Usage of Words Unique to This Book
10. 마지막 한마디 51
Last Words

YOUNGHO AND CHADORI

(Korean–English Bilingual Edition)

Book I: THE DOOR TO THE SPIRIT WORLD

프롤로그·PROLOGUE 61
1. 재수 좋은 구미호와 재치 있는 군만두 71
The Lucky Fox and the Cunning Dumpling
2. 소리 없는 축제 95
A Silent Carnival
3. 여우의 소굴 125
The Fox's Den
4. 먼 옛날의 한 크리스마스 157
Once upon a Time on Christmas Day

5. 어른과 아이 169
A Grown-up and a Child
6. 잃어버린 야구방망이 183
The Lost Baseball Bat
7. 잔인한 토요일 203
The Cruel Saturday
8. 강변의 노을 219
Sunset by the River
9. 하얀 크리스마스 양말 237
The White Christmas Stocking
10. 양들의 합창, 스포츠카, 아기 오리, 그리고 한 권 의 사진첩 267
Singing Sheep, Fast Cars, Ducklings, and a Photo Album
11. 눈부신 빛의 문 287
The Portal of Blinding Light

토론 주제 317
Discussion Topics
영호와 차도리 퀴즈 321
Youngho and Chadori Quiz

작가 소개 325
감사의 글 328
Also By 335

1

작가의 말

AUTHOR'S NOTE

"나는 이다음에 자라면 5개 국어를 유창하게 할 거야!"

중학교에 다니던 어느 날 제가 결심했어요. "그리고 영어는 능숙하다 못해 아예 영어로 책을 쓰고!" 그리고는 저의 새로운 각오를 뿌듯하게 여기저기 알렸죠.

"I will speak five languages fluently when I grow up!"

I decided one day when I was a middle schooler. "And my English will be so good that I'll be writing books in English!" I proudly declared this new resolution to everyone around me.

In the 1980s when I was growing up, there were no laptop computers, of course—no cell phones, and not even a digital dictionary. We had to carry and look up every word in paper dictionaries that were as thick—and almost as heavy—as bricks. For a kid like me back then, that made it a highly ambitious—therefore all the more appealing—goal to dream up. People's reactions generally fell into two groups. Friends (mostly classmates) delighted in my dreams, looking forward to our future with joy and excitement, while others (adults) were skeptical, saying, *"It's challenging enough with English conversation alone—but five languages?"* In fact, it was my mother who remembered those unenthusiastic remarks. As for me, such comments went in one ear and out the other, treasuring only the optimism inherent to dreamers.

Fast forward twenty years... and I made it. Today I speak five languages—Korean, English, French, Spanish, and Norwegian—and including basic conversation and written comprehension, even more. One day, while I was busy at work, it just dawned on me, *Wow! I've actually achieved my middle school dream, and more!*

At the same time, I also realized that speaking a foreign language is not the end of the journey. Rather, it is only the starting point of a longer one—which leads to even more tasks to undertake and dreams to fulfill.

In hindsight, the strength that kept me moving forward in life has always sprung from the simple truth that "dreams can come true."

제가 자란 80년대만 해도 노트북 컴퓨터는 물론이고, 휴대폰은 커녕 전자사전조차 없었어요. 벽돌만 한 종이사전을 가방에 넣어 다니며 단어 하나하나 일일이 찾아야 했죠. 벽돌처럼 무겁게도 느껴졌어요. 당시의 저 같은 아이에게는 대단히 야심만만한, 그러기에 더 멋져 보이는 꿈이었죠. 주위의 반응은 대체로 두 갈래로 나뉘었어요. 기쁨과 설렘으로 함께 미래를 꿈꾸는 친구들이 있었던 반면(주로 같은 반 또래), “영어 회화 하나도 힘든데 무슨 5개 국어냐”며 핀잔을 주는 사람들도(어른들) 있었어요. 솔직히 핀잔은 저희 어머니가 기억하고 계세요. 저는 미래를 꿈꾸는 사람 특유의 낙관으로, 핀잔도 그냥 한 귀로 듣고 한 귀로 흘렸던 것 같아요.

그런데 20년의 세월이 흐르고…… 결국 이뤘어요. 지금은 한국어, 영어, 프랑스어, 스페인어, 노르웨이어, 이렇게 다섯 개 국어에다, 기초 회화나 독해를 합하면 그 이상을 하게 되었으니까요. 직장생활로 분주하던 어느 날 문득 생각해 보니, “앗! 중학교 시절 꿈, 이룩하고도 남았네!” 하는 생각이 들더라고요.

이와 동시에 외국어를 한다는 것 자체가 여정의 끝은 아니라는 것도 깨달았죠. 오히려 더욱 먼 길을 가게 될 출발점에 불과하다는 것, 그리고 해야 할 일들이, 이루어야 할 꿈들이 더 많이 생겼다는 사실과 함께.

돌이켜 보면, 삶에서 저를 이끌어 준 힘은 항상 “꿈은 이루어진다”라는 간단한 진리가 아니었나 생각해요.

It was the slogan of Korea's national soccer team during the 2002 World Cup Games. It was also my mother's creed. She would always encourage me with words like, "You can do it," "If you keep trying, you can achieve anything in the end." And yet, this is my honest confession—in times of difficulties and repeated failures, I often found myself resenting her for what felt like nothing more than "empty words and promises." But as life went on, I came to experience for myself—and witness in those around me—the timeless truth that even dreams which at first seem impossible can, with persistence and effort, eventually come true.

That is perhaps why, among all the literary genres, I love young adult fiction so much—and chose to write it myself—to share and nurture dreams. Just like my younger self who loved books and dreamed galore, I hope today's teens can pause for a moment, take a breath, and spread the wings of imagination through this story. In a world where exams and competition steal away even the time to enjoy a book and dream of the future, wouldn't it be wonderful to have a book that touches the soul and supports learning at the same time? That's exactly the kind of book I wanted to write.

Youngho and Chadori, Book I: The Door to the Spirit World is not just a bilingual edition with side-by-side translations. They are like twin siblings separated at birth and raised on opposite sides of the globe—though identical on the outside, each preserves its own universe of emotions and literary flow.

2002년 월드컵 당시 대한민국 축구 대표팀 슬로건이죠. 또 저희 어머니의 신념이기도 해요. 항상 “너는 할 수 있어.” “뭐든지 노력하면 결국 해낼 수 있어” 라고 용기를 주셨어요. 하지만 솔직히 고백하자면, 힘들고 좌절을 거듭할 때는 “헛된 말로 사람 부추긴” 엄마를 원망할 때도 많았어요. 하지만 결국 “처음에는 불가능해 보이는 꿈일지라도, 꾸준히 최선을 다하면 언젠가는 이루어진다”는 불변의 진리를 직접 경험하고 또 주위에서도 수없이 목격하게 되었어요.

많고 많은 문학 장르 중 유독 청소년 소설을 사랑하고 직접 집필하고자 하는 이유도 바로 그래서인가 봐요. 꿈을 나누며 키우는 일을 하고 싶어서. 책을 좋아하고 꿈이 많던 어린 시절의 저처럼 오늘의 청소년들이 이 작품을 통해 잠시나마 숨을 고르고 상상의 날개를 펼칠 수 있기를 바라는 마음에서. 입시 경쟁에 치여 책 한 권 읽고 미래를 꿈꿀 시간조차 빼앗기는 현실 속에서, 감명 깊게 읽으면서 동시에 공부가 되는 책이 있다면 얼마나 좋을까요? 저는 바로 그런 책을 쓰고 싶었어요.

『영호와 차도리 제1권: 영혼의 세계로 가는 문』은 단순히 번역된 이중언어 작품은 아니예요. 태어날 때 헤어져서 지구 반대편에서 따로 자란 쌍둥이 형제에 가깝다고 할 수 있죠. 겉으로는 똑같아 보여도, 저마다의 감성과 문학적인 흐름을 간직하고 있으니까요.

독자 여러분도 이 책을 통해서, 이야기의 전개뿐만이 아니라 각 언어가 창조해 내는 운율과 정서를 느껴 보실 수 있었으면 해요. 그래서 영어나 한국어 학습을 원하시는 독자들은 그 표현이 문맥에서 어떻게 쓰이는지를 익히고, 또 어휘 습득의 차원을 넘어서 언어만이 생성해 낼 수 있는 감정과 느낌, 그 무한한 가능성을 직접 체험해 보세요. 그렇게 영호와 차도리와 함께 모험을 떠나고, 책장을 덮은 뒤에도 스스로에게 다짐해 볼 수 있었으면 해요.

"나도 언젠가는 내 꿈을 이뤄 내고 말 거야"라고.

I hope readers will not only enjoy the storyline itself but also savor the cadence and tone each language creates. For learners of Korean or English, this book offers more than just vocabulary—it lets you see how expressions are used in context and invites you to experience the feelings and moods that only language can create—its endless possibilities. As you join Youngho and Chadori on their adventure, I hope that you'll be able to close the final page and gain the courage to say:

"One day, I, too, will make my dreams come true."

2

책을 쓰게 된 동기

WHY I WROTE THIS BOOK

『영호와 차도리』의 출발점은 저의 어린 시절이예요.

언제부터인지 부모님 얼굴도 자주 뵙기 힘들었고, 어렸을 때 받던 크리스마스 선물도 모두 끊겨 버렸죠.

The starting point of *Youngho and Chadori* was my own childhood.

At some point, I scarcely saw my parents anymore, and the Christmas presents I used to receive as a little girl stopped altogether.

One year, determined to put up a Christmas tree—and to do it on my own if I had to—I searched the apartment for the plastic tree we used year after year, but I just couldn't find it anywhere. In the end, I decorated and hung one of my father's white socks by my bed—just as Youngho did. The next morning, the sock was empty, but I wasn't all that disappointed—it was more or less expected. I simply laughed it off, and my childish creation faded into oblivion in time.

Years went by, and I eventually got married and settled down. Living in my husband's home country, Norway, I came to develop a special fondness for Christmas. With children at the center, families get together and celebrate the joy of being in one another's company. Of course, it could quickly turn into a routine formality and become stressful for the adults doing the preparations. Still, I found myself thinking how wonderful it would be if every child and teenager could experience such joy and sense of belonging at least once in their lives.

Then one day came a shocking diagnosis: a brain tumor.

A few days later, I had to face yet another tremendous ordeal—a brain hemorrhage that left me hemiplegic. I barely survived a major surgery, only to quit my job and spend more than six long years in rehabilitation. Years crept by in daily rehabilitation efforts, with little progress to show for them.

어느 한 해, 혼자라도 크리스마스트리를 꾸며 보기로 결심하고, 해마다 쓰던 인조 트리를 찾아 아파트를 뒤져 보았지만 아무 데도 보이지 않았어요. 결국 영호가 한 것처럼 아빠의 흰 양말을 장식해서 침대맡에 걸었죠. 다음 날 아침, 양말은 텅 비어 있었지만, 대충 예상하고 있었던 결과라 별다른 실망도 없었던 것으로 기억해요. 그냥 웃으면서 넘어갔고, 나의 어린 시절의 서툰 작품도 시간 속에 묻혀 버렸죠.

세월이 흐르고, 결혼하고 남편의 나라 노르웨이에 정착하고 살게 되면서, 저는 크리스마스에 대한 남다른 애정이 생겼어요. 어린이 중심, 가족 중심으로 함께 모여서 서로의 존재를 즐거워하고 기뻐하는 문화. 물론 그저 형식적인 행사로 변질해 버리는 경우도 더러 있을 것이고, 준비를 해야 하는 어른들 입장에서는 스트레스도 쌓이겠죠. 하지만 자라는 어린이와 청소년들이 이런 기쁨과 소속감을 누구나 단 한 번 쯤은 경험해 볼 수 있었으면 하는 생각이 들었어요.

그러던 어느 날, 뇌종양이라는 충격적인 진단을 받게 되었어요.

또 며칠 뒤 이에 따른 뇌출혈로 반신마비라는 엄청난 시련까지 따랐죠. 대수술 끝에 겨우 목숨은 건졌지만, 다니던 직장도 그만두고, 6년이 넘는 긴 세월을 재활로 보내야 했어요. 수년의 세월을 하루하루 재활에만 매달리며 별 성과도 없이 보냈죠.

하지만 어느 순간부터인지 제 머릿속에는 점차 상상의 꽃망울이 피어나기 시작했어요. 산타 복장을 한 사람들이 하나 둘 눈앞을 스쳐 지나가기 시작했어요. 다들 빨갛고 하얀 색상의 전형적인 산타옷을 입고 있으면서도 각자가 다 달랐죠. 나이·성별·인종·문화·시대를 초월하여 이 세상 모든 사람 하나하나를 상징해 주듯. 그때 어릴 적 장식해 걸었던 하얀 크리스마스 양말이 생각났어요. 그리고는 또 꿈을 꾸기 시작했죠. 어쩌면 어린아이 같은 터무니없는 상상이라고, 심지어는 미쳐 버렸다고 할 수도 있겠지만, 저는 결심했어요.

'이 이야기를 책으로 써야겠다.'

During that time, however, buds of imagination slowly began to form in my mind. Before my eyes, people in Santa costumes flashed past—all clad in the familiar red and white, yet each distinct, as if to embody every single person in the world—every race, gender, age, across all cultures and eras. I then remembered the white Christmas stocking I once decorated and hung as a child, and I began to dream again. Childish? Maybe. Crazy? Definitely. But I decided:

"I must turn this into a story."

3

"제목이 그게 뭐야?"

"ISN'T THE TITLE A BIT OFF?"

"제목이 그게 뭐야?"

영문판이 처음 출간되자마자 어머니께서 하신 말씀이에요. 그리고는 "요새 애들 보기에 좀 구식이지 않니?" 하셨어요. 솔직히 맞는 말이에요.

"Isn't the title a bit off?"

It was the first thing my mother said when the English edition was published. "Isn't it a little old-school for today's kids?" she added. And she was right.

But there was a reason I chose this title in the end. I named the main character "Youngho" because it is a distinctly Korean name, yet one that can be pronounced easily in almost any language as far as I know.

And then, it suddenly struck me: The English spelling "Youngho" ends with "ho," which in American slang can be a shortened form of "whore." I wondered if that might be an issue, but in the end just waved it aside as needless worry. Yet sure enough, I later heard heartbreaking stories of Korean American children with the same name who were teased and bullied at school for that very reason—even forced to change their names in some extreme cases.

That was when I decided: "In that case, 'Youngho' will not only be the name of the hero, but also part of the title. Someday, when my books capture the hearts of readers around the world, the traditional Korean name 'Youngho' will also have become a global one, so that children who bear the name will no longer be mocked, but admired, even envied, by their classmates."

하지만 결국 그런 제목을 선택하게 된 데에는 다 이유가 있죠. 처음 주인공 이름을 '영호'라고 지은 이유는 지극히 한국적이면서도 제가 아는 어느 언어로도 발음이 쉽기 때문이었어요.

그러다가 문득 생각이 들었죠. 영호의 영문 표기 Youngho의 Ho가 미국에서 Whore의 속어로 쓰이곤 하는데, 괜찮을까 하는 생각이 들었어요. 결국 그저 쓸데없는 걱정으로 일축해 버렸죠. 그런데 아니나 다를까, 같은 이름을 가진 한국계 미국인 아이들이 이름 때문에 학교에서 놀림받는 경우가 태반이고, 극단적인 경우에는 이름을 바꾼 사례도 있다는 안타까운 소식을 전해 듣게 되었어요.

저는 그때 결심했어요. "그럼 '영호'를 주인공 이름뿐 아니라 제목으로도 쓰자. 언젠가 나의 책이 세계인의 마음을 사로잡게 되는 그날이 오면, '영호'라는 우리 전통 이름도 세계적인 이름으로 자리 잡게 해 보자. 그래서 그 이름을 가진 아이들이 더 이상 놀림받지 않고, 오히려 반 친구들이 동경하는 부러움의 대상이 될 수 있도록."

영호의 반려견 이름 '차도리'도 같은 맥락이었어요. '차도리'는 역시 우리나라 전통 이름인 '차돌이'를 발음 그대로 표기한 것이죠. 한국에서 아직도 흔히 반려동물 이름으로 쓰이는 전통 이름이 세계인이 즐겨 쓰는 이름이 되면 얼마나 재미있을까 하는 생각을 해 보았어요. 엉뚱한 생각이라고요? 엉뚱한 것이 요즘 제 주특기인가 봐요.

『영호와 차도리』, 평범한 제목에 특별한 꿈을 담아 보고 싶었어요.

The same goes for Youngho's furry friend's name, "Chadori," which is a transliteration of "Chadol-i," another classic Korean name, still commonly used for pets. I started thinking —how fun would it be if one day this old Korean name became a popular name for pets around the world? Too quirky? I know, but "quirky" seems to have become my specialty these days.

Youngho and Chadori—this quaint title carries a special dream for me.

4

'주보경'이 왜 영어로 'B.K. CHU'지?

WHY IS "BO KYUNG CHU"
"B.K. CHU" IN ENGLISH?

제 본명은 주보경이에요.

B.K. Chu는 제 이름 Bo Kyung의 이니셜에 성씨 Chu를 더한 것이죠. 아버지 때부터 영문 성을 Chu로 써 왔기에 자연스럽게 저도 그렇게 쓰게 되었어요.

My birth name is Bo Kyung Chu.

The pen name B.K. Chu simply comes from the initials of my given name combined with my family name. Since my father had already spelled our last name as "Chu" in English, it was natural for me to follow suit.

After I got married, my legal surname changed to that of my Norwegian husband. When it came to my writing career, however, I always knew without question that I would publish under my Korean name.

In early 2020, while I was working on the English edition, the COVID-19 pandemic swept across the globe. Soon after, word spread that the outbreak had originated in China, followed by waves of anti-Chinese sentiment in many parts of the world. "So what?" you may think. "What does that have to do with us Koreans?" But that would be a mistake. To those unfamiliar with the region—its many peoples and diverse cultures—it all looks the same. Whether you are from Korea, Japan, China, or even as far away as Southeast Asia, it often blurs into one single category: "Asia." Instead of turning a blind eye, we need to share the burden and help one another. That's why, while my Korean pen name keeps my cultural identity intact, its English counterpart became B.K. Chu—with initials that make my nationality less apparent.

One day, when my books find their way into the hearts of readers everywhere, I hope such discrimination will also fade away.

결혼 후에는 남편의 성을 따라 법적 이름이 노르웨이 이름으로 바뀌었지만, 작가 활동에 한해서는 의심의 여지도 없이 본명인 한국이름으로 출판하겠다고 항상 마음먹고 있었어요.

한참 영문 집필에 몰두하던 2020년 초, 코로나 팬데믹이 세계를 휩쓸었죠. 곧 그것이 중국에서 시작되었다는 것이 알려지면서, 세계 곳곳에 적지 않은 반중감정의 물결이 퍼져 나갔어요. 한국에서 얼핏 생각하기엔 "그래서? 그것이 우리랑 무슨 상관인가?" 하기 쉽지만, 그렇지 않아요. 동양에 대해, 또 그 다양한 인종과 문화에 대해 모르는 외국인이 얼핏 보기엔, 한중일에서 동남아시아까지 다 그냥 같은 '동양'일 뿐이예요. 나 몰라라 하기보다는 어려움을 함께 나누고 서로 도와야 해요. 그래서 저의 한글 필명은 본명인 '주보경'이지만, 영문으로는 B.K. Chu로 해서 국적을 알아보기 힘들게 했어요.

그래서 먼 훗날 나의 책들이 세계인들에게 사랑받는 그날이 오면, 그런 편견과 차별도 점차 사라지기를 기원하면서.

5

한영 버전, 어떻게 읽을까요?

HOW TO READ THE BILINGUAL EDITION

이 책은 학습 참고서가 아니예요.

무엇보다도 먼저 남녀노소 모두가 즐길 수 있는 소설이죠. 학습자든 원어민이든, 누구나 각자 편한 방식으로 읽을 수 있었으면 해요.

This book is not a study guide.

Above all, it's a novel meant to be enjoyed by readers young and old. Whether you are a language learner or a native speaker, you are free to read whichever way feels most natural to you.

My only advice is this: Read all the way to the end in one language first, before turning to the other, so you can fully savor the story's flow. Along the way, remember to have fun with the illustrations, too, and let the scenes come alive in your imagination. The learning effect becomes much stronger when you truly immerse yourself in the experience and enjoy it. If you come across unfamiliar words or expressions, just underline them and keep reading. Look them up afterward. This will help you practice reading and understanding in context. After all, that's how we all learned our native languages as children—by absorbing words in context.

Here are a few guidelines you might find useful:

· **Beginners and Intermediate Readers:** Start with the language you feel most comfortable in and read the story all the way to the end. Remember to have fun with the illustrations along the way. As you read, underline words or phrases that catch your interest—expressions you might want to learn in the other language. Once you finish, look up those passages and picture them in your mind as you do. You might also find it rewarding to learn the parts that especially resonate with you in the other language!

다만 이야기의 흐름을 제대로 음미할 수 있도록, 한 언어로 끝까지 완독을 마친 뒤에 상대어를 참조해 보세요. 읽는 도중에는 삽화도 함께 보고 즐기면서 장면을 머릿속에 생생하게 그려 보시고요. 그렇게 스스로 체험하고 재미를 느끼는 순간, 학습 효과도 더욱 커져요. 모르는 단어나 표현이 나오면 우선 밑줄만 그어 두고, 다 읽은 후에 찾아보세요. 문맥 속에서 이해하며 읽는 연습이 되니까요. 우리가 어렸을 때 그렇게 문맥 속에서 이해하며 책을 읽고 모국어를 배우던 것처럼.

몇 가지 가이드라인을 한 번 적어 봤으니, 도움이 되었으면 해요.

• **초·중급 독자:** 자신이 가장 편한 언어를 선택해서 먼저 끝까지 읽어 주세요. 읽으면서 삽화도 재미있게 보고 즐기세요. 또 외국어로 알고 싶은 표현이 나오면 우선 밑줄을 그어 놓으세요. 그리고 완독이 끝난 후에 궁금한 문장을 상대어로 확인해 보고, 또 찾으면서 머릿속에 그려도 보세요. 자신에게 특별히 마음에 와닿는 부분을 외국어로 습득해 보는 것도 좋겠죠!

For example, if Korean is your first language, read the Korean first, then refer to the English when needed; if English is your first language—or the one you are more comfortable with—read the English first, then look up the Korean when necessary.

· **Intermediate and Advanced Readers:** Do the same as **Beginners and Intermediate Readers**, but start with the language you want to strengthen. Don't interrupt your reading by dipping into the other language right away—just underline the parts and come back later. (If Korean is your first or stronger language, read the English first, then refer to the Korean when needed; if English is your stronger language, start with the Korean first, then check the English afterward.)

· **Not Comfortable in Either English or Korean:** Then you may need to do as I once did when I first learned English. Choose one language and read little by little. If you get blocked along the way because of the vocabulary and can't follow the story, using a dictionary might be your only option. However, try to build the habit of understanding the text in context—with the help of the illustrations alone. If you don't mind reading the book more than once, why not challenge yourself by trying without a dictionary the second time around?

예를 들어서, 한국어가 모국어인 경우 한국어판을 먼저 읽으신 후 필요한 부분을 영어로 참조하시고, 영어가 더 편하실 경우에는 영어판을 먼저 완독하신 뒤에 필요한 부분을 한국어로 참조하시면 되겠죠.

• **중·상급 독자:** 초·중급 독자처럼 하되, 늘리고자 하는 언어로 먼저 도전해 보세요. 모르는 단어가 나오면 밑줄만 그어 놓고 나중에 확인하는 것도 잊지 마세요. (예: 한국어가 모국어이거나 편한 경우, 영어판을 먼저 읽은 후 필요한 부분을 한국어 참조. 영어가 모국어이거나 편할 경우, 한국어판을 먼저 읽은 후 필요한 부분을 영어 참조.)

• **영어·한국어 둘 다 편하지 않으시다고요?:** 그럼 제가 처음 영어 배우던 것처럼 하셔야 하겠어요. 하나의 언어를 선택해서 조금씩 읽어 주세요. 단어를 몰라서 도저히 이야기를 따라갈 수 없는 경우에는 사전을 사용하시는 수밖에 없죠. 하지만 되도록 문맥에서, 삽화를 보며 이해하는 습관을 들이도록 하세요. 또 혹 다시 읽을 마음이 생기실 경우, 두 번째부터는 사전 없이 도전해 보는 것은 어떨까요?

· **영어·한국어 둘 다 능숙하신가요?:** 대단하세요! 원하시는 방식대로 자유롭게 읽으시면 되겠죠. 다만 제 글을 너무 가혹하게 평가하시지만 말아 주세요.

스스로 특별한 방법을 찾고자 하시는 분들은 자유롭게, 원하시는 대로 하셔도 되겠죠!

· **Proficient in Both English and Korean:** Hats off to you! Feel free to read however you wish—I only hope you won't judge my writing too harshly!

And of course, if you want to experiment with your own special method, please go for it!

6

부록

BACK MATERIAL

이야기를 다 읽고 나서, 책 뒤에 실린 『영호와 차도리』 퀴즈를 풀어 보는 것은 어떨까요?

해답은 bkchu.com에서 확인하실 수 있어요.

Once you finish reading the story, you might like to try the *Youngho and Chadori* quiz at the back of the book.

The answers are available at bkchu.com.

혹 주위 친구들 중에도 『영호와 차도리』를 읽고 있는 사람이 있으면, 토론 주제를 골라 함께 의견을 나눠 보는 것은 어떨까요? 감상문을 쓰거나, 외국어로 말해 보는 것도 좋겠죠.

해답을 찾아볼 때는, 꼭 배우고자 하는 언어로 먼저 확인해 보세요. 궁금한 마음에 학습효과가 팍! 올라가니까요.

If you have a friend who is also reading *Youngho and Chadori,* why not pick a discussion topic and talk about it together? You could even write down your impressions and share them in the language you want to improve.

When you check the answers, be sure to look them up first in the language you're learning. That little spark of curiosity will boost your learning like nothing else.

7

AI—인공지능

AI—ARTIFICIAL INTELLIGENCE

요즘에는 AI가 있어서 언어 학습도 참 편해졌죠.

처음에는 다른 사람 앞에서 외국어를 시도하는 것이 쑥스러울 수도 있어요.

These days, AI makes language learning so much more convenient.

Speaking a foreign language in front of others can feel intimidating at first.

You might want to start by asking AI a question like the example below and chatting in a foreign language at your own pace.

<u>Example:</u>

Type your question in the AI message box and press "Enter." Don't forget to form the question after your needs.

```
Reader:

Let's discuss the following
topic in easy Korean. Please
correct my Korean and explain
the grammar in English so that
even an elementary school kid
can understand. Also use emojis
to make it fun. In Youngho and
Chadori, Book I: The Door to
the Spirit World, who is my
favorite character and why?
```

한번 다음과 같이 AI에게 질문을 던지고, 자신의 방식대로 외국어로 채팅을 해 보는 것은 어떨까요?

예)

AI 메시지 입력창에 다음과 같이 질문을 던지고 Enter 키를 눌러 보세요. 자신의 필요에 따라 메시지를 조정하는 것도 잊지 마세요.

독자:

초급 영어로 다음 주제에 대해서 논하고 싶어요. 내 영어를 교정하고 초등학생도 알아들을 수 있게 한국어로 문법 설명도 해 줘요. 이모지도 써서 재미있게 해요. 『영호와 차도리 제1권: 영혼의 세계로 가는 문』에서 내가 가장 좋아하는 등장 인물은 누구이며 그 이유는?

AI will respond with something like the following. You can continue the conversation as if you were chatting with a human.

AI Partner:

Sure! I will correct your Korean and explain the grammar in easy English, so even an elementary school child can understand. I'll also use emojis to make it fun for you. Please type your answer in Korean.

Reader:

제일 좋아하는 캐릭터는 영호 왜냐하면 용감 남자. ⚔️

AI Partner:

Good try! 👍 Let's fix it a little.

❌ 용감 남자

✅ 용감한 남자

👉 In Korean, when you use an adjective (용감하다 = to be brave) before a noun, you need to add -한.

AI가 다음과 비슷하게 대답을 할 거예요. 그 후에는 사람과 채팅하듯 계속 해서 대화를 나누어 보세요.

AI 파트너:

물론이죠! 영어를 교정하고 초등학생도 알아들을 수 있도록 한국어로 쉽게 문법 설명도 해 드릴게요. 이모지도 써서 재미있게 하죠! 영어로 의견을 써 주세요.

독자:

My favorite character is Chadori because he is funny and he make me laugh. 😂🐶

AI 파트너:

잘했어요! 👍 그런데 한 가지를 고쳐야 해요.

"he make" → "he makes"

👉 영어에서 he, she, it 같은 단어가 주어일 때는, 동사 끝에 -s를 붙여야 해요.

예: I play → He plays 🎲

✅ 고친 문장: My favorite character is Chadori because he is funny and he makes me laugh. 😃✨

AI 파트너:

❌ 영호 왜냐하면

✅ 영호예요, 왜냐하면

👉 You need 예요 to make a polite sentence: "It is Youngho."

✅ Corrected sentences:

제일 좋아하는 캐릭터는 영호예요. 왜냐하면 용감한 남자예요. ✨

Reader (repeats):

제일 좋아하는 캐릭터는 영호예요. 왜냐하면 용감한 남자예요.

AI Partner:

Perfect! 🌟 Very natural now.

독자:

My favorite character is Chadori because he is funny and he makes me laugh.

AI 파트너:

Perfect! 🌟 아주 잘했어요!

Summary: Suggested Prompts

🤖 **Level + Corrections + Explanations:** Let's discuss the following topic in easy (intermediate/advanced) English. Please correct my English (or Korean) and explain the grammar in Korean (or English). (Other requests): (Book title) (Insert discussion topic).

🤖 **Adjusting Difficulty Level:** Please match your answer to my level by using easier (or more difficult) words and sentence structures.

⚠️ **Caveat:** Be mindful that AI can sometimes be wrong—even when it sounds very convincing. Use it as a reference tool, but always remember to double-check important facts.

Keep asking until you get an answer that really makes sense to you!

요약: 권장 프롬프트

🤖 **레벨 + 교정 + 설명:** 초급(중급/상급) 영어로 다음 주제에 대해서 논하고 싶어요. 내 영어(또는 한국어)를 교정하고 한국어(또는 영어)로 문법 설명도 해 줘요. (기타 희망사항): (책 제목) (토론 주제 삽입)

🤖 **난이도 조절:** 더 쉬운(혹은 어려운) 단어(문장구조)를 사용하세요.

⚠️ **주의 사항:** AI는 얼핏 보기에는 맞는 것 같지만 때때로 오류가 있을 수 있어요. 참고용으로만 사용하고, 중요한 내용은 반드시 재확인하세요.

머리에 쏙 들어오는 대답이 나올 때까지 계속 다시 물어보세요!

8

SANTA CLAUS, FATHER CHRISTMAS: 차이가 뭘까요?

WHAT'S THE DIFFERENCE?

같은 산타 할아버지인데, 왜 이름이 다를까요?

간단히 설명하자면 Santa Claus는 미국식, Father Christmas는 영국식 영어라고 할 수 있죠.

It's the same jolly old Saint Nicholas in red—so why the two names?

In short: *Santa Claus* is American English, while *Father Christmas* is British English.

The differences between U.S. and U.K. English show up in small details like this—just as Korean dialects vary not only in pronunciation and intonation but also in spelling and vocabulary. Still, just as people from Seoul can understand the Busan dialect, speakers of different varieties of English can usually communicate without much trouble. Every now and then, though, differences in vocabulary or alternate meanings of the same word can cause confusion.

Broadly speaking, English comes in two main varieties: American and British. In Korea, learners are usually taught American English, largely because of Korea's close ties with the United States. But in the rest of the world, the two types coexist. I myself learned my English in the United Kingdom, so British English comes most naturally to me. When I began working on the English edition of *Youngho and Chadori,* I wrote it in British English without giving it a second thought. As I was drafting a story about Christmas, the contrasts between the two varieties of English became especially striking. Even the affectionate form of an everyday word like "Grandfather" differs: often "Granddad" in the U.S., but mostly "Grandad" in the U.K. Just a single letter apart, but a noticeable shift for a writer.

This bilingual edition of *Youngho and Chadori* is presented entirely in American English. For the British English, the English-only edition follows British English as the standard unless mentioned otherwise.

미국 영어와 영국 영어의 차이는 이렇게 작은 부분에서부터 드러나요. 한국의 다양한 사투리처럼, 발음과 억양뿐 아니라 철자와 단어 선택도 달라지죠. 그래도 서울 사람이 부산 사투리를 알아듣듯, 서로 다른 영어권 사람들 간에도 대체로 큰 어려움 없이 의사소통을 하긴 해요. 가끔 단어 차이나 동일어의 다른 의미 때문에 오해가 생기기는 하지만요.

크게 보면 영어는 미국식과 영국식으로 나눌 수 있어요. 한국에서 보통 배우는 영어는 미국식 영어예요. 한국이 미국과 교류가 많은 탓이겠죠. 하지만 한국 밖의 세계에서는 미국식과 영국식이 공존하고 있어요. 저는 영국에서 영어를 배웠기에 자연스럽게 영국식 영어를 쓰게 되었어요. 그래서 처음 『영호와 차도리』의 영문판 작업에 들어갈 때도 아무 생각 없이 영국식으로 썼죠. 그런데 크리스마스에 대한 이야기를 다루다 보니, 그 차이를 평소보다 더욱 실감 나게 느꼈어요. 또 지극히 일상적인 단어인 '할아버지'의 친근한 표현조차도, 미국은 주로 Granddad, 영국은 대부분 Grandad. 알파벳 하나 다른 스펠링에 불과했지만, 글을 쓰는 사람에게는 큰 차이로 다가왔어요.

『영호와 차도리』 한·영 대역판에서 쓰이는 영어는 전적으로 미국식이에요. 영국식 영어를 원하신다면, 영문 단독판은 별도의 표시가 없는 한 영국식 영어를 기준으로 하고 있어요.

영어 단독언어판은 Amazon, Barnes & Noble, Waterstones, Kobo 등 대부분 해외 온라인 서점에서 찾아보실 수 있으며, Amazon, Apple Books, Google Play 등에서 전자책으로 만나보실 수도 있어요. 영문판은 제2판부터 기본적으로 영국식 철자를 따르되, 어휘는 읽기 좋게 영국식과 미국식을 혼합해 보고자 노력했어요. 한국어판과 보다 가깝게 조율된 개정판은 2026년 2월 출시될 예정이니 참조해 주세요.

그래서 『영호와 차도리』가 어느 독자라도 편하게 즐길 수 있는 책이 되었으면 해요.

You can find the English monolingual edition at most online retailers such as Amazon, Barnes & Noble, Waterstones, and Kobo, or in e-Book format on Amazon, Apple Books, and Google Play. Beginning with the second edition, I have aimed to keep mainly British spelling while blending both British and American vocabulary for readability. A revised edition, more closely aligned with the Korean version, is scheduled for release in February 2026.

My hope is that Youngho and Chadori can be enjoyed with ease by readers everywhere.

9

이 책에서만 특별하게 쓰이는 단어들

SPECIAL USAGE OF WORDS
UNIQUE TO THIS BOOK

『영호와 차도리 제1권: 영혼의 세계로 가는 문』에는 일반적인 사용방식과 다소 다르게 쓰인 단어들이 등장해요.

판타지 이야기니까요.

***Youngho and Chadori, Book I: The Door to the Spirit World* features words used in ways that may seem unconventional.**

It is a fantasy story, after all.

Complete forms of words were chosen even when contractions were available—or even preferred in some cases—for the sake of English learners. Please note that while these usages are not incorrect, they may not be the best choice for everyday conversation or writing.

? ***Would, Had,* and *'d*:** While some contexts clearly prefer the contracted form of "would" or "had"—for example, "I'd love to" instead of "I would love to" in spoken English, or "he'd played" instead of "he had played" in some written contexts—I avoided such contraction in this bilingual edition of *Youngho and Chadori* to avoid confusion for English learners. To see where this contraction is preferred, please refer to the English-only edition.

? **Santas:** The plural of Santa Claus. Traditionally, of course, there is only one Santa, so the plural form is unusual—unless you mean multiple Santa decorations or groups of people dressed as Santa. In *Youngho and Chadori, Book I: The Door to the Spirit World,* I use the term for Santa's helpers in Santa-like costumes, so I chose to use the plural form.

또 학습의 편의를 위한 경우도 있죠. 예를 들면 축약형이 가능하거나 일반적인 경우에도 완전한 형태의 단어를 선택했어요. 틀린 것은 아니지만 일상 회화나 작문에는 어울리지 않을 수도 있으니 유의하세요.

? ***Would, Had, 'd***: 'would'나 'had'는 축약형이 문맥에서 더 자연스러운 경우가 종종 있죠. 예를 들어, 구어체에서 'I'd love to'는 'I would love to'보다 자연스럽게 들리고, 'he'd played'는 문어체에서도 'he had played'보다 자연스러운 경우가 더러 있어요. 『영호와 차도리』 한영대역판에서는 영어 학습 시 혼동을 피하기 위해 되도록 축약형을 사용하지 않았어요. 위와 같은 축약형이 더 자연스럽게 쓰이는 경우의 예를 보시려면 영문 단독판을 참고해 주세요.

? Santas: 산타클로스의 복수형. 전통적으로 산타는 세상에 단 한 분뿐이니 복수형은 맞지 않겠죠. 혹 '장식용 산타 인형 여러 개'나 '산타 복장을 한 사람들 여러 명'과 같은 경우라면 몰라도 말이예요. 『영호와 차도리 제1권: 영혼의 세계로 가는 문』에서는 산타 할아버지와 비슷하게 차려 입은 조수들이 언급되므로 복수를 사용했어요.

? Living soul: 한국어로는 '생혼' 이라는 표현을 사용했어요. 직역하면 '살아 있는 영혼'으로, 단순히 몸이나 영혼만 가진 존재가 아니라, 육체, 생명, 영혼을 모두 담은 의미로 써 보았어요. 영어로는 영적인 뉘앙스로 쓰이기도 하지만, 'I couldn't see a living soul'에서처럼 단순히 '아무도'라는 뜻으로도 종종 쓰여요.

정형화된 방식에서 벗어난 사용법을 택하면서 상당한 짜릿함을 느꼈어요. 판타지 작가만의 많은 즐거움 중 하나죠!

? **Living soul**: In the Korean edition, I used the word *saeng-hon* (생혼), literally "living soul." It signifies more than just a body or a spirit—it designates the union of body, life, and spirit. In English, *living soul* can also mean simply "any person," as in, "I couldn't see a living soul," meaning "there was nobody."

What a thrill it was to play with words beyond their ordinary use—one of the many joys of being a fantasy writer!

10

마지막 한마디
LAST WORDS

『영호와 차도리 제1권: 영혼의 세계로 가는 문』은 한국어판이 원본이예요.

외국어를 배우면 배울수록 저의 모국어인 한글이 너무나도 아름답다는 것을 느꼈기 때문이죠.

Youngho and Chadori, Book I: The Door to the Spirit World **was originally written in Korean.**

The more foreign languages I learned, the more I came to appreciate the beauty of the Korean language—my mother tongue.

As a result, I felt a certain sense of stubborn responsibility that my first book had to be in Korean. Still, publishing a Korean book while living abroad wasn't easy. In the end, I translated it into English myself (I call it "rewriting"), and the English edition was first published at the end of 2020.

Impatient to release my book into the world, I chose the path of self-publishing. That meant not only the translation, but also the cover, illustrations, and even the book design and layout—all under the banner of saving costs. It was an enormous investment of time and effort, but it turned out to be one of the most joyful and meaningful challenges of my life. Yet little did I know that publishing the book itself was only half the journey. Without PR and marketing, I simply couldn't introduce it to the right readers. However, I was exhausted after the arduous publishing process, and *Youngho and Chadori* was quickly buried among the thousands of books released into the world every day.

Finally, five years later, I am both pleased and thankful to be able to bring this bilingual Korean–English edition to readers in Korea. I am deeply indebted to everyone at G-World for their invaluable help and support in making the publication of this bilingual Korean-English edition possible.

따라서 첫 작품만큼은 반드시 한국어여야 한다는 일종의 우직한 사명감이 있었어요. 하지만 해외에 살면서 한국어로 책을 출판하기란 쉽지 않았죠. 결국 영문으로 직접 번역(나에게는 "재집필")하고, 2020년 말 영어판을 먼저 출간하게 되었어요.

한시 바삐 책을 출판하고 싶었던 저는 결국 자가출판의 길을 택하게 되었어요. 비용을 절감한다는 명목으로, 번역뿐 아니라 표지, 삽화, 심지어 도서 디자인 및 구성까지 모두 직접 해야 했죠. 엄청난 시간과 노력을 요하는 작업이었지만, 결국 더없이 즐겁고 뜻깊은 도전이 되었어요. 하지만 책을 출판한다는 것 자체가 단지 여정의 절반에 불과하다는 사실은 미처 몰랐죠. 홍보와 마케팅 없이는 책을 적합한 독자층에게 알릴 수 있는 길이 없었어요. 그러나 고된 출판 과정에 지친 저는 마케팅을 할 기력이 없었고, 『영호와 차도리』는 매일 수천 권씩 세상에 출간되는 책들 사이에 금세 묻혀 버리고 말았어요.

그리고 5년이라는 시간이 지난 지금, 드디어 한영 대역판을 한국에서 출판할 수 있게 되어서 기쁘고 또 감사한 마음뿐이예요. 한영 대역판 출판이 가능하도록 도움과 지원을 아끼지 않으신 좋은땅 출판사 여러분들께 고개 숙여 고마움을 전달하고자 합니다.

글을 쓰고 다듬는 사람들의 부단한 노력과 열정이 있기에 한 언어가 더욱 아름다워지고, 그 글을 읽어 주는 독자 여러분이 있기에 글을 쓰는 사람이 존재할 수 있지 않나 생각해요.

저의 글을 읽어 주셔서 마음속 깊은 곳으로부터 너무나도 감사하다는 말을 드리고 싶습니다.

감사합니다.

2025년 11월 26일,
스타방에르에서,
주보경 드림

I believe that a language becomes more beautiful through the tireless efforts and devotion of those who shape and refine its words, and it is thanks to readers like you that these professions can continue to exist.

From the bottom of my heart, I want to say how truly grateful I am that you are reading my work.

Thank you.

November 26, 2025,
Stavanger,
B.K. Chu

YOUNGHO AND CHADORI

(KOREAN–ENGLISH BILINGUAL EDITION)

BOOK I: THE DOOR TO THE SPIRIT WORLD

어머니와 아버지, 그리고 오빠에게 저의 첫 작품을 바칩니다.

To my mother, father, and brother—I dedicate my first book to you.

저는 크리스마스가 올 때면 항상—그 성스러운 이름과 유래로 인한 종교적 의미를 제외하자면, 아니, 제외가 가능하다면—즐거운 시간, 또 자상하고 너그러워질 수 있는, 인정미 넘치는 좋은 날들을 떠올리곤 한답니다.

— 찰스 디킨스: *크리스마스 캐럴("구두쇠 스크루지")*

I am sure I have always thought of Christmas-time, when it has come round—apart from the veneration due to its sacred name and origin, if anything belonging to it can be apart from that—as a good time; a kind, forgiving, charitable, pleasant time.

— CHARLES DICKENS: *A CHRISTMAS CAROL*

프롤로그·PROLOGUE

아홉 마리의 개와 썰매, 그리고 괴수—NINE DOGS, A SLEIGH, AND A MONSTER

때는 크리스마스 새벽, 세상은 아직도 어둠에 싸여 있고, 막 동이 틀 무렵이다. 기나긴 겨울밤 사이 쌓인 두터운 어두움의 장막을 뚫어 보고자 머리를 들이미는 태양의 힘으로, 검은 밤은 드디어 걷히고 막 검푸른 청옥 같은 새벽이 밝아 오고 있었다.

It was early Christmas morning. The world was still in darkness, with only moments left before daybreak. The sun was forcing its head through the heavy shades of black that had gathered through the long winter night. Finally, the darkness began to lift to unveil the deep sapphirine blue of the twilight hour.

0-1 해와 달·The Sun and the Moon

해가 지평선을 너머 모습을 드러내기도 전에 하늘 저편은 가늘고 희미한 붉은빛으로 먼저 물들어 갔는데, 참으로 기적과도 같은 장면이라고 하지 않을 수 없었다. 시간의 첫 순간부터 하루도 어김없이 지구상의 모든 것에 축복을 내려온—하지만 흔히들 그저 당연한 사실로 잊고 살아가는—기적.

세상은 눈으로 뒤덮여 있었고, 아홉 마리의 개들이 새빨간 썰매를 끌며 달리고 있었다. 금빛 날을 단 썰매에는 한 노인이 타고 있었는데, 유난히도 밝은 얼굴빛과 용맹스러운 기상에도 불구하고 분명 노인임에 의심의 여지가 없었던 것은, 머리가 눈처럼 하얀 백발인 데다가 이마에는 주름이 깊이 패여 있었기 때문이다.

At last, a thin strip of pale orange light emerged along the skyline, although the sun had not yet risen over the horizon. It was such a miracle—often forgotten and taken for granted by most—that had blessed all the occupants of the planet every single day since the beginning of time.

The world was covered in snow. Nine dogs pulled a bright red sleigh with golden blades. It carried an old man whose silvery hair and deep-lined brow gave away his age despite his exceptionally radiant complexion and fearless manner.

He wore a red Santa suit—fittingly enough, given that it was Christmas. There was also a boy around the age of ten or eleven in the sleigh. They stood upright despite the breakneck speed of the charging sleigh. The man bellowed as he raised his fist and thrust it into the air above him:

"Go, go, go! Keep going, and don't look back! We can do it!"

Now, several things might not make sense about this scene. Then again, the world is full of things that simply defy common sense.

In a curious contrast to the Santa outfit the old man was wearing, the boy was still in his pajamas despite the biting cold; his hair was disheveled as if he had just jumped out of bed in a hurry. Even the dogs were not the sorts typically seen pulling a sled. They were all different kinds—from hunting breeds to those often used as police dogs, search dogs, guard dogs, and family pets.

But what was truly extraordinary was that the sleigh ran neither through the snow-covered hills nor across the icy lake. Not even around a school playground or a stadium track. It flew across the sky so high up that the features of the landscape below looked tiny and trivial. At dizzying speed, it had just crossed the vast Eurasian continent and now shot above the sea between China and Korea.

노인은 산타 할아버지 복장을 하고 있었는데, 때가 크리스마스라는 것을 생각해서는 이상할 것이 없었다. 노인의 옆자리에는 열 살에서 열한 살 남짓 되어 보이는 소년이 타고 있었고, 노인과 소년은 엄청나게 빠른 속도로 질주하는 썰매의 속도에도 불구하고 우뚝 서 있었다. 노인이 주먹을 번쩍 들어 공중을 찌르며 외쳤다.

"자, 돌진! 주저 없이 앞만 보고 달리는 거야! 우린 할 수 있어!"

그런데 이 장면에는 상식으로는 도저히 이해할 수 없는 부분이 더러 있다. 이 세상에는 상식적으로 도저히 이해할 수 없는 일들이 참으로 많기도 하다.

소년은 살을 에는 듯한 추운 날씨에도 불구하고 아직 잠옷 차림이었고, 마치 자다가 허둥지둥 뛰쳐나온 사람처럼 머리가 헝클어져 있어 노인의 산타 복장과는 상이한 대조를 이루었다. 썰매를 끄는 개들조차도 일반적으로 썰매를 끄는 종류가 아니었고, 다 같은 종이 아니라 사냥견으로부터 종종 경찰견으로 쓰이는 종, 수색견, 경비견, 반려견 등 종류가 다양했다.

그런데 진정 기이한 일은 이 썰매가 눈으로 뒤덮인 벌판을 달리는 것도, 꽁꽁 얼어붙은 호수 위를 달리는 것도 아니라는 점이었다. 그렇다고 학교 운동장이나 육상경기장 트랙을 돌고 있었던 것도 아니다. 썰매는 온 세상이 장난감처럼 작게 내려다보이는 공중 위를 날고 있었고, 놀라운 속도로 방대한 중국 대륙을 건너 이제 막 서해 상공을 날고 있었다.

뿐만 아니라 썰매는 역시 화살처럼 공중을 가로지르는 그 무언가에 쫓기고 있었다. 집요하게 이들을 추격하는 주체는 사람도 짐승도 아니고 상상 속의 세계에나 있을 법한, 그것도 길고도 어두운 한겨울 깊은 밤 꿈에 나타났다가 아침 첫 햇살과 함께 자취도 없이 사라져 버릴 듯한 그런 괴물이었다. 요괴는 파충류와 같은 녹색이었는데, 머리는 멧돼지에다 몸은 사람의 형상, 발은 공룡의 발을 하고 있었다. 또 한 손에는 커다란 도끼를, 다른 한 손에는 방패를 들었고, 먹구름을 타고 혜성처럼 밤하늘을 가로지르며 손에 든 도끼를 휘두를 때마다 천둥번개가 일었다.

요괴는 사람의 말까지 해서 노인과 소년을 향해 끊임없이 모욕과 비난의 언사를 퍼부었다.

Moreover, something was chasing them at an equally blinding speed. The thing pursuing them relentlessly was neither human nor beast, but a creature so phantasmal it might have sprung from the tenebrous depths of a long winter night's dream—only to vanish without a trace in the first rays of dawn. Green like a reptile, it had the head of a wild boar, the body of a man, and the feet of a dinosaur. It held an ax in one hand and a shield in the other. Cutting across the night sky like a comet, it rode a patch of dark cloud, and every time it wielded the ax, a lightning bolt flashed with a roar of thunder.

It could also speak the human language, continually belittling and insulting the motley group on the run.

0-2 하늘을 나르는 개들·Dogs in the Sky

"Give up your pathetic efforts right now!" cried the monster.

Then it let out a cry like that of a howling beast; the fearsome sound shook the heavens and tore through the atmosphere. Lightning sparked from its ax and darted toward the sleigh, almost striking the pair in flight. Luckily, the sleigh made a quick turn just in time, and they got away by a hair's breadth. The spike of light hit the rear corner of the sleigh, bounced off, and dissipated into nothingness.

"Obey my command and kneel before me!"

A brutal cry of fury filled the sky once more as the monster writhed with rage and leaped into the void. In one terrifying move, it raised the ax and slashed through the air. A single flash of lightning burst forth, followed by a deafening crash of thunder.

"네 이놈들! 이만 순순히 포기하지 못할까!"

요괴가 괴성을 지르자 야수의 포효를 연상케 하는 무시무시한 소리가 천공에 울려 퍼졌다. 하늘을 찢는 듯한 천둥소리와 함께 요괴가 휘두르는 도끼에서 번쩍 한 줄기 번개가 일고, 빛의 창은 가차 없이 노인과 소년이 탄 썰매를 향해 날아가, 거의 명중할 뻔했지만 가까스로 썰매가 방향을 트는 바람에 겨우 뒷부분 모퉁이에 맞고 튕겨 나가 허공에 스러졌다.

"이만 명령에 복종하고 무릎을 꿇으렸다!"

잔혹한 비명 같은 목소리가 다시금 천지를 뒤흔들고, 요괴는 분노에 몸서리치며 공중으로 뛰어올라 도끼를 든 손을 쳐들었다. 이내 도끼가 무시무시한 동작으로 하늘을 가르고, 번쩍 한 줄기 빛이 일더니, 귀청을 찢는 듯한 천둥소리가 울렸다.

1

재수 좋은 구미호와 재치 있는 군만두

THE LUCKY FOX AND THE CUNNING DUMPLING

"김 영호!"

난데없이 화난 여자 목소리가 울린다. 영호는 교실 한복판에 위치한 책상 자리에 앉아 있었다.

"Youngho Kim!" screeched an angry woman's voice. Youngho was sitting at his desk in the middle of the classroom.

1-1 곤경에 빠진 영호·Youngho is in Trouble

잠깐 졸았던 것 같다. 엎친 데 덮친 격으로 지금 영호를 노려보고 있는 사람은 다름 아닌 역사 선생님이자 엄하기로 소문난 박 선생님이었다. 그야말로 끝장이었다.

지금은 오후 마지막 시간. 중간쯤 지날 때부터 살짝 눈이 감기기 시작했다. 몰려오는 졸음에 목에 슬슬 힘이 빠지면서 줄곧 꾸벅꾸벅 목방아를 찧다가, 그럴 때마다 제풀에 화들짝 놀라 목을 다시 꼿꼿이 일으켜 세우곤 했다. 이제 이십 분만 더 깨어 있으면 되었다. 하지만 기를 쓴 노력에도 불구하고 결국 선생님의 낮고 기계적인 목소리가 수면제처럼 작용해 버렸고, 저항이 불가능했던 것이다.

He had dozed off, it seemed. To make matters worse, the teacher glaring at him at this very moment was none other than Mrs. Park—his history teacher and a notorious disciplinarian. In other words, he was in big trouble.

It happened to be the last class of the day, and he had begun to feel quite drowsy halfway through. His neck slowly lost its strength and gave way to the sleep creeping over him. Repeatedly nodding off and jerking his head back up with a start, he had hoped to stay awake for another twenty minutes. Despite his best efforts, however, Mrs. Park's low, mechanical voice worked like a sleeping pill. He just couldn't fight it in the end.

"Stand up at once!" Mrs. Park yelled. "Didn't you get any sleep last night? To fall asleep in class! And this is only an elementary school, for goodness' sake! How on earth are you going to survive when you go on to junior high and high school?"

Youngho gulped in dismay. He was not feeling tired anymore, even though he had had ridiculously little sleep last night. Problem was, he had been up almost all night reading a detective novel—with a flashlight under the blanket so that the light wouldn't leak out of his room and catch Mom's attention. He kept telling himself, *just a little bit more, just a little bit more,* and he ended up reading the whole thing. He would usually do everything on his phone, but Mom had installed an app called *Nighttime Monitor,* which meant that his phone would lock itself and couldn't be accessed after nine o'clock every evening.

Having turned twelve last summer, Youngho was in his sixth and final year attending Jinsung Elementary School on the outskirts of Seoul. It was now December; so he was only about a month short of becoming twelve and a half. While he had black hair and dark brown eyes like most people in the country, he could be easily spotted by his big dreamy eyes that drooped good-naturedly and the permanently sunburned olive-brown skin of someone who spent most of his time outdoors. Though smaller than most other kids of his age, he had unusually big feet for his height; it meant that he wore clothes for younger children but used shoes meant for late teens, sometimes even adults.

"당장 일어서!" 박 선생님이 외쳤다. "어제 잠 안 자고 뭘 했길래 수업 시간에 다 조는 거야! 초등학생이 벌써부터 이러면 곧 중학교, 고등학교 가면 어떻게 버티려고!"

당황한 영호가 침을 꿀꺽 삼켰다. 엄청난 수면 부족에도 불구하고 잠이 확 달아난 것은 물론이다. 어젯밤 늦은 시각까지 추리소설을 읽다가 거의 밤을 새다시피 한 것이 화근이었다. 혹 불빛이 방에서 새어 나가서 엄마에게 들킬까 봐, 이불 밑에서 손전등을 켜고 조금만 더, 조금만 더 하며 계속 읽다가 결국은 끝까지 다 읽고 만 것이다. 평소라면 항상 뭐든지 휴대폰으로 했을 테지만, 엄마가 '나이트타임 모니터'라는 앱을 설치한 이후로 저녁 아홉 시만 되면 화면 잠금 장치가 자동으로 설정되어 무용지물이 되어 버렸다.

영호는 이번 여름에 만 열두 살. 서울 외곽에 있는 진성초등학교 6학년으로, 지금이 12월이니까 한 달쯤만 있으면 만 열두 살 반이었다. 우리나라 사람들 대다수가 그러하듯 검은 머리에 갈색 눈을 하고 있었고, 평소 밖에서 종일 뒹굴며 살다시피 한 결과로 까무잡잡한 피부에, 특징이 있다면 유난히도 크고 꿈을 꾸는 듯한 눈이 살짝 처져 순해 보인다는 점이었다. 또래 아이들 대부분과 비교해 키가 작았지만 키에 비해 거의 비정상적이다시피 발이 커서, 옷은 나이보다 더 어린 아이들용을 입었지만 신발은 청소년용, 때로는 성인용을 신을 정도였다.

He saw himself more like a late bloomer, hoping that he would grow one day to balance out the size of his feet. Someday he was going to grow so tall nobody would recognize him after the summer break.

What he lacked in stature, Youngho more than made up for with an almost prodigious talent—his knack for getting himself in trouble. No matter what he did, he would always find himself in a mess—each time an even deeper one than before. Indeed, it made others wonder how much trouble this small and seemingly harmless child was capable of getting into. Somehow, though, an incredible streak of luck saved him each time. Moreover, he was a sweet-looking child with his doe eyes and shy smile, although he was not aware of it himself. And his innocent looks did help whenever he got himself in deep trouble. He needed all the help he could get, given how often he found himself in trouble.

Embarrassed, Youngho stood up awkwardly from his seat. The whole class turned to stare. Mrs. Park glowered at Youngho over her thick half-moon glasses.

"Okay, Sleeping Beauty! Try answering my question—I'm sure you must know everything if you can sit back and take a nap in my class!"

The class roared with laughter. Mrs. Park paused for a while as if relishing the moment. Youngho thought it was quite uncharacteristic of her to look so enthusiastic.

영호 스스로는 늦게 크는 타입이라고 위안했고, 언젠가는 발 크기에 맞게 키도 자라 주기를 바랄 뿐이었다. 그날이 오면 영호가 크게 훌쩍 자라 버려서 여름방학이 지나고 학교에 가면 아무도 알아보지 못할 정도로.

비록 키는 작았지만 그 부족함 이상으로 채워 주는 것이 하나 있었다. 영호에게는 거의 천재적인 재능이 한 가지 있었는데, 다름 아닌 문제 일으키는 재능이었다. 무슨 일을 하건 간에 항상 혼란 상태로 끝을 맺었고, 매번 문제에서 더 큰 문제의 아수라장으로 이어지고 마는 것이었다. 그야말로 주변 사람들은 도대체 어떻게 이 작고 순해 보이는 아이가 그 많은 문제를 일으킬 수 있을까 의아해하곤 했다. 하지만 항상 일종의 행운이 따라 주어서 결국에는 문제가 더 복잡해지지는 않았다. 게다가 스스로는 모르고 있었지만, 영호는 큰 눈에 수줍은 미소를 띤 미소년이었고, 헤어날 수 없는 문제를 일으킬 때마다 그 순진한 표정이 도움이 되어 준 것은 사실이다. 문제를 일으키는 빈도가 상당히 높았기에 그나마 불행 중 다행이었다고나 할까.

멋쩍어진 영호가 어색하게 엉거주춤 자리에서 일어났다. 반 아이들이 일제히 돌아보고, 박 선생님이 두꺼운 반달 안경 너머로 영호를 쏘아보았다.

“자, 어디 우리 잠꾸러기, 질문에 한 번 대답해 봐. 수업 시간에 편하게 늘어져서 잘 정도면 이미 다 알고 있는 내용인가 봐?”

아이들이 일제히 폭소를 터뜨린다. 선생님은 마치 그 순간을 음미하는 듯 잠시 말을 멈추었다. 이런 열정을 보이는 것도 왠지 박 선생님답지 않다는 생각이 들었다.

"In recent decades, the world has seen rapid development in many areas, such as science, technology, and communications," she began. "It has grown increasingly closer together as a result, becoming ever so 'small,' in the common expression. Now, what do you call such a phenomenon?"

Youngho had absolutely no idea!

He started feeling lightheaded. It was probably something they had covered while he was asleep.

"Well, it must be a breeze for you, for sure, if you can just doze off leisurely in class!" Mrs. Park said with gusto and added tantalizingly, "I'll let you off this once if you get the right answer."

All eyes were on Youngho now. Some with sympathy. Some with curiosity as to whether he could find a way out of this predicament. Mrs. Park's lips curved ever so slightly upward. Youngho wondered if it could be the first time that he had ever seen her smile.

"Yeah, um . . . L-Lemme think—" Youngho tried to come up with something sensible to say, but all he could manage was helplessly stutter a jumble of nonsense.

"No 'ums!' We don't have all day!" Mrs. Park pressed him.

A trickle of cold sweat ran down Youngho's back. If he didn't get the right answer, she was undoubtedly going to call his parents straight away. Mom had caught him once, up late in his bedroom playing computer games. To this day, he regretted that catastrophic mistake.

"최근 몇십 년 사이 과학·기술·통신 등 여러 분야에서는 세계적으로 아주 급격한 발전이 있었지......" 박 선생님의 질문이 시작되었다. "그 결과로 지구촌은 점점 하나가 되고...... 흔히들 세계가 '작아진다'고들 하지. 이러한 현상을 뭐라고 부르나?"

배운 기억이 전혀 없었다!

영호는 머리가 아찔해졌다. 아마도 졸고 있는 동안 다룬 내용인 듯했다.

"자...... 수업 시간에 마음 놓고 자도 될 정도면 이 정도는 당연히 아주 쉽겠지?" 박 선생님이 재미있다는 것처럼 말하고는 약 올리듯 한 마디 보탰다. "만약 맞히면 이번 한 번만은 봐주지!"

아이들의 눈동자가 모두 영호에게로 쏠리고, 더러는 불쌍하다는 듯이, 더러는 과연 영호가 이 위기를 모면할 수 있을 것인지 호기심에 가득 찬 눈초리로 돌아보았다. 선생님의 입가에 야릇한 미소가 돌았다. 박 선생님이 웃는 것을 보는 것도 오늘이 처음이지 않나 싶었다.

"네...... 저...... 새, 생각을 좀......" 아무리 제대로 된 말을 해 보려고 해도 그저 앞뒤 두서없이 버벅대기만 할 뿐.

"뜸 들이지 말고 빨리 대답해 봐!" 선생님이 재촉했다.

영호의 등에서 식은땀이 주르르 흘러내렸다. 제대로 대답 못 하면 당장 집에 전화가 갈 것은 불을 보듯 뻔한 일이었다. 전에도 한 번 안 자고 방에서 PC 게임을 하다가 엄마에게 들킨 적이 있었다. 지금까지도 거의 죽음이었던 그날의 실수가 후회스러웠다.

Come morning, she moved his cherished computer—and every single book he owned—to the living room, except the textbooks and study guides. Of course, they still belonged to Youngho and he had access to them, but he could only use them during certain hours set by Mom. Otherwise, he had to ask for special permission, as if he were in a public library. All he got in return was a single photo album in case he was awake again after bedtime. Then there was the *Nighttime Monitor* app. Youngho called it *Nighttime Monster*—a monster that now haunted him every night—which was installed after the day his beloved computer was forced into exile.

All this pointed to one conclusion: Youngho *had* to find the answer to Mrs. Park's question. The world growing closer together as one—*What was it, again?* He searched desperately through the farthest corners of his brain. He vaguely remembered having seen something similar on TV once. *Or was it in the educational comics I once got for my birthday? Anyway, there's nothing to lose in having a go.* Gingerly, Youngho tried his luck with the first word that came to mind.

"Is it . . . um . . . globalization?"

The faint curve of a smile disappeared from Mrs. Park's lips instantly.

"Correct . . . not bad at all!" she said, looking disappointed.

While Youngho heaved a sigh of relief as quietly as possible, she continued disapprovingly,

다음 날 아침, 엄마는 영호가 애지중지하는 컴퓨터는 물론이고, 교과서와 참고서를 제외한 책이란 책은 죄다 거실로 옮겨 버렸다. 물론 여전히 컴퓨터도 책도 모두 영호 것이었고 사용할 수도 있었다. 하지만 이제는 엄마가 미리 정해 놓은 시간에만 하거나, 특별한 경우에는 마치 공공도서관처럼 따로 허락을 받아야만 하는 신세가 되었다. 그 대가로는 밤에 잠 안 오면 보라고 사진 앨범 하나 달랑 만들어 준 것이 전부였다. 게다가 휴대폰마저 사랑하는 컴퓨터를 압수당하던 그다음 날 엄마가 깔아 놓은 *나이트타임 모니터* 때문에 밤에는 쓸 수 없게 되어 버렸다. 영호에게는 *나이트타임 모니터*가 아니라, 그야말로 *나이트타임 몬스터*였다. 밤마다 나타나서 영호를 괴롭히는 괴물 몬스터.

결국 결론은 하나였다. 박 선생님 질문의 해답을 찾아야 한다는 것. 세계가 점점 하나가 되는 현상. *뭐였더라?* 영호는 필사적으로 두뇌의 구석구석 후미진 곳까지 모두 뒤져 보았다. 얼마 전 우연히 TV에서 비슷한 내용을 보았던 것도 같다. *아니면 이전에 생일 선물로 받았던 교육용 만화책에서 보았나? 어쨌든 밑져야 본전이니 한번 시도나 해 볼까.* 영호는 그냥 머리에 제일 먼저 떠오르는 단어로 조심스레 대답해 보았다.

“세계화…… 아닌가요?”

순간 박 선생님의 입가에 돌던 미묘한 웃음이 사라졌다.

“어—제법인데? 맞았어.” 선생님이 실망한 표정으로 말했다.

영호가 최대한 소리 없이 안도의 한숨을 내쉬는 사이, 선생님이 단호하게 말을 이었다.

"그렇지만 이번은 진짜 행운인 줄 알아! 앞으로 다시는 수업 시간에 졸거나 하는 일 있으면...... 알지!" 선생님은 반 아이들을 둘러보며 다시 한 번 강조했다. "여러분도 모두 명심해요!"

"네!" 모두가 입을 모아 대답한다.

곧 수업의 끝을 알리는 종이 울리고, 아이들이 교실에서 쏟아져 나와 복도를 메웠다. 일부는 뛰어다니고, 크게 소리를 지르며 웃고 떠들었다. 영호도 얼른 책가방을 어깨 한쪽에 걸쳐 멘 채, 단짝인 만우와 함께 서둘러 교실을 나섰다.

"Still, consider yourself extremely lucky this time! If it ever happens again, there'll be consequences!" She looked around at the room full of children and emphasized, "Don't forget that, everyone!"

"Yes, ma'am!" everybody chanted.

Shortly afterward, the school bell sounded, announcing the end of the class. Kids poured out of classrooms and filled the corridor—running, screaming, and laughing. His schoolbag slung over a shoulder, Youngho shot out, too, together with his best friend, Manu.

1-2 세계화·Globalization

It was icy cold outside—cold enough to see the moisture from their breaths freeze and turn into little puffs of cloud. Traces of snowfall from earlier were visible. Trodden and driven over into a gray mass of slush, it had then frozen again and was now littered with gravel and sand, which brought out the gloom against the dull winter sky. However, the boys couldn't care less, dreary as it was. Youngho and Manu strolled lightly down the street along the brick wall enclosing the school.

"Foxy, how did you guess the answer to Mrs. Park's question?" Manu asked, looking incredulous. "I don't think I could've answered that . . . and I'm not the one who was sleeping!"

Youngho often went by the name of Foxy, a nickname created by Manu, which Youngho disliked vehemently. Manu claimed that, if repeated very fast, Youngho's full name with the family name first—Kim Youngho—sounded like *Kumiho,* which was a mythological fox with nine tails in Korean folklore. *Kumiho* was said to take the form of a beautiful woman, often luring unsuspecting travelers to their deaths and eating their livers. Youngho couldn't disagree more and, thoroughly fed up and seriously annoyed, said loud and clear that his name didn't even remotely sound like it. Still, he couldn't stop Manu, who ended up enjoying it even more, and the name kind of stuck.

"I was just lucky, I guess," replied Youngho. "But what's your excuse, Dumpling? Wasn't it something you learned while I was asleep?"

바깥은 매우 추웠다. 내쉬는 숨조차도 순식간에 얼어붙어 작은 구름이 되어 버릴 정도로. 거리에는 그날 눈이 내린 흔적이 여기저기 보였고, 하루 종일 다니는 자동차들과 사람들에게 짓밟혀 온통 잿빛 진창이 되었다가, 또다시 얼어 미끄럼 방지용 돌가루, 모래와 섞여 흐린 겨울 하늘 아래 전체적으로 음울한 인상을 주었다. 하지만 두 소년은 날씨야 음침하건 어쨌건 간에 전혀 개의치 않았다. 영호와 만우는 가벼운 발걸음으로 학교를 둘러싼 돌담 건너편 길을 따라 내려갔다.

"구미호, 너 아까 선생님이 한 질문 정답 어떻게 알았어?" 만우가 휘둥그레진 눈으로 물었다. "안 자구 깨 있던 나두 모르는 걸……"

'구미호'는 만우가 지은 영호의 별명이었는데, 영호는 이 별명이 정말 싫었다. 김영호를 빨리 반복해서 부르면 구미호처럼 들린다는 것이었다. 예쁜 여인으로 둔갑해 멋모르는 행인을 유혹하고 죽음으로 인도한 뒤, 간을 빼먹는다고 전해지는 전설 속의 꼬리 아홉 달린 여우 '구미호'. 영호는 스스로의 이름이 구미호처럼 들린다고는 전혀 생각하지 않았을 뿐더러, 짜증이 나다 못해 진절머리가 나서 내 이름은 전혀 그렇게 들리지 않는다고 벌써 여러 번 단호하게 잘라 말했었다. 하지만 그렇다고 그만둘 만우가 아니었다. 오히려 더 즐겨 부르게 되었고, 결국 별명으로 자리 잡게 된 것이다.

"응, 그냥 재수가 좋았던 것 같애." 영호가 대답했다. "근데 군만두, 넌 변명이 뭐야? 오늘 나 졸고 있을 때 배운 내용 아니었냐?"

Youngho had counter-attacked on the nickname by dubbing Manu "Dumpling," shortened from "Fried Dumpling." In his turn, Youngho also insisted that the word for "fried dumpling" in Korean, *Kunmandu,* sounded like Manu's full name with the family name first—Kwon Manu. Besides, it was a perfect nickname for Manu who loved eating. This nickname had been carefully picked to demean, insult, and irritate endlessly. However, Manu didn't seem to care in the slightest, which was incredibly boring.

"What?" Manu said, shaking his head. "'Just lucky'? How come I never get 'just lucky' like that? We didn't learn it in class while you were taking your beauty nap. That's why everyone was so surprised! Did you see Mrs. Park's face, man?"

Manu squinted at Youngho with a surly expression, clearly imitating the teacher; he did a playful pantomime of lowering imaginary reading glasses and frowning over them. Youngho couldn't help but laugh and elbowed Manu's side in a fake martial arts move. Manu clutched his stomach as if in great pain, his knees slowly bending and hitting the half-frozen ground, with a soundless scream of horror. *Aaaah!*

Youngho and Manu had been neighbors in the same apartment complex ever since they were little, and they grew up playing together all the time. Manu's family had recently bought a house and moved to another neighborhood, but both of them still went to Jinsung Elementary School and found themselves in the same class in their final year, becoming even closer than ever before.

'군만두'는 영호가 보복으로 지은 만우의 별명이었다. 만우의 성을 합친 이름 '권만우'와 발음도 비슷할뿐더러 먹는 것을 밝히는 만우에게 딱 맞는 별명이라고 생각했다. 이 별명은 모멸감을 주고, 수치심, 또 너무너무 견딜 수 없이 거슬리는 느낌을 가져다주는, 뭐 대충 그런 목적으로 엄선한 별명이었다. 그런데 만우는 전혀 개의치 않았고, 한마디로 엄청나게 김이 샜다.

"뭐? '그냥 재수가 좋았었던 것 같애'?" 만우가 고개를 절레절레 흔들며 말했다. "왜 난 '그냥 재수'가 좀 안 따라 줄까...... 오늘 네가 졸구 있을 때 배운 내용 아니라니까. 그러니까 다들 깜짝 놀랐지! 아까 박 선생님 얼굴 봤냐?"

만우가 박 선생님 흉내를 내며 눈을 째리고 영호를 흘겨보다가, 다시 장난스럽게 돋보기를 내리고 그 너머로 얼굴을 찌푸리는 시늉을 한다. 영호는 웃음을 참을 수 없었고, 무술 동작 흉내를 내며 그런 만우의 옆구리를 팔꿈치로 찔렀다. 만우가 엄청난 고통을 느끼는 척 배를 감싸안더니 "우욱!" 하고 소리 없는 비명을 지르며 서서히 반 얼어붙은 맨땅에 무릎을 꿇고 고꾸라지는 척한다.

영호와 만우는 어렸을 때부터 같은 아파트에서 이웃으로 살았고, 언제나 함께 놀며 자랐다. 얼마 전 만우네가 집을 사게 되어 다른 동네로 이사를 가기는 했지만, 둘 다 아직도 진성초등학교에 다닐뿐더러 마지막 학년이 되면서 같은 반까지 되어 오히려 둘 사이는 더욱 가까워졌다.

His face still chubby with baby fat and eyes twinkling with mischief, Manu was half-Chinese from his mother's side and could even speak fluent Chinese. Well, Manu claimed that he did, but there was no way for Youngho to verify if he really did or not. Manu's mother used to be a chef, and every time Youngho went to Manu's house, she would make something delicious—often something he had never tasted before. Youngho's favorite so far was Peking Duck tacos; they were so good and fun to put together. It was no wonder Manu's favorite pastime was eating!

It was winter break soon, and after the spring break next year, they had to change schools to go on to junior high. If they ended up in different schools, they had no choice but to be parted, possibly for good. The decision of which school they went on to depended on a computerized lottery system based on the school district they belonged to. In the end, the odds were not on their side, especially now that they didn't live in the same area. Youngho knew how crushed he would be if they got separated, but they never talked about that, and he just hoped for the best.

But he didn't have to worry about it right now. Youngho and Manu started their play-fight as they always did, performing exaggerated mock martial arts moves. It was Foxy's signature taekwondo side kick versus Dumpling's kung fu maneuvers today. Schoolbags were cast aside right at the start despite the muddy slush, and they even had to take off their thick winter jackets.

만우는 아직도 볼살이 포동포동하고 두 눈이 장난기로 번득이는 개구쟁이였고, 어머니가 중국인이셔서 중국어도 했다. 솔직히 만우 스스로가 유창하게 한다고 주장하기는 했으나, 영호가 확인해 볼 수 있는 방법은 사실상 없었다. 만우 어머니는 전직이 요리사이셨고, 영호가 놀러 갈 때마다 맛있는—종종 영호가 태어나서 처음 먹어 보는—것들을 해 주시곤 했다. 이제까지 영호가 맛본 것들 중 가장 맛있었던 것은 북경 오리구이 타코. 맛있을 뿐만 아니라 직접 싸서 먹는 재미도 있었다. 만우의 취미가 먹는 것인 데에는 다 이유가 있었다!

그러나 이제 곧 겨울방학이고, 새해 봄방학이 지나면 둘 다 중학생이 되어 다른 학교로 진학해야 했다. 만약 제각기 다른 학교에 배정되기라도 한다면, 선택의 여지도 없이 그대로 영영 헤어져 버릴 수도 있었다. 학교 배정은 학군에 따라 컴퓨터가 하는 자동 추첨에 의해 임의로 결정되었고, 특히나 같은 동네에 살지 않는 지금으로서는 아무도 모르는 일이었다. 만약 만우와 헤어지게 된다면...... 정말 생각만 해도 아찔했다. 그러나 둘은 중학교 진학에 관한 얘기는 항상 피해 왔고, 그저 어떻게든 잘 되기만을 바랄 뿐이었다.

하지만 지금 당장 그런 걱정은 할 필요가 없었다. 둘은 여느 때처럼 과장된 동작으로 장난 무술 시합을 벌였다. 오늘은 구미호의 주 무기인 태권 옆차기 대 군만두의 쿵푸 격투술. 눈이 얼다 녹다 해서 생긴 흙탕물에도 아랑곳하지 않고, 책가방은 물론이고 두터운 재킷마저도 곧 길바닥에 그냥 내동댕이쳐졌다.

Pow! Wow! Wham! Bam! Flying tiger side kick!
Hiyah! Kapow! Bang! Smack! Praying mantis strike!

The two boys were sweating profusely in no time and, after a while, picked up their schoolbags and jackets to go home. They were about to turn the corner and say goodbye to each other for the day, when they heard a voice calling out to them. It sounded intimidating and almost sinister.

"Oy, you two! What are you doing here?"

Youngho and Manu stopped short and turned toward the voice; it had come from a tall, lanky boy. He was much bigger than Youngho and Manu, and undoubtedly older too—about fifteen years old by the looks of it. Two others around the same age flanked him. One of the other two wore thick glasses, his face covered in acne scars, while the third had a big mole on his cheek.

"This is our territory!" the lanky one snarled, taking a step forward threateningly. "And you've been fighting here without our permission!"

His deepening voice sounded as if he had something stuck in his throat; it made Youngho cringe with dislike.

"It wasn't a real fight—we were only playing!" Youngho replied at once. "And since when is this your—"

Manu nudged him before he could finish the sentence.

"Play-fighting or fight-fighting, it's the same thing to us!" hissed Lanky.

아자! 헉! 퍽! 받아라! 나르는 호랑이 옆차기!
키야! 와샤! 쿵! 뻥! 사마귀 당랑권!

곧 두 소년은 땀을 뻘뻘 흘리며 치고받고 하다가, 얼마 지나지 않아 다시 책가방과 외투를 주워 들었다. 이제 골목길만 돌면 헤어져서 각자 집으로 향하게 된다. 그때였다. 갑자기 누가 두 소년을 향해 고함치는 소리가 들렸다. 위협적이고 왠지 불길한 예감을 주는 목소리.

"야, 니들 둘! 여기서 뭐 하는 거야?"

영호와 만우는 동작을 멈추고 소리가 나는 쪽을 돌아보았다. 목소리의 주인공은 깡마르고 키가 큰 아이. 영호와 만우보다 몸집도 훨씬 컸고, 열다섯 살 정도로 나이도 더 많아 보였다. 또래의 다른 두 명을 좌우로 끼고 있었는데, 한 명은 두꺼운 안경을 쓰고 얼굴이 여드름 흉터로 덮여 있었고, 나머지 한 명은 한쪽 볼에 큰 점이 있었다.

"여기는 우리 구역이야!" 키다리가 으름장을 놓고는 협박하듯 한 발자국 다가섰다. "그런데 어디서 허락도 없이 싸워?"

변성기 특유의 잠긴 목소리. 목에 무언가 걸린 듯, 혐오감으로 몸을 움츠리게 하는 그런 소리였다.

"진짜로 싸우는 거 아냐. 그냥 장난친 거야!" 영호가 즉시 대답했다. "그리구 왜 이 길이 형들 구역—"

말을 채 끝내기도 전에 만우가 팔꿈치로 영호의 옆구리를 쿡 찌른다.

"장난이든 진짜든! 그게 그거지!" 키다리가 내뱉었다.

The one with glasses agreed with his friend. “You have engaged in the act of violence in our territory,” he declared, “and you must pay the penalty!” The third one with the mole folded his arms and laughed, baring his yellowed teeth.

How could this be their territory? It’s a public street going in and out of school! Youngho thought to himself indignantly, but he decided to keep his mouth shut this time. *What now?* It felt like there was no way out.

All of a sudden, Manu pointed toward the school gate and shouted, “Look! It’s Mrs. Park, heading this way!”

The three bullies turned around at the same time to look. In that instant, Manu quickly grabbed Youngho by the arm and yanked him toward a store on the opposite side of the street. The two boys ran for their lives and, in a split second, disappeared behind the door while the bullies had their backs turned.

안경잡이가 옆에서 말을 거들었다. "우리 구역에서 평화를 깨뜨린 죄로 벌금을 내야지!" 점박이가 팔짱을 끼며 누런 이빨을 드러내고 웃는다.

어떻게 이 길이 자기네 구역이야? 아무나 오고 가는 학교 앞 길인데? 영호는 발끈했지만 이번에는 입을 다물고 잠자코 있기로 했다. *이제 어떻게 해야 하나......* 도저히 빠져나갈 구멍이 없어 보였다.

갑자기 만우가 학교 정문 방향을 가리키며 외쳤다.

"어! 저기 박 선생님 오신다!"

불량배들 세 명이 일제히 뒤를 돌아보는 순간, 만우가 영호의 팔을 덥석 움켜잡고 길 맞은편의 상점을 향해 끌었다. 두 소년은 나 살려라 하고 젖먹던 힘을 다해 뛰었고, 불량배들이 등을 돌린 사이 순식간에 상점문 안으로 사라졌다.

2

소리 없는 축제

A SILENT CARNIVAL

짤랑짤랑 상쾌한 소리를 내며 작은 방울들이 울리고, 허겁지겁 상점 안으로 뛰어든 영호와 만우는 문이 등 뒤로 천천히 닫히자 그제서야 깊은 안도의 한숨을 내쉬었다.

Tiny bells made a pleasant tinkling noise when Youngho and Manu scrambled through the door. They breathed heavy sighs of relief as the door slowly swung shut behind them.

It was a home decor store called Paradise on Earth, which was just a stone's throw away from Jinsung Elementary School. In his six years going to school there, however, Youngho had never once stepped inside the place. Sure, he would take a quick peek at its elegant display window from outside now and then as he passed by, but it just never came across as the type of place he would be interested in. Moreover, the thought of stepping into its neatly ordered interior made him feel uneasy. What if he knocked something over and broke it by accident? Nevertheless, he didn't have much of a choice right now, and a part of him had always wondered what lay beyond the elegant exterior.

Nice and warm, it made a world of difference to enter the store from the cold and desolate street. It was full-on Christmas in here. Exotic aromas—unidentifiable yet wonderful—wafted through the air and made his mouth water. Cheerful Christmas carols filled the space. A magnificent Christmas tree adorned the entrance, with shimmering baubles in red, gold, and silver hanging on its branches; it was decorated with ornaments of all kinds—Santa Claus in a sleigh, Rudolf the red-nosed reindeer, and a snowman wearing a Santa hat. To top it all, a golden star crowned the majestic pine.

A tall, thin man with mop-top hair stood behind the cashier's desk, humming softly along with the music.

"Good afternoon!" he said in a friendly tone, his eyes still fixed on the computer screen. "Welcome to Paradise on Earth! How can I—" When he saw the boys, he stopped in mid-sentence. He obviously knew Manu.

두 소년이 들어간 곳은 '지상천국'이라고 하는 인테리어 상점이었는데, 진성 초등학교에서 엎어지면 코 닿을 거리에 있었지만 영호는 6년 학교생활에서 단 한 번도 들어가 본 적조차 없는 곳이었다. 물론 지나가며 밖에서 흘끗 근사하게 꾸며진 진열장을 들여다본 적은 더러 있었지만, 영호가 특별히 관심을 가져 볼 만한 곳은 아닌 듯싶었다. 게다가 그 깨끗하게 정돈된 실내에 발을 들인다고 생각하면 조바심부터 나지 않을 수 없었다. 잘못해서 뭘 깨거나 부수기라도 하면 어쩌나? 하지만 지금 당장은 선택의 여지가 없었다. 또 항상 그 우아한 디스플레이 뒷면에는 무엇이 있을까 은근히 궁금했던 것도 사실이다.

따뜻하게 난방이 되어 있는 상점 안에 들어오니, 춥고 휑한 거리와는 달리 마치 딴 세상에 온 듯한 느낌을 주었다. 또 온통 크리스마스 장식으로 꾸며져 있는 데다, 이국적인—정확히 무엇이라고 딱 집어 말할 수는 없었지만 감미로운—향기가 은은하게 풍겨나서 입맛을 다시게 했다. 또 즐거운 크리스마스 캐럴이 들리는 입구에는 거대한 크리스마스트리로 꾸며져 있었는데, 가지마다 빨강, 금색, 은색 방울들이 매달려 반짝이고, 썰매탄 산타, 코 빨간 루돌프 사슴, 산타 모자를 쓴 눈사람 등등 갖가지 장식품 위로 꼭대기 높이 금빛 별이 왕관처럼 달려 있었다.

계산대 뒤에는 마른 몸에 키가 훤칠하고 바가지머리를 한 남자가 서서 음악에 따라 낮게 콧노래를 부르고 있었다.

"어서 오세요!" 아저씨는 컴퓨터 화면에서 눈을 떼지 않은 채 상냥한 목소리로 말했다. 그리고는 "'지상천국'에 오신 걸 환영합니다! 어떻게 도와드—" 하다가 두 소년을 보고는 말을 멈추었다. 주인 아저씨는 만우를 아시는 듯했다.

"Oh, it's you, Manu!" said the man as his face brightened into a broad smile. "And you brought a friend today!"

"Good afternoon, Mr. Yang! I thought I might drop by after school," Manu replied lightheartedly, making an exaggerated bow. "It's almost Christmas, isn't it? And I want to give Mom some new ideas," he quickly added, as if trying to find a good reason why he had to be there. Then he gently pushed Youngho toward Mr. Yang. "This is Youngho. We're in the same class at school."

Slightly embarrassed, Youngho managed only a quick nod and mumbled, "H-Hello."

"Welcome, both of you! Feel free to look around and just let me know if you need anything," said Mr. Yang good-naturedly. "Oh, and help yourselves to the gingerbread cookies here!"

He gestured to the heap of cookies on a pink plate at the other end of the cashier's desk.

Finding the store much more interesting than he had expected—and since they had some time to kill until the bullies went away—Youngho decided to look around a little. While Mr. Yang was talking to Manu, he started exploring the store for the first—and probably the last—time.

주인 아저씨는 "어, 너 만우 아니냐!" 하고는 크게 미소를 지으며 얼굴이 밝아지셨다. "오늘은 친구랑 같이 왔구나!"

"안녕하세요, 양 씨 아저씨! 그냥 학교 끝나고 한 번 와 봤어요." 만우가 꾸벅 배꼽인사를 하며 명랑하게 대답했다. 그리고는 재빨리 "이제 곧 크리스마스잖아요! 엄마한테 새로운 아이디어 좀 줘야죠" 하면서 꼭 올 수밖에 없었던 이유를 대려는 듯 둘러대더니, 주인 아저씨를 향해 영호의 등을 살짝 떠민다. "얘는 영혼데요—저희 학교 같은 반 친구예요."

살짝 창피해진 영호는 겨우 고개만 까딱하며 중얼댔다.

"아, 안녕하세요."

"그래, 둘 다 잘 왔다! 마음껏 둘러보구 뭐 필요한 것 있으면 나한테 말만 해!" 사람이 좋아 보이는 양 씨 아저씨가 말했다. "참, 여기 생강 과자—맘껏 먹어!"

아저씨가 계산대 저편 핑크색 접시에 수북이 쌓인 과자를 가리킨다.

상점은 영호가 생각했던 것보다도 훨씬 더 흥미로운 곳인 듯했고—또 어차피 깡패들이 갈 때까지 시간을 때워야만 했기에—한 번 구경이라도 해 보는 것도 괜찮을 듯했다. 영호는 주인 아저씨가 만우와 얘기를 나누고 있는 사이, 평생 처음이자 마지막이라는 생각으로 상점을 둘러보기 시작했다.

Although Youngho hadn't noticed it before, a Christmas garland hung on the glass door through which he had just rushed in. Wrapped in red and gold ribbons, it was peppered with sprigs of holly and pine cones; miniature Christmas stockings and mittens dangled underneath. Another snowman in a Santa hat adorned a corner of the window display by the entrance. Even the ceiling was covered with hundreds—perhaps thousands—of tiny lights that sparkled in different colors, resembling a colorful Milky Way.

Youngho walked further inside. As expected, he found furniture and home decor objects of all kinds, all arranged to look like an elegant living room—sofas, chairs, kitchen tables, carpets, even vases with fresh flowers, and real fruit in fruit bowls. At the same time, the store was unlike anything he had ever seen before. It was like a stylish living room, an upscale grocery store, and even a small museum all at once. Elegant objects, both modern and old, were displayed together in perfect harmony behind the model living room. Tall shelves lined the walls, filled with expensive-looking items from around the world—rare jams, caviar, goose liver, smoked salmon, and exotic spices, to name just a few.

Some of them were things Youngho had never even heard of in his life. One that particularly caught his attention was something called "boysenberry jam." It sounded English, and he was certain it was a kind of jam. *What kind of jam, though? Boys in a berry? Boys and berries? Surely, they don't mean that literally!*

처음에는 몰랐지만 방금 막 허겁지겁 들어온 유리문 위에도 벽트리 가랜드가 걸려 있었는데, 빨간색과 금색 리본으로 치장되어 홀리베리, 솔방울 등이 듬성듬성 박혀 있었다. 또 그 아래편에는 미니 크리스마스 양말과 벙어리 장갑이 대롱대롱 매달려 있고, 입구 유리창 한 귀퉁이에는 눈사람 인형이 산타 모자를 쓰고 서 있었다. 천장에는 수백 개, 아니 수천 개의 아주 작은 전구가 박혀 반짝반짝 색색 가지 빛을 내며 마치 알록달록한 은하수같이 보였다.

영호는 조금 더 안으로 들어가 보았다. 생각했던 것처럼 여러 가지 가구와 인테리어 제품들이 즐비했다. 그 모든 것들은 우아한 하나의 거실처럼 보이도록 배치되어 있었는데, 각종 소파, 의자, 식탁, 카페트 등은 물론이고 싱싱한 꽃까지 꽃병에 꽂혀 있고 과일 그릇에는 진짜 과일도 담겨 있었다. 동시에 상점은 영호가 보아온 그 어떤 곳과도 달랐는데, 마치 세련된 거실, 고급 식료품점, 심지어 작은 박물관까지 다 합쳐 놓은 듯했다. 가구 전시장 뒤로는 갖가지 품위 있는 물건들이 전통과 신세대의 완벽한 조화를 이루며 진열되어 있었고, 벽마다 즐비한 높은 진열장에는 세계 곳곳에서 들여온 고급 수입 식료품들로 가득했다. 희귀한 잼, 캐비어, 거위 간, 훈제 연어, 이국적인 향료 등등.

그중에는 태어나서 한 번도 듣도 보도 못한 것들도 있었다. 특별히 영호의 관심을 끈 것이 있다면 “보이젠베리 잼”이라고 하는 것이었다. 보이젠베리 잼...... 영어 같은데, 분명 잼 종류 중 하나임은 틀림이 없다. *그렇다면 무슨 잼일까?* “보이”는 영어로 소년이라는 뜻이고, “베리”라면 딸기, 블루베리 같은 열매 아닌가? *보이즈 인 베리? 아니면 보이즈 앤드 베리? 열매에 담근 소년? 소년과 열매? 설마 말 그대로는 아니겠지?*

Unaware that his mouth was slightly open, he thought to himself that he liked this peculiar name, even if he didn't quite understand what it was.

Forgetting all about the real reason he was there in the first place, Youngho slowly wandered further and further into the depths of the store, as if in a trance, examining the curious objects and foods that lined the shelves. It was as if he had just found out about a spectacular but silent carnival right next door that had been taking place without him knowing. Youngho started asking himself how he could have overlooked such a marvelous place right under his nose—practically next door to his school!

Toward the back of the store, Youngho discovered a bookcase full of all kinds of fascinating artifacts. For example, he saw wooden carvings of animals that mostly lived on the vast African plains, shaped from all sorts of wood—walnut, mahogany, maple, and pine, to name a few. Among them was a dancing monkey with one foot up, as if about to jump, and palms joined over its head in a clap; a cheering elephant, its trunk twirling upward; a sprinting cheetah suspended in midair with its front and back paws touching; a rhinoceros and a lion, nose to nose, glaring at each other as if about to start a bloody battle; and a giraffe stretching its long neck over them, looking on.

On the other side hung a green-scaled ceramic dragon, a ridge of red dorsal fins running down its spine, writhing and breathing fire over a horde of clay soldiers.

영호는 자기도 모르게 입을 헤 벌린 채, 무엇을 의미하는지 정확히 이해는 안 가지만 어쨌든 마음에 드는 특이한 이름이라고 생각했다.

영호는 애초에 상점에 왜 들어오게 되었는지 진짜 이유는 까맣게 잊은 채, 진열장에 나열된 신기한 식료품과 장식품 구경을 하며 무언가에 홀린 사람처럼 점점 더 깊숙이 상점 내부로 들어가기 시작했다. 마치 바로 옆 집에서 아주 화려한 축제가 영호 모르게 소리 없이 열려오고 있었던 것을 지금 금방 알게 된 듯한 느낌이었다. 영호는 이렇게 멋진 곳을 바로 코앞에 두고도 어떻게 모를 수가 있었을까, 생각해 보지 않을 수 없었다—그것도 거의 학교 바로 옆인 것을!

또 영호는 가게 뒷편에서 온갖 흥미진진한 물품들로 가득 찬 책장을 발견했다. 예를 들자면 드넓은 아프리카 초원에서나 살 법한 동물들의 조각품들이 보였는데, 호두나무, 마호가니, 단풍나무, 소나무 등 소재도 다양했다. 그중에는 한쪽 발을 들고 막 뛰어오르려 하면서 머리 위로는 두 손을 마주하여 박수치고 춤추는 원숭이, 코를 치켜들고 빙글빙글 돌리며 환호하는 코끼리, 공중에 붕 떠서 앞발과 뒷발이 닿도록 질주하는 치타, 곧 피 튀기는 격투라도 시작 할듯 서로 코를 맞대고 노려보는 코뿔소와 사자, 그 위로 기나긴 목을 빼고 지켜보는 기린 등등.

다른 한편에는 녹색 비늘에 등을 따라 적색 지느러미가 능선을 그린 도자기 용이 매달려 꿈틀대며 한 무리의 점토 병사대 위로 불을 토하고 있었다.

Beneath the carved animals lay a decorative skull, painted in a bright kaleidoscope of colors and patterns, side by side with a soccer ball made from an equally splendid patchwork of leather. These were placed together with objects that looked like souvenirs from different countries around the world. Maybe Mr.Yang was a globetrotter himself, or they simply stood for each corner of the earth.

In the same bookcase, small posters and artworks were also on display. There was a portrait of a beautiful dark-skinned woman in colorful clothes and lots of jewels; she was staring back at Youngho, as if her eyes had been following him all along.

One poster showed the profile of an elegant blonde woman wearing a scarlet dress, her long golden hair flowing behind her. She was drinking from a tall, slender wineglass against the backdrop of the Eiffel Tower. The clear, light-gold drink in the glass looked like apple juice with bubbles in it. A little image of a bottle was imprinted at the bottom right corner of the poster. Youngho also saw the same bottles and glasses on the shelves immediately underneath. He tried to get a better look, but they were all locked behind glass doors. He peered through the glass with his nose pressed against it.

"Oh, you like my champagne collection, do you?" sounded Mr. Yang's delighted voice—from right behind him.

Taken by surprise, Youngho jumped and lightly head-butted the glass panel in front of him. Deep in thought, he hadn't heard Mr. Yang approach. To his relief, the glass didn't break, and no damage was done. He could just see a small, round smudge of moisture—probably sweat from his nose.

또 동물들의 조각상 아래로는 알록달록한 색상과 무늬로 장식된 해골 모형, 그리고 역시 현란한 디자인의 가죽을 기워 만든 축구공이 나란히 놓여 있었다. 마치 세계 여러 나라에서 가져온 여행 기념품같이 보이는 것들도 함께 놓여 있었는데, 아마도 양 씨 아저씨의 취미가 해외여행이거나, 아니면 그저 지구 방방곡곡을 나타내려는 것일 수도 있지 싶었다.

같은 책장에는 또 작은 포스터와 미술품 등도 전시되어 있었는데, 한 그림은 갈색 피부를 한 아름다운 여인을 그린 초상화였다. 알록달록한 옷차림에 온갖 보석으로 치장을 한 여인은 영호를 뚫어지게 바라보고 있는 듯했고, 눈이 마치 영호를 따라 움직이는 것처럼 보였다.

한 포스터는 우아한 금발 여인의 옆모습을 담고 있었는데, 선홍색 원피스를 입고 긴 노랑 머리를 뒤로 날리며 에펠탑 앞에서 가늘고 길쭉한 와인잔에 담긴 무언가를 마시고 있었다. 잔에 들어 있는 음료는 맑고 살짝 금빛이 돌아 사과 주스처럼 보였는데, 사이다처럼 기포가 있었다. 포스터 아래편 오른 쪽 구석에는 와인 병 사진이 작게 찍혀 있었는데, 책장 바로 아래 칸에는 똑같은 병과 잔들이 들어 있는 것이 보였다. 영호는 더 자세히 보려고 했으나, 모두 유리문 뒤에 놓여 자물쇠로 잠겨 있었다. 영호는 유리문에 코를 바짝 붙이고 들여다보았다.

“아, 내가 수집한 샴페인 컬렉션이 마음에 드나 보구나!” 주인 아저씨가 영호 바로 뒤에서 감탄한 목소리로 외쳤다.

화들짝 놀란 영호는 움찔하면서 그만 눈 앞에 있는 유리문을 살짝 박치기해 버리고 말았다. 깊은 생각에 잠겨 양 씨 아저씨가 다가오는 소리를 듣지 못한 것이다. 하지만 천만 다행으로 유리는 깨지 않았고 훼손은 없었다. 영호의 코에서 난 땀인지 그냥 작고 동그란 자국이 촉촉하게 묻어 있을 뿐.

"요새는 샴페인을 그렇게 길쭉한 잔에다 마신단다. 거품 빠져나가지 말라구!" 아저씨가 설명하신다.

영호는 양 씨 아저씨가 말씀하시는 동안, 유리문에 아무런 이상이 없기 만을 조용히 바랄 뿐이었다. *그건 그렇고 "산 페인" 이라? 한 번도 들어본 적이 없는데. 저렇게 예뻐 보이는데 이름이 "페인"이라니. 정말?*

"아, 네......" 영호가 어색하게 웃으며 대답했다. 분명 구하기 힘든 수입품일 테고, 또 엄청나게 비쌀 것 같은데...... 하마터면 그걸 다 한꺼번에 박살낼 뻔했다니. 영호의 머릿속은 아직도 그 생각뿐이었다.

"크리스마스 선물루두 아주 운치가 있지. 부모님한테 드리기두 적합하구...... 네가 원하면 아예 넓적한 전통식 잔도 있어."

"Nowadays, champagne is served in elongated flutes like that to keep the bubbles from escaping," Mr. Yang explained.

As Mr. Yang spoke, Youngho silently hoped that he hadn't done any damage to the glass door. *Sham pain, though? Never heard of it. Could "pain" be the name for something that looks so delightful? Seriously?*

"I see," Youngho replied with an awkward smile, still thinking about how close he had come to destroying an exclusive collection of imported—probably very expensive—bottles.

"Champagne glasses can make elegant Christmas gifts—for your parents, for example. I have the classic wide-mouthed coupes, too, of course, if you want!"

2-1 '지상천국'·Paradise on Earth

"Of course. . ."

Christmas? Youngho's family didn't celebrate it anymore. Minji, Youngho's older sister, usually did something with friends, but that was it. Christmas wasn't a traditional Korean holiday, and not everyone observed it, as Mr. Yang surely knew. Some people went to church if they were Christian. Unless they had small kids, of course—small kids loved Christmas regardless of tradition and religion. When Youngho was little, his family used to set up a Christmas tree, and he would also get presents. It all stopped around the time he turned ten, although he couldn't remember exactly why.

Then he thought he saw a faint crack in the glass door, right where he had noticed the sweat mark. It could have been the smudge seen from another angle, but he just wanted to get away from there as soon as possible.

"I'll show you both models if you want," Mr. Yang said excitedly. "Can you take a step away from there, please?"

"It's okay!" Youngho blurted in panic, doing everything he could to draw Mr. Yang's attention away from the glass door.

Before Youngho could stop him, Mr. Yang took him by the shoulders to ease him aside, produced a key from his back pocket, and slipped it into the lock. With an enthusiastic flair, he then turned the key and slid the glass door open. Youngho looked on, his face ashen. The whole world seemed to freeze in that split second.

Before long, the inevitable happened.

"네……"

크리스마스? 영호의 가족은 이제 크리스마스를 쇠지 않았다. 누나인 민지는 보통 친구들과 만나서 무언가 하곤 했지만, 그것이 전부였다. 양 씨 아저씨도 무엇보다 잘 아시겠지만, 크리스마스는 한국 전통 명절도 아니고, 쇠는 사람들도 그다지 많지는 않다. 혹 기독교인이라면 교회에 나가겠지만. 또 어린 애들이 있다면 물론 얘기가 달라졌다. 어린 애들은 전통과 종교를 막론하고 크리스마스를 아주 좋아했다. 영호가 어렸을 때는 가족끼리 크리스마스트리도 세우고 선물도 받고 했었는데, 정확히 어떻게 그랬는지 기억은 잘 나지 않지만 대충 열 살 정도 된 후 그것도 다 멈춰버렸다.

그때였다. 유리문에 땀 자국이 묻은 것을 보았던 바로 그 자리에, 희미하게 금이 간 것이 눈에 들어왔다. 물론 땀 자국을 다른 각도에서 보아서 그런 것일 수도 있었다. 하지만 영호는 그저 그 자리에서 최대한 빨리 벗어나고 싶은 생각밖에 없었다.

"두 가지 종류 다 보여 줄까?" 양 씨 아저씨가 신바람이 나서 말하신다. "거기 좀 비켜 볼래?"

"아니, 괜찮아요!" 당황한 영호가 불쑥 내뱉었다. 영호는 어떻게 해서라도 아저씨의 관심을 유리문에서 돌려보고자 온갖 노력을 다 했다.

하지만 모든 것이 무용지물. 양 씨 아저씨는 영호의 어깨를 두 손으로 잡고 옆으로 살짝 밀더니, 뒷주머니에서 열쇠 하나를 꺼내어 자물쇠에 넣으셨다. 그리고는 과장된 몸짓으로 열쇠를 돌리고는 유리문을 밀어제치셨다. 영호는 얼굴이 백지장처럼 되어 그저 지켜보기만 할 뿐. 온 세상이 그 한 순간에 얼어붙어 버린 것같이 느껴졌다.

얼마 있지 않아 올 것이 오고야 말았다.

It started with a hairline crack, which appeared where Youngho thought he had seen the sweat stain. Then it zigzagged down the panel with a low, sinister creak. In a moment, the whole glass door came down and hit the floor with a resounding *crash!* Splinters of glass flew everywhere.

Mr. Yang let out a cry of horror. "Oh, I'm so sorry!" he said, looking genuinely apologetic. "Are you okay? Thank God it didn't fall while you were still standing there! It has never happened before, oh, no . . ." Then he ran around, sweeping the floor and vacuuming the tiny shards. Luckily, Youngho had been drawn away by Mr. Yang before the glass door collapsed. He was left unscathed—not even a single scratch.

"Are you sure you're okay? I'm truly sorry!" Mr. Yang repeated, looking quite worried.

"Yeah, I'm fine!" Youngho answered hurriedly. "I might actually have—"

"Oh, no, it's not your fault!" Mr. Yang said in alarm, palms raised as if to wave it off. He just didn't give Youngho a chance to explain.

"I suppose these old glass doors need to be replaced," Mr. Yang murmur to himself.

As if abruptly awakened from a delightful dream, Youngho turned around and started looking for Manu. He wasn't surprised to find him by the cash register, munching gingerbread cookies and playing a game on his phone. Youngho was quite sure that the plate had been full when they arrived. It was nearly empty now.

땀 자국이 묻었다고 생각했던 그 자리에서 시작된 미세한 금은 낮게 *뿌지직* 불길한 소리를 내며 유리판 위에 지그재그를 그리며 내려갔다. 그리고는 순식간에 유리판 전체가 *와장창!* 하고 큰 소리를 내며 바닥에 떨어지고, 여기저기 유리 조각을 날리며 깨졌다.

양 씨 아저씨가 당혹한 비명을 지르고는 "어, 쏘리!" 하며 진심으로 미안한 표정을 지으셨다. "어디 다치지는 않았어? 그 앞에 서 있을 때 깨지지 않은 게 천만다행이다! 이제까지 이런 적이 한 번도 없었는데, 이런……" 그리고는 바닥을 쓸고 진공 청소기로 작은 유리 파편을 빨아들이는 등 바쁘게 움직이셨다. 다행히도 영호는 유리문이 깨지기 전에 아저씨가 옆으로 비키도록 한 덕분에 머리 톨 하나도 다친 곳이 없었다.

"정말 괜찮아? 진짜 미안하게 됐다!" 양 씨 아저씨가 걱정된 눈빛으로 거듭 말했다.

"네, 다친 데 없어요!" 영호가 서둘러 대답하고는 덧붙였다. "사실 제가—"

"아니, 네 잘못이 아니야!" 아저씨가 놀란 표정을 지으며 양손을 저었다. 그리고는 아무리 영호가 설명을 하려고 해도 도저히 기회를 주지 않았다.

"유리문이 오래 돼서 새로 바꿔야 할 것 같네." 양 씨가 혼잣말처럼 중얼거렸다.

영호는 좋은 꿈을 꾸다가 갑자기 깨어난 사람처럼 뒤돌아서 만우를 찾아 나섰다. 만우는 예상했던 대로 계산대 앞에 서서 생강 과자를 먹으며 휴대폰으로 게임을 하고 있었다. 가게에 들어올 때만 해도 한 접시 수북이 담겨져 있었던 것 같은데, 이제 거의 텅 비어 있었다.

"Did you get in trouble again, Fox?" mumbled Manu absently through a full mouth. "Try some gingerbread cookies," he continued without waiting for an answer. "They're really good! Your benevolent master has saved the best ones for you, of course!"

Sometimes Manu called himself Youngho's master as if Youngho were his servant, which Youngho mostly ignored. Youngho picked one up and bit into it. Sweet and gingery, it tasted delicious, with a hint of pepper and exotic spices. Youngho took a few more.

"Yeah, you're right, they're good." Youngho had to agree with Manu. "But they're all exactly the same! Best ones, you lying pig!"

Youngho sent him a bogus backhand strike. Manu covered his head with both arms and rounded his mouth in a silent but exaggerated scream of terror. Youngho looked around quickly for Mr. Yang. He was nowhere to be seen, probably still busy cleaning up. Youngho turned back to Manu, and crinkled his nose as if in disdain.

"Are you sure you'll be hungry enough for dinner after all this?" taunted Youngho. "Or are you on a gingerbread diet? Living only on gingerbread cookies up to Christmas, or something!"

"Help yourselves to the cookies!" Mr. Yang's amiable voice sounded from the back of the store. Presently, he reappeared, carrying a mop and a bucket in his hands. "I can always take out more, you know. In fact, I needed your help—I need to get rid of them by Christmas!"

"여우야, 또 사고 쳤냐?" 만우가 한 입 가득 과자를 씹다가 지나가는 말처럼 우물거렸다. 그리고는 영호가 미처 대답하기도 전에, "여기 생강 과자 좀 먹어 봐!" 한다. "진짜 맛있어! 인자하신 주인님께서 너 먹으라고 젤 좋은 것들만 남겨 놨지 않냐!"

만우는 가끔씩 스스로를 영호의 주인님이라고 불렀다. 마치 영호가 무슨 하인이라도 된 것처럼. 영호는 보통 그런 만우를 그냥 무시해 버렸다. 과자 하나를 집어 한입 베어 물었다. 달콤한 생강 맛에 뭐랄까 아주 살짝 톡 쏘는 듯한 이국적인 향료의 맛. 두어 개 더 집어 먹어 보았다.

"응, 진짜 맛있다……" 여기까지는 만우와 동의했다. "근데 전부 다 똑같은데 젤 좋은 것들만 골라서 뭐가 어째, 이 거짓말쟁이 돼지야!"

영호는 손등으로 만우를 치는 시늉을 했다. 만우가 양 팔로 머리를 감싸 안으며 입을 둥그렇게 벌리고 소리 없이 과장되게 공포의 비명을 지르는 척한다. 영호는 재빨리 주인 아저씨가 어디 있는지 돌아보았다. 아직 청소하느라 바쁘신지 보이지 않았다. 다시 만우에게 돌아서서 코를 찌푸리고는,

"과자루 배 채우구 또 저녁은 먹을 수 있냐?"하고 놀려댔다. "아니면 생강 과자 다이어트하냐? 크리스마스 때까지 생강 과자만 먹고 사는 다이어트!"

"과자 마음껏 많이들 먹어라!" 가게 뒤편에서 양 씨 아저씨의 상냥한 목소리가 들리더니, 곧 대걸레와 양동이를 각 손에 들고 나타나셨다. "과자는 또 꺼내 놓으면 되니까. 사실 너희들 도움이 필요하던 참이었다—크리스마스 전에 다 없애야 하거든!"

"Thank you very much, Mr. Yang!" said the two boys in chorus, putting on their sweetest cherubic smiles.

"Shall we go now?" Youngho whispered to Manu. "I've gotta go home soon. Mom's gonna freak out if I come home late without an excuse." Lately, Mom had gotten cranky and anxious about everything.

"All right. They must have left by now," Manu replied as he stuffed the last few cookies into his mouth all at once and gulped them down at an almost supernatural speed.

They? Mesmerized by his discoveries until now, Youngho had almost forgotten about the three bullies, as if the whole thing had been in the distant past. Anyway, there was nothing to lose in being careful. He nodded to Manu.

"Let's use the back door, though—just in case," whispered Manu in Youngho's ear.

As they headed toward the back door, they passed Mr. Yang up on a ladder, stocking the shelves.

"Bye, Mr. Yang! We're leaving!" Manu shouted.

"Bye now! Say hi to your mom!" said Mr. Yang, steadying himself on the ladder while holding several colorful cushions in one hand and a canister full of who-knows-what in the other.

Manu seemed to know the place well. He led Youngho through the narrow labyrinth of boxes, jars, and pieces of furniture crowding the back of the store. Without a word, Youngho followed him out onto the street through the back door.

"감사합니다, 아저씨!" 두 소년이 아기천사처럼 천진난만한 미소를 지으며 동시에 합창하듯 대답한다.

"인제 그만 갈까?" 영호가 만우를 향해 속삭였다. "집에 갈 때도 다 되구. 이유없이 집에 늦게 가면 울 엄마 또 난리 날껄." 엄마는 최근 들어서 왠지 모르게 신경이 날카롭고 뭐든지 걱정이 많아졌다.

"그럴까, 깡패놈들 인젠 갔겠지." 만우가 남은 생강 과자 몇 개를 한꺼번에 입에 쑤셔 넣더니 순식간에 거의 초인간적인 속도로 씹어 삼키고는 대답했다.

깡패? 영호는 지금까지 모든 새로운 발견에 홀려서, 애초에 불량배들을 만났던 것 조차 먼 과거의 일처럼 잊고 있었던 것이다. 하지만 어쨌든 조심해서 나쁠 것은 없다고 생각하고 고개를 끄덕였다.

"그래두 혹시 모르니까 뒷문으로 가자." 만우가 영호에게 귓속말로 속삭인다.

두 소년은 뒷문으로 향했다. 양 씨 아저씨는 가게 뒤편에서 사다리에 올라서서 진열장에 물건을 채우고 있었다.

"아저씨, 저희 가요! 안녕히 계세요!" 만우가 외쳤다.

"그래, 잘 가라! 어머니한테 인사 전하구!" 양 씨 아저씨가 사다리 위에서 한 손에는 알록달록한 방석 여러 개를 들고, 다른 쪽 손에는 무엇인지 가득 찬 통을 들고 서서 아슬아슬하게 균형을 잡으며 대답했다.

만우는 잘 아는 곳이라서 그런지, 영호를 이끌고 가게 뒤편을 빼곡하게 메우고 있는 상자, 병, 가구 등 사이로 굽이굽이 좁은 통로를 따라 빠져나갔다. 영호는 말없이 만우의 뒤를 따라 뒷문 밖의 거리로 나섰다.

As Youngho stepped outside after Manu, his jaw dropped. The door opened onto a pedestrian street lined with stores and cafés. It was a fairly busy street, if not exactly bustling with life. The whole street was decorated in a spectacular Christmas theme now. Of course, Youngho had seen the same area with Christmas decorations before, but it was the first time this year. It looked even brighter, warmer, and more captivating than he had ever witnessed in his six years going to school around here—half his life! It was as if the buildings had been competing with one another to catch the attention of passersby. He had never been inside Paradise on Earth before, so he didn't know that there was a shortcut through the back door either.

"Wow, Dumpling! How did you know there was a back door?" Youngho said, eyes still on the dazzling street.

"Well, you don't need to be so impressed, Foxy," replied Manu matter-of-factly. "I come here quite often with my mom. I'm her proferssional shopping-bag porter, you see. She thinks I've been gifted with exceptional physical strength!" Manu said, playfully flexing his muscles.

"Are those actual muscles, though?" Youngho joked. "Or just bulging fat? Hahaha!"

Before Manu had time to react, Youngho put an arm around his shoulders, nodded solemnly, and said, "But that was some serious reflexes back there, Dumpling! I give you that!" Then he quickly added, "I didn't know pigs also had reflexes! Hehe!" and took off, laughing loudly.

만우를 따라 밖으로 나선 영호는 입이 저절로 벌어지지 않을 수 없었다. 뒷문 쪽 골목은 여러 가지 상점과 카페 등이 줄지어 서 있는 보행자 전용 거리였는데, 굳이 번화가는 아니더라도 나름대로 활기 넘치는 거리였다. 그 골목 전체가 크리스마스를 테마로 화려하게 꾸며져 있었던 것이다. 물론 같은 거리에 크리스마스 장식이 되어 있는 것을 이전에도 보았지만 올해는 처음이었고, 이제까지 6년—영호의 반 인생!—동안 오고 가며 보아왔던 그 어느 해보다도 더 밝고 따사롭게 눈을 사로잡았다. 마치 건물들이 지나가는 사람들의 관심을 끌기 위해 서로 경쟁이라도 하듯. 예전에는 '지상천국' 안에 발을 들인 적이 한 번도 없었으므로, 상점 뒷문에서 나오는 지름길이 있다는 것도 알지 못했다.

"우와, 군만두, 넌 뒷문이 있는 건 어떻게 알았냐?" 영호가 화사하게 꾸며진 거리에서 눈을 떼지 않은 채 말했다.

"어, 그렇게 감탄할 것 없어, 여우야." 만우가 아무렇지도 않게 대꾸한다. "우리 엄마 따라서 자주 오는 곳이야. 내가 이래봬두 울 엄마 쑈핑빽 나르는 데 전문 아니냐! 이 몸이 힘 한바탕 쓴다구 생각하걸랑!" 만우가 장난스럽게 근육을 돋우어 보이는 시늉을 했다.

"어, 근데 그거 근육 맞어?" 영호가 농담으로 받아친다. "그냥 지방이 튀어나와서 그런 거 아냐? 하하하!"

만우가 미처 반응을 보기도 전에, 영호는 만우의 어깨에 팔을 두르고 엄숙하게 고개를 끄덕이며 말했다. "근데 아깐 정말 순발력 대단했어, 군만두! 그거 하나는 인정한다." 그리고는 다시 재빨리, "돼지두 순발력이 있다는 건 미처 몰랐네! 히히!" 하더니 큰 소리를 내고 낄낄 웃으며 도망쳤다.

2-2 크리스마스 거리·The Christmas Street

"뭐라구! 여우 너 일찍 죽을려구 작정했냐?" 만우가 소리를 지르고는 그 뒤를 쫓아 달려간다. 그러다가 갑자기 멈춰 서더니 영호의 등 뒤를 가리키며 말했다. "어, 저기! 너 여자친구 온다...... 신지선!"

"거짓말!"

"거짓말 아니야......"

지선은 영호가 흠모하는 같은 반 여학생이었다. 누가 물어도 주저 없이 학교 전체에서 가장 예쁘다고 대답할 수 있었다. 당연히 다른 애들도 좋아하는 애들이 많았다. 게다가 착하기까지 했다—예뻐도 잘난 체하고 속이 썩어 문드러진 그런 여자애들과는 달리. 하지만 아쉽게도 지선은 영호의 여자친구는 아니었다. 뿐만 아니라 사실은 그다지 친하지도 않았다.

"What! You wanna die young, Fox?" Manu shouted, running after him. Then he stopped dead and said, "Look! It's your girlfriend, Jisun!"

"Liar!"

"I'm not lying . . ."

Jisun was a girl from their class Youngho liked. If anybody asked him, he would reply without hesitation that she was the prettiest in the whole school. Naturally, she had other admirers too. Plus, she was kind as well—unlike some other girls who were pretty outside but stuck-up and rotten inside. Unfortunately, though, she was not his girlfriend. Far from it—they weren't even that close, in fact.

Youngho even wondered if she would even notice if he got sick and missed school one day.

Manu had been telling the truth. Jisun and two other girls came out of one of the stores, giggling and completely ignoring the two boys. Instantly, Youngho stopped running away from Manu, his gaze following Jisun's back. Her shiny, straight hair swayed from side to side behind her as she disappeared into the distance.

"Stop drooling and close your mouth, will ya?" Manu snickered.

"Shut up, you burnt pork dumpling! You got a death wish, or what?"

The boys launched into another mock fight. They were only playing, but Youngho hit harder this time.

Nooooo! Manu rounded his lips in a dramatic scream without sound, clawed at the air, and staggered a few steps.

It was then that something caught Youngho's eye. He spotted a miniature Christmas tree with toy presents underneath in one of the display windows along the street. The tiny gold and silver gift boxes were tied with pink and sky-blue ribbons.

"Dumpling, do you still get Christmas presents, by any chance?" Youngho murmured, coming to a stop.

"No, it's been ages!" Manu said, his hand still raised in midair as if frozen in time, yet ready to deal a bogus blow at any moment. "I'm struggling to get even St. Manu's Day presents these days, you know. How 'bout you?" Manu called his own birthday "St. Manu's Day."

영호는 만약 어느 날 아파서 결석을 한다 해도 지선이 알기라도 할까 하는 생각도 해 보았다.

만우의 말은 사실이었다. 지선은 다른 여학생 두 명과 함께 어느 가게에서 나오다가 꺄르르 웃음을 터뜨리고는, 두 소년을 본 척도 하지 않았다. 영호는 순간 만우에게서 도망가기를 멈추고 지선의 뒷모습을 바라보았다. 윤기 나는 긴 생머리가 등 뒤로 찰랑찰랑 흔들리며 멀어져 갔다.

"야, 침 떨어지겠다. 입 좀 닫아라!" 만우가 키득키득 웃으며 한마디 한다.

"우씨, 다 타 버린 돼지 군만두! 너 죽구 싶어서 그러냐?"

둘이는 다시 치고 박고 장난을 시작했다. 영호는 장난이긴 했지만 이번엔 좀 더 세게 때렸다.

만우가 *으악!* 하며 입을 벌려 과장되게 소리 없는 비명을 지르더니, 손을 뻗어 허공을 거머쥐고는 휘청휘청 몇 발짝 뗀다.

그러다가 길가 어느 진열대 유리창 안에 놓인 미니 크리스마스트리와 그 밑에 놓인 모형 선물 꾸러미가 영호의 눈에 들어왔다. 금색 은색 포장지에 핑크색과 하늘색 리본이 둘러져 있었다.

"군만두, 너 혹시 아직두 크리스마스 선물 받냐?" 영호가 장난을 멈추고 물었다.

"아니, 안 받은 지 오래지!" 만우가 시간이 정지해 버리기라도 한 듯, 하지만 언제라도 금세 공격을 가할 수 있도록 허공에 주먹을 쥐어 든 채 대답했다. "만우절 선물두 받을까 말깐데. 너는?" 만우는 스스로의 생일을 '만우절'이라고 불렀다.

"Same here . . . it's been a while," Youngho muttered pensively.

He knew that Christmas wasn't a traditional Korean holiday, and it was probably a thing of the past now that he was almost in his teens. Yet he missed the times when his family would set up a tree and celebrate it—as well as the music, warmth, and laughter. Those were happier times.

Youngho and Manu started wandering up and down the street, looking at Christmas decorations and grading them from best to worst. After a while, they headed home to make it in time for dinner.

“나두…… 꽤 됐지.” 영호가 생각에 잠긴 듯 말했다.

물론 크리스마스가 한국 전통 명절이 아니라는 것도 알았고, 또 거의 십 대가 다 된 지금에 와서는 이미 한 물 건너간 이야기라는 것도 알았다. 그럼에도 가족이 함께 트리를 장식하고 크리스마스를 쇠던 때가 그리웠다. 크리스마스 음악, 그때 느꼈던 따스함, 웃음 등과 함께. 참 행복했던 시절이었던 것 같다.

두 소년은 그렇게 길을 왔다 갔다 하며 크리스마스 장식 구경을 했고, 가장 잘 꾸민 집, 못 꾸민 집 순위로 점수를 매기다가 저녁 식사 시간에 늦지 않게 각자 집으로 향했다.

3

여우의 소굴

THE FOX'S DEN

영호네 집은 아파트 11층이었는데, 15층 건물 3개로 구성된 아파트 단지에 지하 주차장, 공용 잔디밭, 놀이터 등의 시설이 구비되어 있었다.

Youngho's family lived on the eleventh floor of an apartment complex that consisted of three fifteen-story buildings with an underground parking garage, a shared lawn, and a playground.

Within walking distance of Jinsung Elementary School, the apartment had three bedrooms, a living room, an open-plan kitchen connected to the living room, two bathrooms—including the one in the primary bedroom that Mom and Dad used—and a small utility room. Two balconies joined together in an L-shape. Youngho felt especially lucky that, from his bedroom window, he had a beautiful view over the park and the river. The bedroom faced west, and although Minji said a window was best facing south—hers next door also faced west—Youngho loved watching the sunset over the park. He also took Chadori, the family dog, there on walks every day.

It was Sunday evening at last. Youngho liked Sundays. It would be Monday tomorrow, which meant he would be going back to school. Hurray! Jokes aside, he did like Sundays a lot. While his family rarely saw one another during the week, they always got together for dinner on this one evening. The truth was that they now had almost all their meals separately. Everybody was just so busy all the time doing their own things—work, school, friends, colleagues—that nobody seemed to care about being a family anymore.

Well, except Mom. Youngho knew that Mom still cared; she had recently quit her job and had a whole lot more time on her hands. Yet it didn't change things very much, apart from the fact that she was at home most of the time now and Youngho didn't have to eat dinner alone.

또 진성초등학교에서 걸어서 얼마 되지 않는 거리에 위치해 있었다. 방 세 칸, 거실, 거실과 연결되어 트인 부엌, 욕실 두 개—엄마 아빠가 쓰는 안방에 있는 것까지 합해서—그리고 작은 다용도실 하나가 있었고, 베란다 두 개가 'ㄱ'자를 그리며 연결되어 있었는데, 영호가 특히 행운이라고 생각했던 것은 방 창문에서 공원과 강이 내려다보여 경치가 좋다는 점이었다. 영호의 방은 서향이었는데, 누나는 남향이 가장 좋은 창문 방향이라고 했지만—영호 옆방을 쓰는 누나의 창문도 역시 서향이었다—영호는 공원 너머로 해가 지는 것을 구경하기를 즐겼고, 그 공원으로 반려견 차도리를 데리고 매일 산책을 가기도 했다.

드디어 일요일 저녁. 영호는 일요일 저녁이 좋았다. 내일 월요일이 찾아오면 다시 학교에 갈 수 있으니까. 만세! 농담은 제쳐놓고, 정말로 일요일 저녁이 참 좋았다. 가족들이 주중에는 서로 얼굴 보기도 힘들었던 반면, 일요일 저녁만은 꼭 함께 모여 저녁을 먹었기 때문이다. 사실 영호네 가족은 이제 거의 매일 밥도 각자 따로 먹었다. 모두가 제각기 직장, 학교, 친구, 동료 등으로 항상 바빴기 때문이다. 이제 다들 가족 생활에는 전혀 관심이 없는 듯했다.

엄마를 빼면 말이다. 그래도 엄마는 아직 가족을 챙겼고, 최근 직장을 그만두고 시간이 상당히 넉넉해졌다. 하지만 그 후로 특별히 달라진 것은 없었다. 엄마가 이제 거의 대부분 집에 있고, 영호가 저녁을 혼자 먹지 않아도 된다는 것을 제외하면.

And Youngho liking Sunday evenings didn't mean that he disliked school. True, some teachers complained that he wasn't focused enough on the lessons, but Youngho himself enjoyed the classes and mostly got on with everybody. Even when teachers caught him playing silly pranks or distracting others in the class, they couldn't be mad at him for very long; they just had to take one look at his cheeky but harmless face and they would see at once that his smile was genuine.

Nevertheless, when he got into his downward spiral of getting into one mess after another, there was no stopping him. Like the time he had been running around the classroom with Manu during a break—Manu said something annoying just to get on his nerves and dashed to the front of the class. They started chasing each other, jumping from desk to desk; all the other kids in the room were watching and cheering them on.

For some stupid reason—without thinking at all, obviously—Youngho hurled his lunch box full of food at Manu while Manu was jumping up and down on a desk near the classroom door. Youngho flung it high over Manu's head, of course, as the purpose—if there had been any—was just to scare him a bit, not to knock him out. As intended, it didn't hit Manu. Instead, it slipped from Youngho's hand, flew a little too high, and hit the wall over the door; the plastic lid popped off and its contents, including *kimchi*—pickled vegetables in chili and garlic brine—tumbled all over the place.

그리고 영호가 일요일 저녁을 좋아한다고 해서 학교가 싫어서 그러는 것은 아니었다. 물론 선생님들은 수업시간에 제대로 집중을 하지 않는다고 나무라는 경우도 더러 있었지만, 영호 스스로는 수업이 재미있었고, 반 친구들과도 대부분 잘 어울렸다. 혹 수업시간에 실없는 장난을 치거나 학습 분위기를 흐리다가 선생님께 들키더라도, 그 노여움이 오래 가지는 못했다. 맹랑할지라도 악의는 없는 영호의 얼굴을 보면 그 미소가 진실된 것임을 단번에 알 수 있었던 것이다.

하지만 영호가 일단 잇따른 문제의 소용돌이에 한번 휘말리기 시작하면 도저히 멈출 수 있는 방법이 없었다. 얼마 전 쉬는 시간에 만우와 교실에서 뛰어다니다가 있었던 일처럼. 만우가 뭐라고 장난으로 영호를 놀리고는 교실 앞쪽으로 재빨리 도망갔었다. 두 소년은 책상에서 책상으로 뛰어다니며 쫓고 쫓기기 시작했고, 같은 반 아이들까지 모두 구경하며 함성을 질렀다.

그러다가 영호가 생각 없이 바보 같은 일을 저지르고 말았다. 만우가 교실 앞문 옆 책상 위에서 방방 뛰고 있었을 때였다. 영호가 음식이 가득 찬 도시락통을 만우를 향해 내던진 것이다. 물론 만우의 머리 위로 높이 던졌다. 전혀 생각 없이 저지른 일이기는 했지만, 목적이 있었다면 단순히 겁을 좀 주려는 것이었지, 만우를 때려잡자는 것이 아니었기 때문이다. 어쨌든 의도했던 바와 같이 만우의 머리에 맞지는 않았지만, 대신 살짝 영호의 손에서 빠져나가 좀 너무 멀리 위로 날아가 버렸다. 도시락통은 문 위 벽에 부딪혔고, 플라스틱 뚜껑이 열리면서 그 안에 들어있던 밥, 반찬—김치를 포함한—이 여기저기 흩어졌다.

In a panic, Youngho rushed to the bathroom, found a bucket, and spent the rest of the break frantically cleaning up his spilled lunch before the next class started. However, most of the *kimchi* had fallen on top of the doorframe. Since Youngho was not particularly tall, he had to drag the podium toward the door and balance precariously on top of it to clean up the mess—the stinky, fermented, garlicky vegetables dripping blood-red chili brine—into the bucket. He thought he was being clever when he left some room between the podium and the door, planning to slip out through the gap to get rid of the bucket afterward.

After a while—having cleaned up just about everything—he was tiptoeing dangerously on the podium and leaning almost entirely against the door to keep his balance as he prepared to jump down. At that exact same moment, the door slid open and Mr. Choi burst in. The unsuspecting math teacher walked straight into the podium, which fell with a deafening *crash!* At the same time, Youngho lost his balance and toppled helplessly, with the bucket falling upside down over the poor teacher's head. Youngho found out afterward that Mr. Choi came back to fetch the reading glasses he had forgotten at the end of the previous class. Instead of his glasses, Mr. Choi received the crown of an upturned bucket *and* the baptism of Youngho's lunch pouring down on him.

놀란 영호는 허둥지둥 화장실로 달려가 양동이를 찾아오고, 남은 쉬는 시간 내내 다음 시간이 시작되기 전 흔적을 없애기 위해 흘린 도시락을 줍고 닦고 했다. 하지만 김치 대부분은 앞문틀 위에 떨어졌고, 키가 작은 영호의 손이 닿지 않아 교단을 문 앞에 끌어다 놓고 그 위에서 아슬아슬하게 균형을 잡으며 치우는 수밖에 없었다. 신내를 풍기며 시뻘건 피같은 국물이 뚝뚝 떨어지는 김치를 양동이에 주워 담았다. 영호는 문과 교단 사이에 나중에 다 치우면 양동이를 들고 빠져나갈 만한 자리를 조금 남겨 두었고, 스스로 똑똑한 처신이라고 생각했다.

조금 뒤, 교단 위에서 내내 위태롭게 까치발을 하고 쫑쫑대던 영호가 대충 다 치우고 막 교단을 뛰어내리려는 찰나였다. 영호가 몸을 굽히면서 균형을 유지하기 위해 교문에 거의 완전히 기대었다. 바로 그때 갑자기 미닫이문이 쓱 열리면서 멋모르는 수학 담당 최 선생님이 들이닥쳤고, 순간 교단과 정면으로 충돌했다. 교단이 쿵! 하고 큰 소리를 내며 쓰러지고, 이와 동시에 중심을 잃은 영호가 앞으로 고꾸라졌다. 그리고는 그만 손에 들고 있던 양동이로 수학 선생님의 머리를 덮어씌우고 만 것이다. 나중에 알게 된 바에 의하면 최 선생님은 전 시간이었던 수학 수업이 끝나고 놓고 간 돋보기 안경을 가지러 왔던 것이라고 했다. 최 선생님은 안경 대신 엎어진 양동이 왕관을 쓰게 되었고, 음식물 세례까지 함께 받은 것이다.

As if that wasn't enough, Miss Lee, Youngho's homeroom teacher, happened to be walking by. When she heard the podium falling and kids screaming, she rushed into the room to find her class in chaos and Mr. Choi with a bucket over his head, dripping what she believed was blood. She ran screaming to call the ambulance and bring the school nurse. In the end, nobody was injured and no real damage was done. However, the unfortunate Mr. Choi reeked of *kimchi* for weeks after that. Not surprisingly, Youngho was summoned to the principal's office and severely scolded. By the end of that day, the whole school knew about it, too, including all the teachers. Everybody whispered and exchanged looks whenever Youngho walked by—for at least a month. It was so bad that he was lucky to get away with just a scolding. It could have been far worse. Mom found out, too, of course, and grounded him for a few weeks.

Back to the present now. Apart from Sunday evenings, Youngho was not such a fan of weekends these days. During the weekends, time just crawled ever so slowly, with nothing much to do except sleep all day or watch TV. While he enjoyed having enough time to read or take long walks with Chadori, that was pretty much the only highlight of his weekends lately. Sometimes, he got so bored that he felt as though he had spent the whole weekend counting the ticks of the clock. He used to think that he couldn't possibly get in trouble on the weekends, at least, since he was not doing much.

그것으로도 부족했는지, 마침 그 순간 영호네 반 담임 선생님인 이 선생님이 지나가다가, 교단 넘어지는 소리에 연이어 아이들의 비명 소리를 듣고는 교실로 달려 들어왔고, 반 전체가 아수라장인 데다 최 선생님이 머리에 양동이를 쓰고 피 같은 것을 뚝뚝 흘리는 것을 본 것이다. 임 선생님은 비명을 지르며 달려가서 응급차를 부르고 보건교사를 데려왔다. 결국에는 아무도 다친 사람도 없고 실질적인 피해도 없었다. 그날 따라 운이 따라주지 않았던 최 선생님만 몇 주 내내 김치냄새를 풍겼을 뿐. 말할 것도 없이 영호는 교장실에 불려 가서 호되게 꾸중을 들었다. 게다가 그날 학교가 끝날 즈음에는 선생님들을 포함한 학교 전체가 그 사건에 대해서 알게 되었고, 그 뒤로 최소한 한 달 동안은 영호가 지나갈 때마다 서로 눈짓을 주고받으며 속닥거렸다. 상황이 아주 심각했기에 그냥 꾸지람을 듣고 끝난 것만으로도 천만다행이었다. 엄마에게 연락이 간 것은 당연지사였고 몇 주 동안 등교를 제외한 외출 금지령이 내렸다.

현재로 돌아와서, 영호는 이제 일요일 저녁을 제외하고는 주말을 그리 좋아하지 않게 되었다. 주말이 되면 시간이 너무도 천천히 꾸물꾸물 기어가는 듯했고, 하루종일 잠만 자거나 TV를 보는 것을 제외하고는 별다르게 할 일이 없었다. 마음껏 책 읽을 시간, 차도리와 오랫동안 산책할 수 있는 시간이 넉넉한 것은 좋았지만, 최근에 들어서 주말에 기억에 남을 만한 일은 그것이 전부였다. 어쩔 때는 너무도 지루하다 못해 주말 내내 시계 바늘 소리만 세며 보낸 것 같은 생각마저 들 정도였다. 처음에는 그나마 아무 것도 하는 일이 없으니 주말에는 최소한 문제는 일으키지 못하겠지 하고 생각했었다.

하지만 웬걸, 영호의 문제 일으키는 재주 하나는—아무 것도 하지 않고 있을 때조차도—그야말로 상상을 초월했다. 점심으로 먹으려고 끓이던 라면 태우는 일부터 시작해서 화장실 변기에 휴지를 너무 많이 채워서 거의 폭파할 정도까지 간 것 등등.

주말이 항상 이렇게 따분했던 것은 아니다. 주말이 오기만을 기다리던 때도 있었다. 옛날 한때는 엄마 아빠가 비록 주중에는 항상 꽤 바빴어도, 주말에는 아빠와 야구나 축구경기를 보러 가기도 하고 가족끼리 하이킹도 하고 여행도 다니고 했었다. 하지만 지난 몇 년 사이 그런 가족 활동은 서서히 줄어들다가 아예 전멸해 버렸다.

Still, the amount of trouble he could make for himself was unbelievable—even when he wasn't doing much—from burning instant noodles he was boiling for lunch to nearly exploding the toilet bowl after stuffing too much toilet paper inside.

The weekends hadn't always been as tedious as this. Youngho used to look forward to them. There were times when Dad took him to baseball or soccer games, his family went on hikes or just away for the weekend—although Mom and Dad were always pretty busy during the week. Over the past few years, such family activity gradually died out.

3-1 엎어진 양동이 왕관·The Crown of Upturned Bucket

Everybody was just too busy. Mom—until Mom stopped working—and Dad, of course, had their full-time jobs. They both worked in the same company—Happy Electronics—Mom in marketing and Dad in accounting. That's how they met in the first place, which was not so surprising since they never seemed to have time to do anything else outside their jobs. Even Minji was busy all the time. Now in her second year of junior high, she was only two years older than Youngho. However, she was already acting as if she always had something going on. Minji had her high school entrance exam coming up, of course, but it was still more than a year away. Even though she was supposed to be so busy, she spent an astounding amount of time and energy on her looks—from hair, skin, and nails to clothes, bags, and shoes. Plus, she talked to her friends on her phone for hours on end when they weren't constantly texting each other.

Sundays now seemed to be the only time when all four members of his family were together in one place—Mom, Dad, Minji, and Youngho himself. Youngho took after Mom, and Minji looked like Dad. They were all kind of small—all four of them! Grandpa had been quite lean and tall, while Grandma—Youngho was told—was tiny. Dad was somewhat shorter compared to the family norm as a result; with Mom not particularly tall, either, Youngho and Minji came out even more vertically challenged. That was, more or less, the family's recent history in brief. Or the history of the family made short, one might say!

모두가 그저 너무 바빴다. 엄마와 아빠는 물론 직장을 다니니까—엄마가 직장을 그만두기 전에는—그렇다고 치자. 엄마와 아빠는 둘 다 같은 회사—해피전자—에 다녔고, 엄마는 마케팅, 아빠는 회계 부서에서 일했다. 처음 만나게 된 것도 회사라고 했다. 직장 외에는 딱히 다른 일을 할 만한 시간이 없었을 테니 그리 놀랄 만한 일도 아니다. 하지만 누나까지도 항상 바빴다. 누나는 이제 중학교 2학년이었고 영호보다 겨우 두 살 위였는데, 벌써부터 항상 할 일이 많은 것처럼 행동했다. 물론 얼마 있지 않아 고등학교 입학 시험이 있기는 했지만 아직도 일 년 이상이나 남았고, 그렇게 바쁜 척하면서도 머리, 피부, 손톱 발톱부터 시작해서 옷, 가방, 신발 등등까지 외모에 엄청난 시간과 노력을 쏟았다. 또 그러면서도 친구들과 쉬지 않고 문자 메시지를 주고받거나 그렇지 않으면 몇 시간이고 전화로 수다를 떨었다.

어쨌건 이제 영호네 가족이 한 자리에 모일 수 있는 날은 일요일 뿐인 듯했다—엄마, 아빠, 누나, 그리고 영호. 영호는 엄마를 닮았고, 누나는 아빠를 닮았다. 영호 가족은 네 명 모두 키가 작은 편이었다! 할아버지는 상당히 호리호리하고 키가 크셨지만, 영호가 듣기에 할머니는 아주 아담하셨다고 했다. 따라서 아빠는 친척들 기준에 비해 좀 작게 나왔다. 또 엄마도 키가 그리 크지 않은 편이다 보니, 영호와 민지까지 조금 더 조그만해졌다. 대충 그것이 최근 가족의 짤막한 변천사였다. 아니면 가족이 짤막해진 역사라고 해야 옳을까!

They used to be a family of five until last year. Grandpa had always lived with Youngho's family as far as Youngho could remember—but he passed away last December. Grandpa had practically raised Youngho since he was a baby because Mom and Dad both had full-time jobs. Youngho and Grandpa even shared a bedroom. Then he suddenly suffered a heart attack, and a few days later, he died in the hospital. Youngho was devastated—he had never cried so much in his life. It came as a shock since Grandpa had been in excellent health for his age up to that point. Mom and Dad tried their best to make Youngho feel better by saying things like, "death is only a natural part of life, just like birth"; "such is the law of the universe"; "it was a great blessing that Grandpa enjoyed good health right until the end and that death claimed him quickly and painlessly." True, they were all fair points, but it didn't change the fact that Grandpa's death had dealt a tragic blow to Youngho. Even now, one whole year later, he still missed him terribly.

Anyway, that was how they became four.

No, they were still five, of course! You could say that they had gone from six to five, including Chadori. He was lying on the floor by the entrance, half sleeping, half observing the family. He was watching them watch TV! Chadori was a medium-sized spaniel hunting breed with reddish-brown-and-white fur and large, drooping ears. Seen from behind, his hanging ears with soft fur made him look as if he were a redhead with a bob, while the white part covering his snout and forehead was precisely the shape of Mom's white vase.

작년까지만해도 영호네는 5인 가족이었다. 영호가 기억할 수 있는 한 항상 할아버지도 영호네 가족과 함께 사셨는데, 그만 작년 12월에 돌아가시고 말았다. 엄마 아빠가 풀타임으로 맞벌이를 했으니 할아버지가 영호를 애기 때부터 거의 도맡아서 키우다시피 하셨고, 영호와 방도 같이 썼다. 그러다가 갑자기 심장마비로 쓰러지셨고, 며칠 지나지 않아 병원에서 돌아가셨다. 영호는 너무나도 큰 슬픔에 빠졌고, 태어나서 그렇게 많이 울어본 것도 처음이었다. 할아버지가 그때까지 나이에 비해서 너무나도 정정하셨기에 충격이 아닐 수 없었다. 엄마 아빠는 "죽음도 탄생처럼 자연스런 인생의 일부이다." "그것이 우주의 법칙이다." "할아버지처럼 최후 마지막 순간까지 건강하게 계시다가 빨리 고통 없이 가실 수 있었던 것도 사실은 더할 수 없는 복이다." 등등의 말로 영호를 위로했다. 사실 모든 것이 다 맞는 말이긴 했지만, 그럼에도 불구하고 영호에게는 그야말로 청천벽력으로 다가왔고, 일 년이 지난 지금까지도 할아버지가 너무도 보고 싶었다.

어쨌든 그것이 지금 가족이 네 명으로 줄게 된 이유이다.

아니, 아직도 물론 다섯 명이었다! 차도리까지 합하면 여섯에서 다섯이 되었다고 볼 수 있었다. 차도리는 지금 현관문 앞 바닥에 엎드려서 반 졸다시피 하며 가족을 지켜보고 있었다. 가족이 TV 보는 것을 보고 있었다고나 할까! 차도리는 스패니얼 종류의 중형 사냥견이었는데, 흰 털과 붉은 밤색 털에 큰 귀가 양쪽으로 늘어져 있었다. 특히나 보드라운 털을 한 귀가 축 처져서 뒤에서 보면 마치 빨강 머리 여인이 단발을 하고 있는 것처럼 보였다. 또 주둥이와 이마를 덮은 흰 털은 엄마의 하얀 꽃병과 모양이 흡사했다.

From time to time, it fooled Youngho into thinking that Chadori was staring at him—wanting to go out, for example—when Youngho was trying to take a nap on the sofa. More often than not, however, it just turned out to be the white vase on the coffee table. In truth, Chadori lay at the other end of the living room, having his own blissful nap.

Chadori was short-haired apart from his chest and most of his tail, where he was covered in long, soft, feathery fur. His fur was especially long on top of his tail. Whenever he wagged it, it looked as if a huge duster was sweeping back and forth. And he had freckles—loads of them! He had light gray-brown spots everywhere—not only on his snout and legs, but also on his shoulders and even on his belly. Chadori was a handsome dog from any angle, but it was his freckles that made him so cute. Moreover, seen from behind, Chadori had a white spot on the right side of his rear, which meant Youngho could recognize him even from far away!

Chadori was already fully grown when he came to live with Youngho's family. He was from Bristol, England, where Uncle Bongsoo lived and adopted him as a puppy. When his owner eventually had to return to Korea, Chadori made the long journey with him. Not long afterward, Uncle Bongsoo had to move to yet another country, and things got complicated.

"Of course, we'll take good care of him for you. You can adopt a kangaroo in the Outback instead!"

Dad said he had reassured his childhood friend and promised to take Chadori in without a second's hesitation.

때때로 영호는 소파에 누워서 낮잠을 자려고 하다가 차도리가 계속 뻰히 쳐다보고 있다고 생각하고—예를 들면 밖에 나가자고 조르느라고—일어나 보면 십중팔구 탁자 위에 놓인 하얀 꽃병이었고, 실제로 차도리는 거실 반대 편에 누워 나름대로 편안하게 낮잠을 자고 있기가 일쑤였다.

털 길이는 대체적으로 짧은 털에, 가슴과 꼬리 부분만 솜털같이 부드러운 긴 털로 덮여 있었다. 꼬리 윗부분은 특히나 털이 길어서, 꼬리를 한 번 흔들면 마치 커다란 먼지털이가 왔다 갔다 하는 것처럼 보였다. 또 차도리는 주근깨가 아주 많았다! 코 언저리와 다리는 말할 것도 없었고, 심지어는 어깨와 배에까지도 옅은 밤회색 점이 온 데 흩어져 있었다. 차도리는 어느 각도로 보아도 잘 생긴 개임이 분명했지만, 한층 더 귀엽게 느낄 수 있었던 것은 주근깨 때문이라고 생각했다. 또 뒤에서 보았을 때 궁둥이 오른 쪽에 하얀 점이 있어서, 멀리서도 차도리인지 대번에 알아볼 수 있었다.

차도리가 영호네 집에 오게 된 것은 성견이 다 되어서였다. 차도리는 영국 브리스톨 출신이었는데, 봉수 삼촌이 그곳에 사시다가 강아지 적부터 데려다 키우셨다. 그러다가 한국으로 돌아오시면서 차도리도 주인을 따라 먼 길을 오게 되었다. 그런데 얼마 지나지 않아 봉수 삼촌이 또 다시 다른 나라로 옮겨 가게 되면서 일이 복잡해진 것이다.

“차도리는 당연히 우리가 잘 보살펴 줄 테니, 아웃백에서 대신 캥거루나 한 마리 데려다 키워!”

걱정하는 어릴 적 친구를 이렇게 위로하고 단번에 주저 없이 차도리를 데려다 기르기로 약속했다고 아빠가 말했었다.

3-2 브리스톨에서 온 아빠친구·Dad's Friend from Bristol

하지만 현실적으로 매일매일 하루 종일, 게다가 주말까지 직장 근무로 바쁜 아빠가 개를 돌볼 만한 여유는 없었다. 사실상 차도리를 보살피는 자잘한 일들은 처음엔 주로 할아버지가, 할아버지가 돌아가신 이후로는 영호가 도맡아 하게 되었다. 먹이 주는 일부터 목욕시키는 일, 매일 산책시키면서 똥 치우는 일까지. 어쩌다가 차도리가 속이 좀 안 좋거나 해서...... 상상에 맡기겠지만, 어쨌든 그럴 때면 뒤도 닦아 줘야 했다. 그때는 엄마도 직장생활로 아주 바빴기에 그다지 도움이 되지 못했다. 하지만 워낙 동물을 좋아하고 항상 반려견을 원했던 영호에게는 오히려 엄청나게 운이 좋았다고 생각되었다. 만약 봉수 삼촌이 아니었다면, 개를 기르자고 부모님을 설득시키는 것은 어림도 없는 일이었다.

In reality, though, he had no spare time to care for a dog, as he was so busy with his job—all day, every day, and even on the weekends. In practice, it was Grandpa who had to do all the work at the beginning, and Youngho after he passed away. From feeding and washing him to walking him every day and cleaning up after him—even wiping his backside sometimes when his stomach was a little . . . you get the picture. Mom hadn't been much help either, since she was also so busy with work then. Still, Youngho felt incredibly lucky. He loved animals and had always wanted a dog. If it hadn't been for Uncle Bongsoo, it would have been impossible to convince his parents to get one.

Especially a big dog like Chadori! When they stood side by side, Chadori's head came up above Youngho's waist. According to Uncle Bongsoo, he was even larger than average for his breed.

Minji loved Chadori as well in her own way, but she never seemed to have enough time to handle his daily care. Every time she needed to leave the house, she spent hours in front of the mirror, trying to make herself look a little different. She would always end up looking more or less the same, though! She also picked every last dog hair off her clothes whenever she stepped outside. All this puzzled Youngho and felt like a total waste of time, but he was more than happy to have Chadori to himself—especially since Grandpa had passed away.

It was dinnertime at last. Everybody sat on the floor, clustered together around the coffee table, leaving the dining table and sofa empty. Admittedly, the real reason behind the family gathering was a popular TV series called *The Fortune-teller*. It aired at six o'clock on Sunday evenings—around dinnertime, in other words. It was something everybody could enjoy together, regardless of age, and quickly became a favorite for the whole family. It was also popular with his classmates, and it was hard to join a conversation at school on Mondays without having seen the latest episode. Maybe it wasn't the purest of motives for having a family dinner, but it did allow them to get together, share a meal, and talk to one another like a family.

특히나 차도리처럼 큰 개는! 영호와 차도리가 나란히 서면 차도리는 머리가 영호의 허리 위로 올라왔다. 더더구나 봉수 삼촌 말에 의하면 차도리는 같은 종 평균보다도 크다고 했다.

누나도 나름대로 차도리를 예뻐하긴 했지만, 매일 일일이 보살필 여유는 없는 듯했다. 그도 그럴 것이 집을 나설 때면 몇 시간이고 거울 앞에 서서 뭔가 다르게 보이려고 지성을 들였다. 그런데 결국에는 항상 특별히 달라지는 것이 없었다! 또 밖에 나갈 때마다 몸에 묻은 개털을 마지막 한 톨까지 세세히 모조리 떼어 내었다. 그러한 누나의 행동이 영호로서는 전혀 이해가 가지 않았고 시간 낭비라고 느껴졌지만, 차도리를 독차지하게 된 것에 대해서는 오히려 쾌재를 불렀다. 특히나 할아버지까지 돌아가시고 안 계신 지금은 더더욱 그랬다.

드디어 저녁 먹을 시간. 영호네 가족은 식탁과 소파는 휑하니 비워둔 채 거실 탁자 주변 마루에 옹기종기 모여 앉아 저녁을 먹었다. 사실 가족이 한 자리에 모이는 진짜 이유는 따로 있었는데, TV에서 하는 인기 드라마 "점쟁이 아가씨" 때문이었다. 일요일 저녁 6시 방영으로 말하자면 대충 저녁 먹을 시간이었고, 남녀노소 누구나 함께 재미있게 볼 수 있어서 곧 온 가족이 즐겨 보는 프로그램이 되었다. 반 친구들 사이에서도 너무나 인기가 좋다 못해 어쩌다 한 편을 놓치고 월요일에 학교에 가면 대화에 끼어들기가 힘들 정도였다. 가족이 함께 저녁을 먹는다는 순수한 동기는 아닐지 몰라도 어쨌든 식구답게 한자리에 모여서 밥도 먹고 얘기도 나눌 수 있는 구실은 되어 주었다.

Today's main dish was tofu soup, with a side of grilled mackerel, parboiled spinach salad, and *kimchi*. Ordered takeout as usual—even the rice—the soup was already lukewarm by the time it arrived and the fish was almost cold, but nobody bothered to heat them up again. All in all, it wasn't too bad, but nowhere near what Mom used to make. Although she had much more time on her hands now that she didn't work anymore, the dinner menus remained more or less the same as before—rice, *kimchi*, and one or two side dishes, perhaps more on the weekends. They still ate a lot of takeout meals from the local supermarket—even *kimchi*, something Korean moms often made at home with great pride. Youngho couldn't see the real benefit to Mom quitting work as far as food was concerned.

To be precise, however, she hadn't quit her job—she had been fired. Youngho overheard Mom and Dad talking about all the big firms "tightening their belts" and laying people off. He didn't mean to eavesdrop—he just happened to step out of his bedroom at that moment.

Youngho remembered thinking it was kind of creepy that Mom and Dad were speaking hush-hush in low voices while sitting in the living room. He even made more noise than usual as he approached them so that they could hear him coming. Why were they being so secretive? It didn't sound like anything special. He couldn't understand why Mom and Dad seemed so serious.

And why did Mom look so sad?

오늘의 저녁 메뉴는 두부찌개. 반찬으로는 고등어 구이, 시금치 무침과 함께 김치—항상 그렇듯 밥까지 모두 배달주문시켜 온 것이었는데, 음식이 도착했을 때에는 찌개는 이미 다 식어 있었고 생선구이는 거의 차가울 정도였다. 하지만 아무도 다시 데우려고 신경 쓰지 않았다. 전반적으로 뭐 그런 대로 먹을만 했지만, 엄마가 직접 하던 음식과는 비교도 되지 않았다. 엄마는 직장을 그만 둔 이후로 시간이 아주 넉넉해졌지만, 저녁 식단은 그럭저럭 예전과 달라진 것이 없었다. 밥, 김치, 그리고 반찬 한두 개. 주말에는 좀 더 오를까. 영호네는 아직도 반찬 대부분을 동네 슈퍼에서 사다 먹었다. 엄마들이 서로 뽐내듯 직접 담근다는 김치까지도. 음식으로만 봤을 때에는 엄마가 직장을 그만 두고 특별히 좋아진 것이 없었다.

정확히 말하자면 엄마는 직장을 그만둔 것이 아니라 잘린 것이었다. 엄마랑 아빠랑 나누던 얘기를 들은 바에 의하면 대기업들이 다 "허리띠를 졸라매고" 인원을 감축하는 추세라고 했다. 일부러 엿들으려고 한 것은 아니었다—막 방을 나서던 참에 그냥 우연히 듣게 된 것이었다.

거실에 앉아서 낮은 목소리로 쉬쉬하며 말하는 소리가 왠지 어색하게 느껴져서, 일부러 들으라고 평소보다 요란하게 소리를 내며 나갔던 기억이 난다. 그다지 비밀스러운 말도 아닌 것 같은데 왜 그랬을까? 엄마 아빠가 왜 그렇게 심각해 보였는지 잘 이해가 가지 않았다.

또 엄마의 표정은 왜 그렇게도 슬펐던 걸까?

Whatever the reason, Youngho didn't mind the small changes in his daily routine that resulted—he liked that Mom was there when he came home from school; he didn't have to eat dinner alone, although Grandpa was no longer with them.

He couldn't say much about the quality of food, however. Mom was an excellent cook when she put her mind to it. She just never seemed to have the time to set foot in the kitchen —although she didn't have that excuse anymore.

At the end of it all, Youngho thought it was far better now than when he hardly saw her. She used to work late, sometimes even on weekends. She would say she had no choice since the economy was so bad. When she lost her job, she seemed very upset.

"Youngho will be going to junior high soon," Mom said almost every day ever since. "We would have been able to afford private lessons for him, English conversation or math, at least. If only I still had my job!"

Honestly, Youngho was more than happy that he got away without having to take private lessons after school, like most of his classmates were doomed to—especially math! No, thanks! He loved having enough time to go for long walks with Chadori, read all the comics and detective novels he wanted, and lose himself in computer games with Manu after school. He learned more than enough English from his computer games, after all!

이유야 어쨌건 간에 영호에게는 이로 인한 일상의 작은 변화들이 싫지는 않았다. 영호가 학교에 다녀오면 엄마가 집에 있는 것도 좋았고, 이제는 저녁을 혼자 먹지 않아도 되어서 또 좋았다. 특히나 할아버지가 없는 지금으로서는 더더욱 그랬다.

하지만 음식의 질을 보았을 때는 크게 할 말이 없었다. 엄마는 사실 하려고 마음만 먹으면 요리를 아주 잘했는데, 그저 부엌에 발 디딜 틈도 없는 듯했다—이제는 그 구실조차 없어졌지만 말이다.

결국 거의 엄마 얼굴조차 보기 힘들던 예전과 비교해서는 지금이 훨씬 더 좋다고 생각되었다. 잦은 야근에다 주말조차 툭하면 직장에 불려 나가던 때보다는. 그럴 때마다 엄마는 경제상황이 좋지 않아서 어쩔 수 없는 일이라고 했다. 엄마는 직장을 그만두게 된 것에 대해 상당히 우울해하는 눈치였다.

"이제 우리 영호 중학교에 입학할 날두 얼마 안 남았는데 말이야." 엄마가 그 이후로 거의 매일 되뇌이는 말. "최소한 영어회화나 수학 개인 교습은 시킬 수 있었는데…… 내가 직장에서 해고만 되지 않았어두!"

솔직한 심정으로 영호는 학교가 끝난 후에 대부분 급우들의 불쌍한 운명처럼 개인 교습을 하지 않아도 되는 것이 천만다행이라고 생각되었다. 더군다나 수학을…… 절대 사절이었다! 차라리 차도리와 한가하게 오랫동안 산책도 하고, 만화책과 추리소설도 마음껏 읽고…… 학교 끝나고 만우와 PC 게임에도 몰두하고 하는 것이 좋았다. 영어는 PC 게임하면서 충분히 배우고도 남았다!

An endless chain of commercials showed on TV before the day's episode began. One of them was about a Christmas promotion in a downtown department store. Youngho suddenly remembered Paradise on Earth—the extraordinary home decor store he discovered with Manu after school the other day, not to mention its back door opening out to the lavishly decorated Christmas street.

"How come we don't celebrate Christmas anymore?" Youngho blurted out without giving it any thought. "No Christmas presents, either!"

Dad gulped, looked at Youngho, and replied with a patronizing smile,

"Christmas! Aren't you a little too old for that now?"

Minji also had something to say, of course,

"Seriously, he has no idea how things are these days!" she exclaimed. "Well, you're still such a baby, aren't you?"

This was unexpected. Immediately regretting having spoken at all, Youngho was about to drop the whole thing when Dad put an arm around his shoulders.

"Listen . . . it's not a bad idea in itself," he said. "I don't want to disappoint you, Youngho, but it's all so commercial these days, you see . . . Do you know why Santa Claus even wears red and white? It's because—"

At that moment, Mom broke her silence and cut him short mid-sentence.

"Stop it, all of you!" she said in a low but firm voice, then added in a softer tone, "You're right, Youngho! Mom and Dad have been far too busy to think of Christmas. Now that I have more time, we can put an end to all that!"

TV에서는 드라마 프로가 시작되기 전 광고가 끝도 없이 줄을 지어 나왔는데, 그중 하나는 시내 백화점에서 하는 크리스마스 행사에 대한 내용이었다. 불현듯 영호는 며칠 전 만우와 학교가 끝나고 우연히 들렀던 인테리어 상점 '지상천국'과 그 뒷문에서 나갔던 거리의 화려한 크리스마스 장식이 떠올랐다.

"우린 인제 왜 크리스마스 안 쇠는 거야?" 영호가 별 생각 없이 문득 말을 떼었다. "크리스마스 선물두 안 주구……"

아빠가 밥을 꿀꺽 삼키더니 영호에게 고개를 돌려 네가 아직 덜 컸구나 하고 훈계하려는 듯한 웃음을 지으며 대답했다.

"크리스마스! 다 큰 녀석이 크리스마스는 무슨 ……"

누나도 옆에서 당연히 한 말 거든다.

"참 나, 얘 세상 물정을 몰라도 한참 모르네!" 그리고는 한숨을 내쉬며, "너 초딩 티 내냐, 진짜?"

뜻밖의 반응이다. 애초에 말을 한 것 자체가 후회된 영호가 그냥 없었던 일로 하려던 참에 아빠가 영호의 어깨에 한 팔을 두르며,

"아니…… 생각은 좋은데 말이지" 하고 말했다. "뭐 영호 너 실망시키려구 하는 얘기는 아니지만 말이야, 요새는 다 상업적으로 팔아먹으려고들 하는 거야…… 그 왜, 산타 할아버지가 입고 다니는 옷도 왜 빨갛고 하얀지 아냐? 그게 말이지—"

그때까지 잠자코 있던 엄마가 침묵을 깨고 아빠의 말을 끊었다.

"다 그만들 좀 해!" 조용하지만 단호한 한마디. 그리고는 좀 더 부드러운 목소리로, "그래, 영호 말이 맞네…… 그동안 엄마 아빠가 너무 정신 없이 바쁘다 보니까 크리스마스 같은 건 다 잊구 살았네. 이젠 엄마두 시간이 넉넉해졌으니까 좀 달라져 볼게." 했다.

그리고는 다시 영호를 보며 덧붙였다.

"아직두 크리스마스트리 하기 늦지 않았어! 장식세트두 상자에 담아논 거 어디 있을 꺼야. 우리 영호 참 멋진 생각이다!"

"누구는 좋겠다...... 아들이라구 편 들구...... 막내라구 위하구 ......" 누나가 찌개를 떠 가면서 들으라는 듯 궁시렁거렸다.

마침 광고는 스포츠 용품으로 바뀌고, 골프채와 관련용품들이 화면에 뜨자 아빠가 갑자기 비상한 관심을 보이며 검지손가락을 입에 대고 "쉬!" 한다.

Then she looked at Youngho and said,

"It's not too late to put up a Christmas tree. I think we still have the ornaments lying in a box somewhere too. It's such a good idea, Youngho!"

"Favoritism, as usual . . . because he's a boy, because he's the youngest," Minji murmured audibly, helping herself to more soup.

The commercial had switched to sporting goods by now; golf clubs and accessories flashed on the screen. Dad suddenly showed a keen interest and silenced everybody, bringing an index finger to his lips.

3-3 차도리의 먼지털이 꼬리·Chadori's Duster Tail

"Can we just watch the TV, please?" said Dad in frustration. "Minji, is it you against the entire world, all of a sudden?" Then he added, "Well, you're a teenager, after all . . . that fits the definition!"

"Dad!" retorted Minji.

Mom quietly laid a hand on Minji's arm, as if to appease her, and cast Dad a murderous glance.

"What's wrong with you guys?" muttered Youngho, quite irritated at this point. "I didn't mean we *had to* do it. It was just an idea!"

His face flushed red, Youngho tried to calm everybody down. Luckily, the program started shortly afterward and their focus shifted. When it was over, Youngho shot up from his seat and left the house with Chadori to walk him for the evening.

아빠는 "아, 테레비 좀 보자!" 하며 짜증을 팍 내더니 다시, "민지 넌 갑자기 온 세상에 불만이 왜 그렇게 많냐?" 하고 한 마디 보탰다. "맞아—인제 너두 그 사춘기지...... 그 정의에 따악 맞네!"

"아빠!" 민지의 항의.

엄마가 말없이 누나를 달래듯 팔에 손을 얹고는 아빠에게 눈을 흘겼다.

"아, 다들 왜 이래 진짜!" 기분이 상한 영호가 투덜댔다. "뭐 꼭 해야 된다는 게 아니구. 그냥 한 번 해 본 말이야!"

영호는 얼굴이 빨개져서 가족들을 진정시키려고 했다. 다행히 곧 드라마가 시작되었고, 모두의 관심이 그쪽으로 쏠렸다. 연속극이 끝을 맺자 영호는 재빨리 자리에서 일어나, 차도리를 데리고 저녁 산책을 시키러 집을 나섰다.

4

먼 옛날의 한 크리스마스

ONCE UPON A TIME ON CHRISTMAS DAY

이미 눈이 내려와 있었고, 저녁 공기는 차지만 맑았다. 영호와 차도리가 아파트 건물을 나섰을 때는 이미 어둑어둑해진 후였고, 벌써 밤의 여행길에 나선 보름달은 말할 것도 없이 하늘에는 별이 총총 떠 있었다.

It had snowed earlier, leaving the evening air cold but clear. It was already dark when Youngho and Chadori stepped outside the apartment complex; the sky was strewn with stars, not to mention the full moon that had already begun its nightly journey.

The boy and his companion followed their usual route through the park, which was only about a five-minute walk from where they lived. It was the same park Youngho could see from his bedroom window. It stretched all the way down to the river and continued along the well-lit area by the riverbank. They would always make a good trip out of it—half an hour, at least.

Most of the time, Chadori didn't even need a leash inside the park since he was so well-trained. They walked side by side this evening, too, leash-free. Despite the winter darkness, the park was brightly lit. The radiance from the streetlights cast an ethereal glow over the relatively fresh snow, which gave a beautiful but strangely lonely impression under the bluish light of the fluorescent lamps. The park was always empty at this time on Sundays, but Youngho was not afraid of walking in the dark. He had Chadori with him; although he was not an aggressive dog, other people didn't know that. When Grandpa was alive, he usually walked Chadori. At first, Youngho used to tag along simply because he thought it was fun. Now that Grandpa was gone, Youngho began to enjoy his solitary walks with Chadori—just walking for walking's sake, with no particular end or aim.

Youngho couldn't take his mind off what had just happened at home. It seemed like a pattern these days—his family couldn't be together for more than five minutes without arguing; one of them would invariably find something petty and insignificant to pick on.

둘은 항상 그렇듯 집에서 5분 정도 되는 거리의 공원길을 따라 갔다. 영호 방 창문에서 보이는 바로 그 공원이었는데, 강까지 쭈욱 가서 환하게 밝혀진 강둑길을 따라 걸으면 항상 넉넉하게 산책이 되었고, 최소한 30분 정도는 걸을 수 있었다.

차도리는 워낙 훈련이 잘된 개라서 공원 안에서는 보통 리드줄이 필요 없었고, 오늘 저녁도 마찬가지로 줄 없이 둘이 나란히 걸었다. 겨울 저녁은 어두웠지만 공원은 환하게 불이 밝혀져 있었다. 금방 내린 깨끗한 눈 위에 비친 가로등 불빛은 마치 이 세상의 것이 아닌 듯한 신비로운 느낌을 주었고, 푸르스름한 형광등 불빛 아래 아름다우면서도 묘하게 쓸쓸한 인상을 남겼다. 일요일 저녁 이 시간에는 보통 공원이 텅 비어 있었지만, 영호는 어두워진 후 산책하는 것이 무섭지 않았다. 차도리가 함께 있었고, 사나운 개는 아니었지만 다른 사람들은 그 사실을 몰랐기 때문이다. 할아버지가 살아 계셨을 때에는 차도리 산책을 도맡아 하셨었다. 영호는 처음에는 그저 재미있으니까 따라다녔지만, 할아버지가 계시지 않은 지금은 혼자 차도리와 특별한 이유도 목적도 없이 마냥 걷는 것이 좋아졌다.

영호는 방금 집에서 있었던 일이 생각에서 지워지지 않았다. 요즘 들어서 매일같이 있는 일이었고, 영호네 가족은 싸우지 않고 조용히 5분 이상 함께 있지를 못했다. 항상 꼭 누군가 사소하고 하찮은 구실을 찾아내서는 티격태격 언쟁으로 번지곤 했다.

This time, it was Youngho himself who had sparked the brawl, simply by asking why they no longer celebrated Christmas. *Just great!* he thought to himself. He succeeded in bringing about yet another mindless disaster. He didn't mean for it to end like this, though.

There had been times when they celebrated Christmas, just naturally without anybody having to remind the others, as if it were part of their tradition like Thanksgiving or New Year's Day. Every year, Mom would prepare amazing meals and Youngho watched her with his mouth watering. It was not exactly what you would call a traditional Christmas dinner, but Mom would always make something delicious, regardless of the menu, and they used to turn it into a grand feast.

As he walked along the deserted path through the snow-covered park, Youngho recalled with misty eyes how happy they had been together as a family back then. He remembered one particular Christmas when he was seven, shortly after Chadori had come to live with them. There was the Christmas tree, of course. Twinkling lights and tinsel adorned the tree like in that home decor store; Christmas presents lay under it in shiny wrapping paper, tied with colorful ribbons. They sang Christmas songs together, too, smiling and laughing, and Youngho and Minji even danced to the songs. Grandpa and Chadori were also there.

All six of them.

Mom made turkey *jjim*, a Korean stew; she would normally have made it with chicken, but she used turkey that day.

이번에는 영호가 크리스마스를 왜 안 쇠는지에 대해 물었던 것이 불씨가 되었다. *참 잘 했다, 잘 했어!* 영호가 스스로에게 말하듯 생각했다. 별 생각 없이 또 하나의 문제를 일으킨 것이다. 하지만 처음부터 그러려는 의도는 아니었다.

이전에는 누가 따로 얘기하지 않아도 그냥 자연스럽게, 추석이나 설날 같은 전통 명절처럼 크리스마스를 쇠던 때가 있었다. 매년 엄마는 아주 맛있는 음식을 만들곤 했고, 영호는 군침을 흘리며 엄마가 요리하는 모습을 지켜보았다. 딱이 전통 크리스마스 요리는 아니었지만, 저녁 메뉴가 무엇이던 엄마의 요리는 항상 맛있었다. 그렇게 항상 온 가족이 대잔치를 벌였다.

영호는 눈쌓인 공원 텅 빈 길을 따라 걸으며 온 가족이 함께 행복하던 때를 기억하고는 눈물이 글썽해졌다. 영호가 일곱 살 때의 크리스마스—그러니까 차도리가 영호네 가족과 함께 살게 된 지 얼마 지나지 않아서—가 문득 떠올랐다. 물론 크리스마스 트리도 있었고, 며칠 전 인테리어 상점에서 보았던 것처럼 반짝반짝 빛나는 전구를 달고 틴셀을 두르는 등 장식도 했었다. 트리 밑에는 빛나는 포장지에 쌓여 색색 가지 리본을 두른 예쁜 선물 꾸러미들이 놓여 있었고, 다 함께 크리스마스 캐럴도 부르며 웃음이 넘쳐났다. 영호와 민지는 노래에 맞춰 율동까지 했다. 할아버지와 차도리도 있었다.

여섯 명 모두 다.

엄마는 그날 저녁으로 칠면조찜을 했는데, 평소라면 닭고기를 사용했겠지만 그날은 칠면조 고기를 사용했다.

"Hope the turkey adds a little Christmas twist!" She smiled brightly, throwing her head back. She did that when she was in a really good mood. Youngho couldn't remember when he had last seen her do that.

Turkey drumsticks filled the casserole amid large chunks of potatoes, red onions, broccoli, carrots, and bell peppers in every color. Thoroughly braised meat was almost falling off the bones, all tender and juicy; piping hot, the gravy was thick with crumbling potatoes.

And the smell—it exuded such a wonderful mixture of soy sauce and sesame oil. And tasting it was like . . . yummmmm, heaven! It made his mouth water just thinking about it now, minutes after eating dinner.

Apart from the turkey *jjim,* the table was heavily laden with all kinds of food: double-boiled egg mousse, silky smooth and so soft it defied its original names—steamed eggs or *gyeran jjim*—sprinkled with thinly sliced scallions and toasted sesame seeds; a seafood pancake that wasn't too spicy, its edges golden and crisp; a mango salad where sweet and tangy flavors blended to perfection; and at least three kinds of kimchi—including one pan-fried in butter. Youngho still remembered them vividly because many of them became his all-time favorites.

After dinner, when everybody had eaten so much that they couldn't have one more spoonful—even Mom, who was on a permanent diet to lose weight—finally came the moment Youngho had been waiting for: Christmas presents!

"칠면조 고기를 써서 좀 크리스마스 분위기가 날까!" 엄마가 밝은 미소를 지으며 머리를 뒤로 제쳤다. 엄마가 기분이 아주 좋을 때 하는 행동이다. 엄마가 그렇게 웃는 것을 본 지가 얼마나 되었을까.

칠면조 다리와 함께 크게 듬성듬성 썬 감자, 빨간 양파, 브로콜리, 당근, 색색 가지 피망 등이 냄비를 가득 채웠고, 고기는 푹 익다 못해 뼈에서 저절로 떨어질 정도로 부드럽고 촉촉했다. 또 아직 김이 모락모락 나는 따끈한 국물은 익어 부스러진 감자로 걸쭉했다.

또 간장과 참기름이 적당히 어우러진 그 향기의 완벽한 조화...... 그리고 그 맛을 음미하는 것이란...... 냠냠...... 그야말로 천국이 따로 없었다. 저녁을 먹은 지 불과 몇 분 되지 않은 지금도 생각만 하면 입에 군침이 절로 돌았다.

칠면조찜 말고도 밥상은 각종 요리와 반찬으로 상다리가 부러지게 차려져 있었다. 예를 들면 계란찜이라고 하기엔 너무나도 부드러운, 송송 썬 파와 볶은 참깨가 솔솔 뿌려진 계란 중탕 무스, 너무 맵지 않고 둘레가 노릇노릇 아삭아삭하게 구워진 해물파전, 새콤달콤한 맛이 완벽한 조화를 이룬 망고 샐러드, 게다가 버터에 볶은 김치를 합해서 김치도 최소한 세 가지는 되었던 것 같다. 그날 먹었던 것 대부분이 지금까지도 영호가 가장 좋아하는 음식으로 남아 있었기에 아직도 생생히 기억했다.

저녁식사가 끝나고 다들 단 한 숟가락도 더 들어갈 자리가 없을 정도로 잘 먹고 난 후—살 뺀다고 항상 다이어트 중인 엄마까지도—드디어 영호가 가장 기대하던 시간이 왔다. 바로 크리스마스 선물!

4-1 먼 옛날의 크리스마스·Once upon a Time on Christmas Day

영호는 빛나는 은색 포장지에 싸여 빨간 리본을 두른 네모난 선물 꾸러미를 받았다. 또 포장지 위에는 봉투가 하나 붙어 있었는데, 반짝이가 솔솔 뿌려진 수제 크리스마스카드가 들어 있었다. 들뜬 영호가 성급하게 봉투에서 카드를 꺼내자, 반짝이가 떨어져 여기저기 흩날렸다. 반짝이 바람을 들이마신 영호가 *에취!* 하고 재채기를 하자 또 하나의 작은 반짝이 폭풍이 일어 영호와 주위 사람들 모두에게로 몰아쳤다.

"어머나! 산타 할아버지는 반짝이를 아주 좋아하시나 봐!" 엄마가 함박미소를 지으며 말했다.

온 가족이 웃음을 터뜨리자 차도리도 또 반짝이로 뒤덮인 꼬리를 흔들어 다시 꼬리 주변에 반짝이 회오리 바람을 일으키고…… 그걸 보고 또 더 웃고……

He received a square box wrapped in shiny silver-colored paper, tied with a red ribbon. There was also an envelope attached to the wrappings with a handmade Christmas card inside, sprinkled with glitter. When Youngho pulled the card from the envelope, eager and impatient, he sent the glitter scattering everywhere. He even breathed some in and sneezed *Achoo!* which sparked off another little storm of glitter all over himself and everybody around him.

"Oh, no! Santa Claus must love glitter!" Mom said, smiling broadly.

Everybody burst out laughing; Chadori started wagging his tail, also covered in glitter. They laughed some more watching Chadori, who stirred up his own flurry of glitter around his tail.

Youngho tore open the package. He received a soccer ball; soccer became his favorite sport from then on.

Even now, years later, Youngho still remembered how happy he had been that day. Of course, it was great getting Christmas presents, but it didn't matter what was inside the box in the end. Just getting something from somebody, the expectation, and opening the package was pure happiness in itself. Minji received a doll; Chadori also got a little bundle with a doggy treat inside. The two children munched on gingerbread cookies afterward while playing with their Christmas presents. Not far away, Chadori chewed on his ham bone, watching them play.

Then, Minji ran around trying to help her "baby brother" wipe the glitter off his face, even though she wasn't much bigger herself. She fetched water, wet a towel, and rubbed his face, spilling the water everywhere. Youngho's lips curled up in an absent smile as he reminisced about the happy past.

"Oh . . . look at the dog! He's so beautiful!" a woman's voice chirped dramatically behind Youngho.

영호는 허겁지겁 선물을 뜯어보았다. 영호의 크리스마스 선물은 축구공이었고, 그 이후로 축구는 영호가 가장 좋아하는 스포츠가 되었다.

몇 년이 지난 지금도 그날 얼마나 행복했었는지 아직 기억에 생생했다. 물론 크리스마스 선물 때문도 있었지만, 결국 무엇을 선물로 받느냐 하는 것은 그리 중요하지 않았던 것 같다. 누군가로부터 무엇을 받는다는 것, 그 기대감, 그리고 선물을 뜯어 본다는 것이 순수한 행복 그 자체였다. 누나는 인형을 받았고, 차도리도 애완견용 간식이 들어 있는 작은 꾸러미를 선물로 받았다. 잠시 후 두 아이가 생강 과자를 먹으며 크리스마스 선물로 받은 장난감을 가지고 노는 사이, 차도리도 근처에서 역시 그날 받은 간식용 뼈다귀를 갉아먹으며 아이들이 노는 것을 지켜보았다.

그러다가 누나가 갑자기 '우리 애기 동생' 얼굴에 묻은 반짝이를 닦아 주겠다며 분주하게 왔다갔다했다. 그 당시 누나 스스로도 그다지 크지 않았었는데도 말이다. 그렇게 물을 떠오고 수건을 적셔서는 영호의 얼굴을 박박 문지르면서 여기저기 물을 뚝뚝 다 흘렸었다. 영호는 과거의 행복했던 추억을 떠올리며 무의식 중에 입가에 웃음이 번졌다.

"어머, 이 개 좀 봐...... 너무 멋지다!" 영호의 등 뒤에서 과장된 소프라노의 여자 목소리가 들렸다.

5

어른과 아이

A GROWN-UP AND A CHILD

가던 길을 멈추고 갑자기 K-POP 스타처럼 멋지게 차려입은 미남미녀 한 무리에게 둘러싸인 영호와 차도리. 다들 이십 대 초반 정도의 나이로 보이는 것이 남자 둘에 여자 두 명이었고, 집 근처 대학교에 다니는 학생들인 듯했다.

Youngho and Chadori stopped on their way and found themselves suddenly surrounded by a group of young people —all very good-looking and dressed up like K-pop stars. Probably in their early twenties, they were two men and two women, likely students from the local university.

"He looks like he's just popped out of a movie set!" said the same woman judging from the voice, admiring Chadori from head to toe. "What kind of breed is he?"

"Yeah, well . . . um . . . he is a kinda rare breed in this country," Youngho replied with a timid smile—slightly embarrassed, but more than happy with all the attention. "We took him over from his previous owner, my Dad's close buddy. He was living in Bristol, England, and—"

He went on while the other girl, perhaps scared of dogs or just in a rush, walked far ahead and waited for the rest of the group. Laughing and chattering boisterously, the rest of them had also moved on before Youngho finished his explanation. It happened very often that people stopped on their way to stare at Chadori from afar, and some would even come up and pet him, asking details about his breed and origin. Chadori didn't seem to mind the attention from strangers at all. In fact, he looked as if he quite enjoyed it.

Youngho still remembered the first time he met Chadori, down to the last detail. He was afraid of Chadori at the very beginning, not only because Chadori was larger than him, but also because Youngho had never had close contact with an animal—apart from those in cages in a pet store or the zoo. It was not long after he started at Jinsung Elementary School. They were the same age, Youngho and Chadori! By then, Chadori was already a full-grown adult dog, while Youngho was just a little boy. Chadori was even taller than Youngho if he stood on his hind legs.

"어디 영화 찍다가 나온 개 같다!" 목소리의 주인공인 듯한 누나가 차도리를 머리부터 발끝까지 샅샅이 살피며 말했다. "얘는 무슨 종이니?"

"아, 네...... 저...... 국내에는 좀 드문 종류인데요...... " 영호가 쑥스러우면서도 한편으로는 또 으쓱하기도 해서 수줍게 웃으며 대답했다. "원래 우리 아빠 친한 친구분이 기르던 개였는데요, 그분이 영국 브리스톨에 사시다가—"

영호가 말을 계속하는 사이 누나 중 한 명이 개가 무서운 건지 그냥 가는 길이 급해서인지 저만치 앞서 가서 일행을 기다렸다. 나머지 청년 무리 또한 영호가 설명을 채 끝내기도 전에 벌써 히히호호 웃고 떠들며 저만큼 멀어져 갔다. 사실 길 가던 행인들이 가던 길을 멈추고 차도리를 멀찍이서 쳐다보는 것은 아주 흔히 있는 일이었고, 직접 다가와서 쓰다듬거나 종류 원산지 등에 대해 샅샅이 캐묻는 경우도 태반이었다. 차도리도 모르는 사람들의 관심을 싫어하지 않았을뿐더러, 사실은 상당히 즐기는 듯했다.

영호는 처음 차도리를 만났을 때를 아직도 자세히 생생하게 기억했다. 처음에는 차도리가 무서웠다. 차도리가 영호보다도 몸집이 컸기 때문도 있었지만 영호는 애완동물 가게나 동물원 우리 안에 갇힌 동물을 제외하고는 가까이서 동물을 접하는 것 자체가 태어나서 처음이었으니까. 영호가 진성초등학교에 입학한지 얼마 되지 않았을 때이다. 영호와 차도리는 나이가 동갑이었다! 하지만 영호가 아직 어린애였던 것에 비해 차도리는 늠름한 성견이었고, 뒷발을 딛고 일어나면 영호보다도 더 키가 컸다.

Of course, Grandpa was still around at that time. He saw that Youngho felt uneasy.

"Say 'sit' and give him the treat when he follows your command," he said, putting a treat in Youngho's hand. "You can even try and pet him on the back afterward if you want."

In his day, Grandpa trained and worked with dogs in the military, so he had good knowledge about dog training. Youngho did as Grandpa said, but even before Youngho had the chance to say the command, Chadori heard Grandpa and sat down at once, like a soldier standing to attention. Then, he waited patiently while Youngho hesitated, his little hand clutching the treat and trembling.

"Don't be afraid! He is a well-trained dog," Grandpa reassured him. "You can open your hand now and give him the treat!"

Youngho followed Grandpa's advice and unwrapped his fingers, but he took his hand away as soon as he felt Chadori's breath on it. The treat fell on the floor, but Chadori didn't even touch it. He sat there and waited patiently, wagging his tail. Youngho picked up the treat and tried again. Twice. Three times. Several tries later, Youngho was not afraid anymore, even when Chadori licked his fingers. Before long, Youngho began to love the feel of Chadori's tongue on his skin. It felt smooth, but a little rough at the same time. Warm and moist. And it tickled! Every time he felt Chadori's tongue on his cheek, Youngho broke into an uncontrollable chortle. Before long, he plucked up the courage to pet him on the head, hug him around the neck, and rub his cheeks against the soft, down-like fur under his collar.

물론 그때는 할아버지도 살아 계셨었다. 불안해하는 영호의 마음을 아신 할아버지.

"'앉아' 하구 말 한 다음에 명령을 따르면 먹이를 줘 봐!" 할아버지가 영호의 손에 개 간식을 쥐어 주시며 하시던 말씀. "그리고 나서 등을 쓰다듬어 줘도 되구!"

할아버지는 한때 군대에서 군견 훈련을 담당하신 적이 있어서 개 훈련에 대해서 아는 것이 많으셨다. 영호는 할아버지가 시키는 대로 해 보았지만, 차도리는 채 명령을 내릴 틈도 없이 할아버지의 설명을 듣자마자 그대로 앉아 버렸다. 마치 차렷 자세를 취하는 군인처럼. 그리고는 먹이를 꼭 쥔 영호의 작은 손이 떨리며 머뭇거리는 사이에도 차도리는 참을성 있게 기다렸다.

"무서워하지 말고...... 잘 훈련 받은 개니까 괜찮아." 할아버지가 옆에서 거드셨다. "이제 손 펴고 먹이 줘도 돼!"

영호는 할아버지의 말씀대로 살며시 손바닥을 폈다가, 차도리의 입김이 손바닥에 느껴지자 무서운 나머지 재빨리 손을 치웠고, 먹이는 바닥에 떨어졌다. 차도리는 먹이가 바닥에 떨어져도 건드리지 않고 그저 앉아서 꼬리를 흔들며 참을성 있게 기다렸다. 영호는 떨어진 먹이를 주워 다시 시도해 보았다. 두 번. 세 번. 여러 번 반복해서 먹이를 줘 보았고, 차도리가 손바닥을 핥아도 무서워하지 않게 되었다. 뿐만 아니라 차도리의 혓바닥이 피부에 와닿는 느낌을 좋아하게까지 되었다. 차도리의 혓바닥은 부드러우면서도 조금 까칠했고, 따스하고도 촉촉했다. 또 너무 간지러웠다! 차도리의 혓바닥이 영호의 볼을 핥을 때마다 영호는 키득키득 저절로 웃음이 나왔다. 곧 용기를 내어 차도리의 머리도 쓰다듬어 보고, 목을 껴안고 그 풍성하고 부드러운 목털에 볼을 부벼 보기도 했다.

A short distance away, Grandpa watched them play with a smile on his face.

Soon, Youngho and Chadori were inseparable. Chadori never growled or snapped, even when Youngho's play had gone a little too far. Youngho and Chadori. Chadori and Youngho. From then on, it was always the two of them together. After a while, Youngho even began to love Chadori's smell. In general, people don't mean anything nice when they say something "smells like a dog." For Youngho, though, the scent of Chadori's fur brought the snuggest and coziest feelings in the world. Whenever he buried his face in Chadori's fur and breathed in, he felt so safe, as if no harm could ever come to him as long as Chadori was there—as if the smell of his fur had formed a magic bubble around him.

One exception was Chadori's farts. Oh yes, Chadori could fart! Whenever he passed his potent gas, the whole house stank so terribly that the windows had to be opened at once to let in fresh air, and everybody had to evacuate immediately as if a toxic gas bomb had just gone off.

"Phew . . . we're gonna need gas masks from now on. I was about to pass out in there!" Minji said the last time Chadori farted. "Youngho! What are you feeding him?"

And Chadori loved playing soccer. He made the perfect practice partner for Youngho, who loved the game—even if the partner was a dog.

할아버지는 옆에서 그저 흐뭇한 표정으로 둘이 노는 모습을 지켜보셨던 것 같다.

그 이후로 영호와 차도리는 뗄레야 뗄 수 없는 가까운 사이가 되었다. 차도리는 영호가 아무리 장난을 치고 못살게 굴어도 으르렁거리거나 사납게 굴었던 적이 단 한 번도 없었다. 영호와 차도리. 차도리와 영호. 둘은 금세 단짝이 되었다. 얼마 지나지 않아 영호는 하다못해 차도리의 냄새까지도 좋아하게 되었다. 보통 누가 어디서 "개 냄새가 난다"고 하면 그다지 좋은 뜻은 아니다. 하지만 영호에게는 그 냄새가 더없이 포근하고도 아늑하게만 느껴졌다. 차도리의 털에 얼굴을 묻고 숨을 들이쉬고 있노라면, 차도리가 곁에 있는 이상 그 어떤 것도 영호를 해하지 못할 것 같은—마치 차도리의 털냄새가 마법의 보호막이라도 만들어 준 듯—안전한 느낌이 들었다.

단 차도리의 방귀 냄새만은 절대 예외였다. 차도리의 방귀 냄새는 그야말로 지독했다! 어쩌다 차도리가 방귀 한 번 뀌면 온 집 안에 그 냄새가 진동을 해서, 즉시 창문을 열어 환기시키는 것은 물론이고 마치 독가스 폭탄이라도 금방 터진 것처럼 온 가족이 대피해야 할 정도였다.

"윽…… 인제부터 우리 방독면 써야 할 것 같다. 질식하는 줄 알았네!" 얼마 전 차도리가 방귀를 뀌었을 때 누나가 한 말. "야, 영호 너 도대체 애 뭐 먹이길래 이러는 거야?"

또 차도리는 축구를 아주 좋아했고, 축구를 좋아하는 영호의 공 차기 파트너—비록 그 파트너가 개일지라도—로 딱 안성맞춤이었다.

5-1 아빠는 식물인간·Dad is a Zombie

영호가 어렸을 적에는 아빠가 축구공 직선으로 차기, 야구공 던지기, 자전거 타기 등등도 가르쳐 주고 종종 함께 놀아 주었지만, 어느 순간부터인지 아빠는 항상 저녁 늦은 시각에, 그것도 영호가 이미 잠든 후 들어왔고, 이제는 아예 얼굴조차 보기 힘들었다. 어쩌다 아주 드물게 주말에 집에 있으면, 하루종일 식물인간처럼 소파에 누워 노트북 컴퓨터를 들여다보거나 낮잠만 잤다.

특히 엄마까지 직장 근무로 바빴을 적에는 마치 할아버지와 차도리가 영호의 가족 전부인 것처럼 느껴졌다. 할아버지를 포함한 세 명은 어디든 함께 다녔다.

Dad often played with Youngho when he was little, teaching him how to kick the soccer ball in a straight line, throw a baseball, or ride a bike. In recent years, though, Dad always came home late at night, mostly after Youngho had gone to bed. Now he just never saw him anymore—well, almost. On the rare weekends when Dad was actually home, he was like a zombie, lying on the sofa with his laptop or sleeping away the whole day.

When Mom also turned into a workaholic, it felt almost as if Grandpa and Chadori were the only family Youngho had. The three always hung out together.

When Grandpa came across a friend or wanted to sit down for a brief rest, Youngho and Chadori played soccer together. Youngho kicked the ball to Chadori, who dribbled it back to him with his snout; they just kept passing the ball to each other, back and forth. Above all, what mattered most was that they did it together—united as one. Almost without exception, though, Chadori would dart off with the ball in the middle of a game so that Youngho had no choice but to run after him. Then their soccer game suddenly turned into football.

All that changed when Grandpa passed away last year. Youngho and Chadori stopped playing soccer after that. Moreover, it was now up to Youngho alone to take care of Chadori's needs—such as his daily walks and occasional baths. Nobody told him to do it, but it felt like the natural thing to do. After all, it was what Youngho wanted more than anything. Looking after Chadori somehow helped him carry the weight of the grief that burdened his shoulders, the sorrow that was simply too much for him to bear on his own.

When they first met, Youngho and Chadori started as simple playmates. Little by little, Chadori became the only one to whom Youngho could open up completely. Of course, Youngho couldn't talk to Chadori about how his day had been at school or ask which color socks to wear. But it was precisely because of this that he could confide his innermost feelings to him, happy or sad—Chadori didn't judge or ask for a reason.

산책길에 할아버지가 아는 분을 만나거나 잠시 앉아 휴식을 취하실 때, 영호와 차도리는 축구를 하며 놀았다. 영호가 차도리에게 공을 차면 차도리가 받아서 주둥이로 몰아 영호에게로 다시 보내고, 또 반복해서 서로 패스하고...... 하는 식이었다. 어쨌든 가장 중요한 것은 하나로 호흡을 맞추며 함께 뛴다는 것이었다. 그런데 항상 그렇게 잘 나가다가는 꼭 차도리가 공을 입에 물고 혼자 뺑소니쳤다. 영호는 또 하는 수 없이 그 공을 빼앗으러 차도리의 뒤를 쫓아가고...... 그렇게 영호와 차도리의 축구는 순식간에 럭비로 돌변하곤 했다.

그러다가 작년에 할아버지가 돌아가시면서 모든 것이 바뀌어 버렸다. 그 뒤로 영호와 차도리는 축구를 한 적이 없다. 더군다나 이제는 매일 시키는 산책이나 드물게는 목욕 등 차도리 돌보는 일을 영호 혼자 도맡아 하게 되었고, 또 누가 시킨 것은 아니었지만 그냥 자연스레 그렇게 되었다. 무엇보다도 영호 스스로가 원하는 일이기도 했다. 영호 혼자서는 도저히 감당해 낼 수 없었던, 그 어깨를 짓누르는 슬픔의 무게도 차도리를 돌봄으로해서 어느 정도 견뎌 낼 수 있었다고나 할까.

차도리는 처음 만났을 때만 해도 그저 단순한 놀이 동무였지만, 점점 무엇이든 모두 털어놓을 수 있는 유일한 벗이 되어주었다. 물론 학교에서 있었던 일에 대해 얘기하거나 오늘 무슨 색 양말을 신을지 물어볼 수는 없었다. 하지만 그럼으로써 더더욱 마음속 깊은 곳에 숨어 있는 기쁨과 슬픔을 함께 나눌 수 있었다—차도리는 잘잘못을 가리거나 이유를 따지지 않았던 것이다.

Slowly and quietly, their silent talks grew into a bond like no other in the world. Not a word of explanation was necessary, even for something that a thousand words couldn't possibly describe. Chadori was just there for him—supportive, no matter what. Youngho always felt so serene and calm whenever he was with Chadori and he was certainly thankful for that. Even his knack for getting into trouble again and again seemed to be under control when they were together. Of course, Mom and Dad were there for him, and he also had Manu. But for some reason, Youngho didn't want to show this kind of fragile side of himself to them. Maybe he was embarrassed. Maybe he was afraid of disappointing them.

Then, an ominous cry came from nowhere and jolted Youngho out of his reverie.

"Oy, you! Stop right there!"

With horror, Youngho realized that he recognized the voice.

점차 조용히 영호와 차도리의 말 없는 대화는 이 세상 그 무엇과도 바꿀 수 없는 두터운 우애로 굳어져 갔다. 아무리 수많은 단어를 써도 표현하기 힘든 말이 있을 때에도, 차도리는 그 어떤 설명 하나 필요 없이 그저 위해 주고 함께해 주었고, 그런 차도리와 함께 있으면 항상 마음이 차분하게 안정되었다. 영호는 그런 차도리가 고맙게만 느껴졌다. 차도리와 함께 있으면 하다못해 영호의 문제 일으키는 재주까지도 잠잠했다. 물론 영호의 곁에는 엄마 아빠도 있고 만우도 있었지만, 그런 약한 모습은 왠지 보이기 싫었다. 멋쩍어서였을까. 아니면 실망시키기 싫어서였을까.

느닷없이 사뭇 불길한 목소리가 영호를 몽상에서 흔들어 깨웠다.

"야, 너 거기 서!"

이미 들어 본 적이 있는 목소리였다. 그러기에 더욱 반갑지 않은……

6

잃어버린 야구방망이

THE LOST BASEBALL BAT

전에도 들어 본 목소리—목이 살짝 갈라진 듯한, 거의 쇠소리가 나다시피 하는 변성기의 목소리로 왠지 무언가 불쾌한 것을 연상시켰다. 이미 알고는 있지만 전혀 친근하지 않은 목소리였다. 영호는 내키지 않았지만 몸을 돌려 목소리의 주인공과 대면하지 않을 수 없었다. 온몸의 세포 하나하나에서 몸을 돌리기 싫어 저항하는 것이 느껴졌다.

Youngho had heard it before—the deepening voice of an adolescent boy with a slight crack in the throat; almost metallic, it reminded him of something unpleasant. Familiar, yet not friendly. Reluctantly, Youngho turned to face it. Every single cell in his body seemed to resist the effort.

As he had feared, the gang of three bullies stood before him—the same ones he had met and dodged with Manu the other day. They looked like they had been playing baseball somewhere; the lanky guy held a baseball bat.

In no time, they surrounded Youngho and Chadori, as if to make sure that they didn't get away.

"Well, well, well . . . what have we got here?" said Lanky, one corner of his mouth curled up in a lopsided smile. A bleached canine tooth peeped through. "Speaking of the fox, hey?"

"Not the fox—the devil! Speaking of the devil!" whispered the one wearing glasses—Goggles—in Lanky's ear. It wasn't really a whisper, though, since Youngho could hear everything that was said, and so could the third of the pack—Spot, the one with a big mole on his cheek. Tossing a ball in and out of his glove, he smirked conspicuously. Lost for what to do, Youngho kept looking around for a way out; unfortunately, he spotted none.

"Who cares if it's the devil or the fox!" Lanky growled at his friends. "Does it matter? It's all the same!"

Turning back to Youngho again, he was screaming almost hysterically. "You won't get as lucky today as you and the little piggy did last time!" he snapped, baring his teeth.

Youngho felt the world slowly collapse under his feet. Last time, he had Manu with him, but he was all alone today. To make things worse, he couldn't see anyone else in the park either. He felt lightheaded and his legs started shaking.

역시 우려했던 바대로 며칠 전 만우와 마주쳤다가 가까스로 따돌렸던 바로 그 불량배 세 명이었다. 어디서 야구를 하고 오는 듯했고, 키다리는 야구방망이를 들고 있었다.

절대 도망가지 못하게 단단히 막으려는 것인지 세 명이 순식간에 영호와 차도리의 주위를 둘러쌌다.

"이것 좀 봐라? 너 참 잘 만났다!" 키다리가 입 한 쪽으로 비뚤어진 미소를 지으며 말했다. 표백한 송곳니가 빼꼼히 드러나 보였다. "뭐 여우 새끼도 제 말하면 나타난다더니...... 으흐흐!"

"여우가 아니고 호랑이! 호랑이도 제 말하면 온다!" 안경잡이가 키다리의 귀에 급히 속삭였다. 정작 속삭인다고는 해도 말하는 것이 다 들렸다. 세번째 불량배—볼에 큰 점이 있는 점박이—도 들었는지, 야구공을 글러브에 던져 넣었다 뺐다하며 손장난을 치다가 소리 내어 헤헤 웃었다. 눈앞이 막막해진 영호가 어떻게 빠져나갈 구멍이 없을지 주위를 둘러보았으나 아무리 찾아보아도 방도가 없는 듯했다.

"그래, 호랑이든 여우든 간에!" 키다리가 양쪽 두 명에게 한바탕 성깔을 부린다. "뭐면 어때? 다 거기서 거기지!"

그리고는 다시 영호에게 돌아서며 거의 히스테리성 목소리로, "지난 번에는 네 친구 돼지새끼랑 잔꾀를 부려서 달아났지만 오늘은 절대 그렇게 못 할걸!" 하며 이빨을 드러내고 으름장을 놓았다.

영호는 두 발 밑에서 땅이 서서히 꺼지는 것같이 느껴졌다. 지난번에는 만우라도 같이 있었지만 오늘은 혼자였다. 하필이면 공원에는 지나가는 사람조차 없었다. 머리가 아찔해지고 다리가 후들후들 떨려 왔다.

6-1 예기치 못한 만남·An Unexpected Encounter

물론 차도리가 있기는 했지만, 워낙 성질이 순한 데다 철저하게 훈련까지 받은 차도리가 사람을 조금이라도 위협할 리는 절대 없었다. 역시 우려했던 바와 같이 차도리는 깡패들을 보고도 꼬리를 흔들기 시작했다—행인들이 가던 길을 멈추고 쓰다듬어 줄 때 항상 그러듯.

“좋은 말할 때 순순히 들어!” 키다리가 내뱉었다. “가진 돈 있으면 다 내놔! 반항하믄 알지!”

“며칠 전 안 내고 튄 돈에 대한 이자, 벌금까지 다!” 옆에서 안경잡이가 키다리의 협박을 거든다.

“나 가, 가진 돈 없는데……” 영호가 말을 더듬으며 간신히 대답했다.

“아, 짜아식 푼수 아냐! 그럼 딴 거라두, 우씨!” 키다리가 으르렁댄다. “휴대폰, 시계…… 가진 건 다 내놔!”

He had Chadori with him, of course, but he was a gentle dog. Plus, he was strictly trained not to show the slightest sign of aggression toward people. Just as feared, Chadori started wagging his tail at the bullies—as he always did when people stopped to admire him on the street.

“I’ll say this only once,” spat Lanky. “Give up every last miserable penny on ya—or else!”

“Including the interest *and* the penalty on the part you dodged last time!” said Goggles, adding to Lanky’s threats.

“I d-don’t have any cash on me . . .” Youngho stammered.

“Anything, then, you idiot!” snarled Lanky. “Your phone, watch—just gimme everything you got!”

He ranted on some more, making threats of terrible violence and untimely death. Youngho's head started spinning. Could he avoid trouble today like last time? He kept eyeing the baseball bat in Lanky's hand. It had the air of a weapon. *What if he started swinging that!* The three of them were all taller and most probably stronger than Youngho. He felt the world closing in around him.

Then Lanky's attention shifted to Chadori. "And what's this, hey?" he said in a slightly changed tone. "Look at this mutt! Well, it's not a bad-looking mutt, is it?" Then he looked Chadori up and down for a while as if oblivious to what he had been doing. Goggles gave him a brusque nudge. Visibly embarrassed, Lanky quickly changed the subject. "Quite unlike his owner!"

The three bullies cackled loudly. Youngho had been silent up to that point. This time, he retorted indignantly.

"Chadori is not a mutt!" he said defiantly. "He is a pedigree dog all the way from Bristol, England!"

Lanky's face distorted. Youngho instantly regretted speaking at all, but it was already too late.

"What did you say?" growled Lanky through clenched teeth, taking one step closer to Youngho and towering menacingly over him.

"If I say it's a mutt, then it's a mutt, isn't it? A pedigree from where?"

From a closer angle, he appeared even bigger and more intimidating.

키다리는 계속해서 그렇게 너 맞을래, 죽을래, 한참 협박을 계속했다. 영호는 머리가 빙빙 돌기 시작했다. 오늘도 과연 전처럼 이 순간을 모면할 수 있을까. 키다리의 손에 들린 야구방망이를 거듭 곁눈질하지 않을 수 없었다. 야구방망이가 무기처럼 보였다. *저걸 휘두르기라도 하면 어쩌나!* 다들 영호보다 키도 훨씬 컸고, 힘도 분명 셀 것이다. 하늘이 무너져 내리는 것처럼 느껴졌다.

그러던 중 키다리가 차도리를 보고는, "근데 이건 또 뭐야? " 하며 목소리가 살짝 바뀌었다. "이 똥개 좀 봐라? 어쭈, 똥개 치고는 그래도 좀 생겼는데?" 하더니 금방 영호를 협박하던 사실도 잊은 듯 차도리를 위아래로 한참 훑어본다. 그러다가 안경잡이가 옆구리를 툭 치자, 몹시 당황한 듯 얼른 말을 돌렸다. "흠! 주인이랑은 전혀 다르게 말이야!"

세 명의 불량배가 큰 소리로 낄낄 웃었다. 그때까지 잠자코 있던 영호. 그러나 이번에는 자신도 모르게 발끈해서 대꾸했다.

"우리 차도리 똥개 아냐! " 영호가 반박했다. "영국 브리스톨에서 데리고 온 족보 있는 순종이란 말야!"

키다리의 표정이 일그러졌다. 아차 싶었지만 이미 쏟아진 물이었다.

키다리가 이빨을 드러내며 "뭐가 어쩌구 어째?" 하더니, 영호에게 한 발짝 더 다가서며 협박하듯 내려다보았다.

"아니, 내가 똥개라면 똥개지! 뭐 어디서 온 순종?"

가까이서 보니 생각했던 것보다 훨씬 더 덩치도 크고 위협적으로 보였다.

"You little piece of . . . you just wanna die, don't ya?" Lanky said and shoved Youngho's shoulder with one hand.

Youngho's small body swayed easily, and he staggered back a few steps.

"Haha! The mutt doesn't even know his owner is in danger," said Goggles, pointing at Chadori. "Look at that! It's still wagging its tail!"

Aghast, Youngho turned around. Sure, Chadori's tail had lost its eagerness, but it was still swaying in a slow, back-and-forth, windshield-wiper motion. Chadori looked quite confused. Were the boys merely play-fighting, like he had seen Youngho do many times before? Or was it real danger?

"It's not just a mutt, but a stupid one, or what!" Lanky sneered, gloating triumphantly.

The three bullies guffawed raucously. Youngho's mind went blank. He couldn't think straight anymore—he was at a dead end now.

"You heard him!" spat Goggles. "Pay your freakin' toll while you still have a chance, or else!"

Reassured that Chadori wouldn't attack him, Lanky acted bolder than ever now and pushed Youngho's shoulders once more—this time with both hands. Youngho's body lost its balance again. With a shriek of distress, he fell backward in a puddle of slush. The three bullies roared with braying laughter like a pack of hyenas. Thanks to the cushion of snow, Youngho wasn't hurt by the fall except that his pants were soaked in filthy ice water. Yet, he was in utter despair. *How am I going to escape this mess?*

그리고는 "이 짜아식이...... 너 죽구 싶어? " 하며 한 손으로 영호의 어깨를 떠밀었다.

영호의 작은 몸은 쉽게 휘청했고, 뒤로 몇 발짝 주춤했다.

"하하하! 똥개가 주인이 위험에 처한 지도 모르네!" 안경잡이가 차도리를 가리키며 비아냥거렸다. "저거 꼬리 흔들고 좋아하는 것 좀 봐!"

영호는 아찔하여 뒤돌아보았다. 차도리의 꼬리는 물론 평소처럼 활기차게는 아니었지만 자동차 앞 유리 닦개 돌아가듯 천천히 왔다갔다 움직이고 있었다. 차도리도 상당히 혼동이 되는 듯 보였다. 영호가 항상 그러듯 이번에도 장난 싸움을 하는 것일까? 아니면 정말 위험에 빠진 것일까?

"이 건 똥개도 아주 멍청한 똥개 아냐!" 키다리가 의기양양해서 빈정거린다.

세 명의 불량배가 다시 요란하게 웃어대고, 영호는 머리가 텅 빈 것처럼 느껴졌다. 이제 아무런 생각도 나지 않고, 도저히 이 상황에서 빠져나갈 수 있는 구멍이란 없는 듯했다.

"너 들었지!" 안경잡이가 쏘아붙인다. "좋은 말할 때 순순히 내놔, 말 안 들으면 알지!"

한편 차도리가 덤비지 않을 것이라고 확신한 키다리가 이제는 의기가 양양하다 못해 하늘을 찔러서, 한 번 더—이번에는 양손으로—영호의 어깨를 떠밀었다. 영호의 몸은 다시 중심을 잃었고, *악!* 소리와 함께 그만 얼다 만 진탕물 속에 주저앉아 버리고 말았다. 깡패들 셋이 하이에나 떼 짓듯이 웃어댔다. 영호는 그나마 다행히 눈 위에 나가떨어졌기에 더러운 얼음물에 바지 적신 것 외에는 다친 곳이 없었다. 하지만, 눈앞이 캄캄했다. *어떻게 이 곤경에서 빠져나갈 수 있을까?*

Until then, Chadori had been nothing but gentle and friendly. As soon as the cry of anguish slipped through Youngho's lips, though, he started baring his teeth—snarling. Youngho was in utter shock. It could very well be the first time in Chadori's entire life that he ever growled at anyone.

"What's that? Was it a meow?" said Lanky, trying to sound calm, but his voice shook even as he said that. "This mutt has rabies, or what?"

The other two also stopped laughing. Lanky waved his baseball bat at Chadori. In turn, Chadori went beyond growling now and began barking ferociously, as though he were about to jump on them at any moment.

"Help! A mad dog's killing us!" Lanky squawked pathetically.

The three bullies ran for their lives back the way they had come, with Chadori chasing them and barking fiercely. Lanky seemed to be running short of breath after a while. He stopped suddenly, turned around, and swung the baseball bat at Chadori. The sudden force threw it out of his grip; the bat flew to meet Chadori's flank with a dull *thump*. With a yelp of pain, Chadori fell to the ground. Lanky stopped on his way and looked back, seeming to hesitate, but took off again, leaving the baseball bat lying around in the park. The three of them were gone in a flash.

지금까지 순하게 잠자코 있던 차도리. 그러나 영호의 입에서 외마디 비명소리가 들린 그 순간, 이빨을 드러내며 으르렁대기 시작했다. 영호 스스로도 대단히 놀라지 않을 수 없었다. 특히나 사람을 보고 으르렁대는 것은 아마도 차도리가 태어나서 생전 처음이지 않을까 싶었다.

"어쭈, 이건 또 뭐야? 얘 지금 '야옹'했냐?" 키다리가 멀쩡한 척 말은 그렇게 하면서도 목소리가 떨렸다. "이 똥개 광견병 걸린 거 아냐?"

나머지 두 명도 더 이상 웃지 않았다. 키다리는 차도리를 향해 야구방망이를 휘저어 대기 시작했고, 차도리는 이제 으르렁거리는 것을 넘어서서 금방 물어뜯을 듯이 공격적으로 짖기 시작했다.

"사람 살려! 미친 개가 사람 잡는다!" 키다리가 과장되게 비명을 질렀다.

세 명의 불량배는 왔던 방향으로 다시 줄행랑을 치고, 차도리는 그 뒤를 쫓아가면서 사납게 짖어 댔다. 그러던 중 달아나던 키다리가 숨이 찬지 갑자기 멈춰 서더니, 휙 돌아서서는 달려오는 차도리를 향해 야구방망이를 휘둘러 댔다. 야구방망이는 순간적인 힘에 의해 키다리의 손에서 빠져 날아가고, *퍽!* 하고 둔한 소리를 내며 차도리의 옆구리에 맞고 말았다. 차도리가 *깨갱!* 하며 나자빠지고, 키다리가 뒤를 돌아보고는 달아나던 걸음을 멈추고 잠시 망설이는 듯했다. 그러다가 야구방망이도 공원에 내팽개친 채 다시 달아났고, 세 명의 불량배는 순식간에 꽁무니를 빼고 자취를 감추었다.

영호는 가슴이 덜컥해서 차도리에게로 달려갔다. 그러나 가까이 다가가자 차도리는 아무 일도 없었다는 듯 몸을 일으켜 세우고는, 꼬리를 흔들며 영호의 손을 핥았다. 차도리가 비록 겉보기에는 아무 상처도 없었지만, 아무래도 엄마가 자세히 살펴보도록 하는 것이 낫겠다는 생각이 들었다.

영호는 그 길로 바로 차도리를 데리고 공원을 나섰고, 서둘러서 곧장 집으로 돌아갔다. 키다리가 팽개치고 간 야구방망이가 얼핏 눈에 들어왔지만, 왠지 손도 대서는 안 될 불길한 물건 같은 예감이 들었고, 또 불량배들이 다시 찾으러 올지도 몰라 겁이 나기도 했다. 결국 한시 바삐 그곳을 벗어나고 싶은—또 차도리를 안전하게 집으로 데려가야겠다는—생각뿐이었다.

Alarmed, Youngho rushed over to Chadori. But as Youngho approached him, he got up as if nothing had happened and licked Youngho's hand, wagging his tail. On the outside, Chadori had no apparent injury, but Youngho thought it best to have Mom check him more thoroughly.

At once, he left the park with Chadori and rushed back home. His eyes caught sight of the bat Lanky had left behind, but it almost felt like a dangerous object he shouldn't even be touching; he was also afraid that the bullies might come back for it. After all, he just wanted to escape the scene as soon as possible—and take Chadori home safely.

6-2 차도리 화났어요·*Chadori is Angry*

Mom was sitting alone at the kitchen table when Youngho and Chadori arrived home.

"You are back early this evening!" she chirped cheerfully as her eyes shifted from the book she had been reading. In an instant, her grin turned into a look of concern when she noticed that something was not right.

"What's the matter?" she said immediately, alarmed. "Are you okay?"

Youngho explained what had happened.

"Oh, no!" Mom said with a screech of horror. "You poor thing! Are you hurt? I *knew* it! It's too dangerous for you to go out alone in the evening—even if you have Chadori with you!"

Then she examined Youngho from head to toe, treating him as if he were a baby.

Youngho tried his best to shrug it off. Frankly, he was quite unworried about himself, and simply wanted to make sure that Chadori was all right. Mom's reaction, on the other hand, was anything but. She was in full defense mode, bordering on hysterical, and didn't seem to be worried about Chadori at all.

"Chadori seems just fine!" she said, enraged. "It's you I'm worried about! Tell me everything you remember about them—anything! I'm going to find out which school they go to and make sure they get punished for what they did!" she raved on. "They deserve to be expelled at the very least. Oh, and we must contact the police, of course!"

영호와 차도리가 집에 도착했을 때 엄마는 부엌 식탁 앞에 혼자 앉아 있었다.

"오늘은 평소보다 빨리 왔네!" 엄마가 읽던 책에서 눈을 떼며 명랑하게 말하다가, 무언가 잘못된 것을 알아채고는 금세 미소가 걱정된 표정으로 변했다.

"아니, 왜 그래?" 엄마가 놀라서 당장 물었다. "무슨 일 있었어?"

영호는 자초지종을 대충 설명했다.

"악!" 소리와 함께 공포에 질린 목소리로 엄마가 말했다. "큰일 날 뻔했구나! 그래, 어디 다친 데는 없어? 어쩐지, 그럴 줄 알았어! 너 저녁 시간에 혼자 나다니기는 너무 위험해서 안 돼—아무리 차도리가 있어두 그렇지!"

그리고는 마치 영호가 갓난아기라도 된 듯, 머리부터 발끝까지 샅샅이 살폈다.

영호는 되도록이면 별일 없었던 것처럼 지나가려고 했다. 솔직히 스스로는 그다지 걱정되지 않았고, 그저 차도리가 어디 다치지는 않았는지 확인하고자 했을 뿐이었다. 한편 엄마의 반응은 정반대였다. 그야말로 완전 방어 태세를 넘어서서 거의 히스테리에 달하는 수준이었다. 게다가 차도리는 전혀 걱정되지 않는 듯했다.

"차도리는 다친 데 하나 없어 보이니까 걱정 끊어!" 엄마가 신경질적으로 말했다. "니 걱정이나 해! 인상착의 기억 나는 대로 다 얘기해 봐—전부 다! 정확히 어느 학교 다니는 누구인지 알아내서 반드시 저지른 일에 대한 벌을 받게 해야 돼!" 엄마가 그렇게 한동안 계속했다. "최소한 퇴학은 시켜 버려야 돼. 당연히 경찰서에 신고두 해야지!"

6-3 고양이 화나면 지옥보다 무서워요·Hell Hath No Fury like an Angry Cat

엄마가 그렇게 노발대발하는 것을 보는 것도 처음이다. 이제는 오히려 영호가 엄마를 진정시켜야 할 정도였다. 엄마는 그렇게 순순히 가볍게 지나가지 않을 성싶었다. 일단 지나고 보니, 사실 엄마가 생각하는 것만큼 그렇게 심각하지는 않았던 것도 같았다. 게다가 순식간에 일어난 일이라 세세하게 기억이 나지도 않았다. 단 한 가지 어렴풋이 생각나는 것이 있다면, 야구방망이에 무언가 써져 있는 스티커가 붙어 있었다는 것이다. 그것이 혹시 이름과 전화번호가 아니었을까.

영호는 엄마와 함께 아빠가 집에 오기를 기다려서—아빠는 저녁 식사 후 복권을 사러 잠깐 밖에 나갔었다—셋이서 영호가 불량배들을 만났던 자리에 가 보았다. 하지만 불량배들이 이미 찾아갔는지 야구방망이는 온데간데없었다.

Youngho couldn't remember seeing her so angry before—ever. Now it was Youngho who had to calm her down; she didn't look like she was going to let it go that easily. Thinking it over, in fact, it wasn't as dreadful as Mom made it out to be. Moreover, things happened so fast; Youngho couldn't quite recall every single detail. One thing he vaguely remembered, though, was a label on the baseball bat with something written on it—possibly a name and phone number.

Youngho and Mom waited for Dad to come home—he had gone out after dinner to buy a lottery ticket—and then the three of them went together to the spot where Youngho met the bullies. There was no trace of the bat, however. Maybe the bullies got there first.

Mom was quite upset that they couldn't find the bat, which she claimed was a crucial piece of evidence, but Youngho was somehow relieved. It was almost as though all the bad things that had happened would go away if he could just forget about everything and leave it at that.

After that day, Mom decreed that Youngho and Chadori take their evening walks before dinner rather than afterward —and avoid late evening hours at all costs. To Youngho's relief, however, she didn't go so far as to call the police.

As for Chadori, he was perfectly fine on the outside, but he had almost entirely stopped eating since the incident and couldn't poop either. In the end, Youngho got Mom to agree to take Chadori to the animal hospital. At twelve, he was not exactly in his prime in dog age—a check-up at the vet's was long overdue.

Just in case.

엄마는 야구방망이가 결정적인 물증이라며 찾지 못한 것을 한탄했지만, 영호에게는 차라리 다행스럽게 느껴졌다. 왠지 그냥 그렇게 잊고 내버려 두면 나쁜 일이 있었던 사실 자체가 사라져 버릴 것만 같아서였다. 그날 이후로 차도리의 산책은 저녁 먹은 후가 아니라 저녁 먹기 전—반드시 늦은 저녁 시간을 피하여—시키라는 엄마의 엄명이 떨어졌다. 하지만 다행히도 엄마는 경찰서 신고까지 가지는 않았다.

한편 차도리는 겉보기는 멀쩡했지만, 그날 이후로 밥도 거의 안 먹고 똥도 누지 못했다. 결국 영호는 엄마를 졸라 차도리를 동물병원에 데려가 보기로 했다. 이제 차도리도 열두 살로 개로서는 젊은 나이가 아니었고, 건강 진단을 한 번 받을 때도 되고도 한참 지났기 때문이었다.

만약을 대비해서 말이다.

7

잔인한 토요일

THE CRUEL SATURDAY

공원에서 있었던 그 일 이후로 일주일 조금 넘게 지났을까. 이제 차도리는 많이 좋아져서 밥도 먹고 물도 마셨다. 하지만 여전히 똥은 누지 못했다. 누려고 시도는 계속했으나 정작 아무것도 나오지 않는 것이었다.

More than a week passed since that terrible day at the park. Chadori was much better now. He started eating and drinking again, but he still couldn't poop. He did try again and again, but nothing came out.

7-1 SOS! 차도리가 풍선처럼 부풀어요!·Help! Chadori Is Bloating like a Balloon!

걱정되는 것은 이렇게 가다가는 몸이 초대형 풍선처럼 부풀어 오르지 않을까 싶었다. 한쪽으로 들어가기만 하고 다른 쪽으로는 나오는 것이 없으니……

영호는 여느 때처럼 차도리와 산책을 하고 돌아왔다. 엄마의 명령대로 저녁 먹기 전. 산책을 하면서 차도리의 변비에 대해 곰곰이 생각을 해 보았다. 차도리 같은 사냥개가 하루 한 번 산책으로 부족했던 것은 아닐까. 사냥개들은 충분히 뛰고 운동량도 많아야 한다는데…… 생각에 생각을 거듭한 영호는 결국 결론에 도달했다. 차도리와 함께 달려 본 지도 한참 지난 것 같았다.

It bothered Youngho—if this went on much longer, Chadori might start bloating like a huge balloon. Something going in one end and nothing coming out the other . . .

Youngho went for a walk with Chadori as usual, but before dinnertime as Mom had ordered. During the walk, he brooded on Chadori's constipation. He wondered if their daily walks were enough for his four-legged brother. Chadori was a hunting dog, after all. Hunting breeds were meant to run around and get loads of exercise. Youngho pondered this and concluded that it had been far too long since the last time they ran around together.

They could start playing soccer again, for example. He remembered how much fun it was; he made a mental note to take it up again—when the snow melted—as he opened the door and stepped in. He stopped at the entrance to wipe Chadori's feet, when he heard Mom's voice:

"Youngho, is that you?" she said in a suspiciously formal tone. "Can you come over here and sit down for a bit?"

"Sure, Mom," replied Youngho, but something wasn't quite right.

She often spoke in a weird, stiff voice like that when she had either bad news to break or something to tell him off about. Youngho started wondering, *What have I done this time?*

Unwillingly, Youngho walked past the bedrooms that lined the corridor—dragging his feet—then turned right toward the living room. Mom was sitting on the far end of the light-pink synthetic-leather sofa, near the glass doors leading to the balcony. She wasn't doing anything in particular: The TV wasn't on; There wasn't a book or a magazine on the coffee table either—not even a cup of coffee or tea.

Mom was always doing something incessantly, deeming a minute of pause as time wasted. *Ah, well, that's a first!* Youngho thought and sat gingerly at the other end of the sofa, as far from her as possible. *Judging from the soft expression on her face, though, it doesn't look like I've done anything wrong. It's even freakier that she looks kind of depressed. About what . . . ?*

"It's okay. Come closer," Mom said, gently patting the seat next to her.

예를 들어서 같이 축구를 다시 시작해 볼 수도 있지 않을까. 차도리와 축구를 하던 그때 정말 너무도 재미있었던 것 같다. 영호는 눈이 녹는 대로 다시 시작해 보겠다고 다짐하며 문을 들어섰다. 막 현관에 멈추어 서서 차도리 발을 닦아 주려는데 엄마 목소리가 들려왔다.

"영호, 왔니?" 왠지 수상하게 형식적인 목소리였다. "여기 와서 좀 앉아 볼래?"

"네" 대답하면서도 무언가 예감이 이상했다.

보통 엄마가 꺼내기 어려운 말 또는 무슨 꾸지람할 일이 있을 때 잘 쓰는 딱딱하고 어색한 말투였다. *내가 이번엔 또 무슨 일을 저질렀지?* 하는 생각이 들었다.

가기 싫었지만 어쩔 수 없이 현관 앞 복도를 따라 줄지어 선 방문들을 지나—발을 질질 끌며—오른쪽으로 돌아 거실로 향했다. 엄마는 연분홍색 인조가죽 소파 맨 가장자리 베란다 유리문 쪽에 앉아 있었다. 특별히 하고 있는 일도 없어 보였다. TV도 꺼져 있고, 탁자 위에 책이나 잡지조차도 보이지 않았다—하다못해 커피잔이나 찻잔도 하나 없었다.

엄마는 언제나 끊임없이 무언가를 하면서 단 일 분의 휴식도 시간 낭비로 간주하는 성격이었다. *정말 살다 보니 별일이네!* 생각하며 엄마와 최대한 거리를 두고 소파 반대쪽 끝자리에 조심스레 앉았다. *부드러운 표정으로 봐서는 내가 뭘 잘못해서 그러는 것 같지는 않은데...... 왠지 울적해 보이는 것이 더 수상하다. 왜 무엇 때문에 그러는 거지?*

"괜찮아, 이리로 가까이 와서 앉아 봐......" 엄마가 손바닥으로 소파 옆자리를 살짝 두드리며 말했다.

Not totally convinced, Youngho grudgingly shuffled along the couch, inching toward her without even lifting his seat. It almost felt as though he were wiping the sofa clean with his backside—not that it needed more cleaning, of course. The apartment was always in immaculate condition, especially now that Mom had more time on her hands. Her eyes fixed on the empty space ahead, Mom rested one hand on his shoulder. He quickly looked around in the same direction, but he didn't find anything there—nothing but the empty coffee table and bare wooden floor.

If it isn't me, is it because of Chadori? Has he done something wrong? Perhaps he couldn't hold it anymore and just had to go? It must have been bucketloads by now since he hasn't been able to do it for almost ten days!

But wait—Chadori would never do that—he's house-trained, and that's a fact! Plus, the house smells fine . . . Youngho could still detect the scent of lemon from the cleaning wipes Mom used to mop the floor. Not a single strand of dog hair was visible.

"I got a call from the vet this morning," she started gingerly.

Youngho felt the floor vanish from beneath him. With a jerk of his head, he turned to face her. Her sad look was already telling him everything there was to know.

Youngho suddenly understood.

Mom told him about the phone call in detail. They got the test results back and found the real cause of Chadori's recent change in behavior.

영호는 마음이 내키지 않았지만 하는 수 없이, 궁둥이를 소파에서 떼지도 않은 채 조금씩 굼실굼실 엄마 옆으로 옮겨 갔다. 마치 엉덩이로 소파를 닦고 있는 듯한 느낌이었다—물론 소파는 더 이상 닦거나 할 필요는 없었지만 말이다. 집 전체는 항상 티끌 하나 없을 정도로 깨끗했다. 특히나 엄마가 시간이 더 넉넉해진 지금은 더더욱. 엄마는 눈 앞의 허공을 응시한 채 영호의 어깨에 손을 올렸다. 영호는 재빨리 엄마가 보고 있는 쪽을 돌아보았지만, 텅 빈 탁자와 나무 바닥 외에는 아무 것도 없었다.

나 때문에 그런 게 아니라면...... 차도리 때문인가? 차도리가 집에서 무슨 일이라도 저질렀나? 혹시 더 이상 참지 못하고 그냥 싸 버린 건가? 거의 열흘 동안 누지 못한 것이 쌓여서 한 바가지 나오고도 넘었을 텐데!

그런데 잠깐, 차도리는 똥오줌 가리는 건 기본인데 설마 그랬을 리가. 게다가 아무 냄새도 안 나는데...... 거실에는 아직도 엄마가 바닥 닦을 때 쓰는 청소포의 레몬향이 풍겼고, 개털 하나 보이지 않았다.

"오늘 아침에 동물병원에서 전화가 왔는데......" 엄마가 조심스레 말을 꺼냈다.

발 밑에서 땅이 꺼지는 것 같았다. 영호는 순간적으로 엄마를 돌아보았다. 엄마의 슬픈 표정이 이미 모든 것을 다 말해 주고 있지 않은가.

영호는 갑자기 모든 것을 알아차렸다.

엄마가 통화 내용에 대해서 자세히 설명했다. 검사 결과가 나왔는데, 최근 차도리가 행동이 이상해진 진짜 이유를 알아냈다는 것이다.

The problem was not the baseball bat—but that he had terminal cancer. It was the real reason he had trouble eating and couldn't "go to the bathroom," as Mom put it. Cancerous cells had already spread through his body beyond control, making any kind of treatment a lost cause—not to mention the considerable cost. Even if they went ahead with the surgery against all odds, the procedure would be extremely tough on Chadori—and there was no guarantee it would work. If it worked, he probably had only a few months to live; he would spend those months in pain. All things considered, it was best to put him down—for Chadori's sake more than anything.

In a numb shockwave, Youngho's mind went empty. He simply couldn't think at all. He got up from the sofa and rushed back to the front door. Paws still wet from the walk, Chadori sat there exactly as Youngho had left him, waiting.

"Youngho!" Mom's anxious voice called out behind him.

Without saying a word, Youngho stormed out the door with Chadori. He just wanted to get away—as far away as possible.

Far away from reality.

Youngho led Chadori back on their daily walk through the park. Chadori, not knowing the reason, trotted along, just happy to get another walk.

문제는 야구방망이에 맞아서가 아니라, 암 말기라서 그렇다고. 또 차도리가 밥도 잘 못 먹고 엄마의 말을 빌려서 "화장실을 못 가는" 이유가 사실은 그래서라고. 게다가 몸 전체에 암세포가 퍼질 대로 퍼져 완전한 치료 자체가 불가능하며, 혹 엄청난 비용을 감수하고 치료를 받는다고 해도 수술 자체가 차도리에게 대단히 힘들뿐더러 성공을 기대할 수도 없다는 것이었다. 또 성공한다고 해도 몇 달 더 살 수 있을지 모르는 데다가, 그 몇 달마저도 고통 속에서 보내야 하니, 이 모든 것을 고려했을 때 안락사를 시키는 것이 최선의 방법이라고 했다—무엇보다도 차도리 스스로를 위해서.

영호는 충격에 마비되었는지 머릿속이 텅 빈 것 같았고, 아무 생각도 나지 않았다. 그리고는 그대로 자리를 박차고 일어나 다시 현관으로 뛰쳐나갔다. 차도리는 아직도 산책하다가 젖은 발 그대로 앉아서 영호를 기다리고 있었다.

"얘, 영호야!"

엄마의 안타까운 목소리가 등 뒤에서 들려왔지만, 영호는 말없이 차도리를 데리고 문을 뛰쳐나갔다. 그냥 멀리, 할 수 있는 한 아주 멀리 도망쳐 버리고 싶었다.

현실에서 아주 멀리.

집을 나선 영호는 그냥 차도리와 평소 산책하는 공원으로 향했다. 차도리는 영문도 모르고 얼떨결에 산책을 한 번 더 하게 되어 신이 나서 따라왔다.

Youngho trudged on until, after a while, he got too tired to walk more. Eventually, they sat on the snow-covered steps by the river, watching the sun go down over the mountains behind the high-rise buildings on the other side of the river. The evening air was crisp with cold; the sky was clear, dappled with red and pink from the sunset, which gradually turned purple and orange.

It was beautiful—the kind of intense beauty that made you cry without knowing why. Youngho wrapped an arm around Chadori's body, buried his face in the feathery fur on his head, and breathed in the familiar, cozy scent.

A smell that could warm.

Tears streamed down his face. Chadori licked the tears from Youngho's cheeks. Did he know the trouble he was in? *It's me that usually gets in trouble, not you!* Chadori's tongue tickled Youngho's cheeks just like the first day they met. It was soft and rough at the same time—and it made him smile. Then his smile turned into a chortle of delight before his face crumpled again, covered in tears that streaked down his cheeks, leaving a salty taste on his lips.

Youngho and Chadori sat there until the sun went down. It was already getting dark when they headed back home. Under normal circumstances—especially after the incident with the bullies—all hell would have broken loose if Youngho came home after sunset. Today, though, Mom didn't say anything and quietly set the table for him.

걷고 또 걷다가 더이상 걷지 못할 정도로 지친 영호는 차도리와 함께 강변 눈 쌓인 계단에 앉아 강 건너 고층 빌딩들 뒤 산 너머로 지는 해를 바라보았다. 저녁 공기는 찼다. 하늘은 맑았고, 노을에 붉은색, 핑크색으로 물들었다가 또 보라색, 주황색으로 젖어 갔다.

너무나도 아름다웠고, 왠지 모르게 그 아름다움으로 인해 더더욱 코끝이 찡해졌다. 영호는 옆에 앉아 있는 차도리의 몸을 한 팔로 끌어안은 채, 차도리의 머리 위 부드러운 털에 얼굴을 묻고 숨을 들이쉬었다. 영호가 너무나도 잘 알고 있는 아늑한 냄새가 느껴졌다.

따스함을 주는 냄새.

눈에서는 눈물이 주르륵 흘러내렸다. 차도리는 영호의 뺨에 흘러내리는 눈물을 핥아 주었다. *차도리는 지금 자기가 어떤 처지에 놓여 있는지 알기나 할까? 보통 궁지에 몰리는 사람은 나지, 네가 아냐!* 차도리의 혓바닥이 영호와 처음 만나던 그날처럼 뺨을 간지럽혔다. 부드러우면서도 깔끄러운 그 느낌—저절로 얼굴에 미소가 퍼졌다. 미소는 주체할 수 없는 웃음으로 변하고, 그렇게 웃다가 영호의 얼굴은 또 일그러지고 말았다. 두 뺨이 그렇게 다시 눈물로 얼룩지고, 입술은 소금기로 절어 갔다.

영호는 차도리와 함께 그냥 그렇게 앉아 있다가 해가 지고 어두워질 때쯤에야 집으로 향했다. 평소 같으면—특히 불량배들과 있었던 그 일 이후로—해가 진 후에 집에 들어갔다가는 꾸지람을 듣고도 남았을 것이었지만, 오늘만은 엄마도 아무 말 하지 않고 그저 말없이 영호의 밥상을 차려 주었다.

차도리가 최후의 주사를 맞기로 한 운명의 토요일은 단 한순간의 오차도 없이 빨리도 찾아왔다. 차도리는 지난 며칠간 다시 식음을 전폐하고 있었기에 마르고 쇠약해져 있었고, 털조차도 윤기를 잃고 또 많이 빠졌다. 영호네는 온 가족이 함께 동물병원에 갔지만, 그 누구도 아무런 말도 하지 않았다. 나갈 준비를 하는 동안에도. 동물병원으로 향하는 차 안에서도. 차도리도 그런 분위기를 눈치 챈 것인지, 단지 힘이 없어서 그런 것인지, 평소와는 달리 아주 침울해 보였다. 일단 동물병원에 도착한 후에는 순식간에 모든 것이 끝나 버렸다. 차도리는 모든 것을 포기한 듯, 시술 침대 위에 누워 힘없이 꼬리를 흔들었다.

The fateful Saturday when Chadori was scheduled to receive the final injection came far too soon, without a second's delay. Having stopped eating altogether again, he had thinned considerably; even his fur had lost its luster and volume. Youngho's family all went to the vet together, but nobody spoke a word. Not while they were getting ready. Not in the car either. Maybe Chadori sensed something, too—or he was just unwell. He looked unusually gloomy. Once at the vet's, things happened very quickly. Lying on the examination table, Chadori moved his tail weakly in apparent resignation.

7-2 노을을 바라보며·*Watching the Sunset*

Youngho laid his hand on his furry best friend as the fatal injection was administered—he could feel his warmth under his palm. Tears ran down his face and fell over Chadori's body, which suddenly went limp and began to lose its warmth.

Slowly. Comfortably.

Youngho and his family left the vet's office in silence, leaving Chadori's rapidly cooling body behind. They drove home without a word. When they arrived, they had dinner in silence, trying to avoid eye contact with one another. The evening news was on, but nobody was really watching.

차도리에게 마지막 주사가 놓일 때, 영호는 그 몸 위에 손을 얹었다. 차도리의 따스한 온기가 손바닥에 느껴졌다. 두 눈에서는 눈물이 하염없이 흘러내려 차도리 위로 떨어졌다. 순식간에 그 몸에서 남은 기운마저 빠져나가고, 그렇게 몸이 식어 갔다.

서서히. 안락하게.

영호 가족은 급속하게 식어 가는 차도리의 몸을 뒤로하고, 아무 말도 주고받지 않은 채 묵묵히 동물병원을 나섰다. 집에 오는 길 차 안에서도 그 누구도 말 한마디 하지 않았다. 집에 도착해서는 함께 침묵 속에 저녁을 먹었고, 그러면서도 애써 서로의 눈을 피했다. TV에서 저녁뉴스가 흘러 나왔지만, 사실상 보는 사람은 아무도 없었다.

8

강변의 노을

SUNSET BY THE RIVER

"야구미호! 어디 가냐, 주인님 놔두구?" 만우가 영호의 뒤를 허겁지겁 따라오며 외쳤다. "너 또 치사하게!"

지난 며칠간 그래 왔듯이, 오늘도 영호는 학교가 끝나자마자 곧바로 혼자 교실을 나섰다.

"Yo, *Kumiho*! Where are you going without your master?" shouted Manu, hurrying after Youngho. "Again! Shame on you!"

Youngho darted straight to the exit once his classes were over—alone, like he had done for the past few days.

By the time he caught up with Youngho, Manu was gasping for breath. Under normal circumstances, they would always leave the classroom together. Since Chadori's death, however, Youngho morphed into a ghost. He showed up to school all right, but he just came and went silently without saying anything beyond a monosyllabic *hi* and *bye*. He simply didn't want to connect with anybody—least of all joking and laughing like before. That was probably why he shunned even his best friend. While Manu was saddened by Youngho's sudden change, he knew what had happened to Chadori. Without saying much, he just hoped that Youngho would heal in time.

But today was different—the long, forty-day winter break had just begun. They probably wouldn't see each other for weeks. What was more, the boys had to change schools to enter junior high shortly after the break. The school they would be assigned to depended entirely on the luck of the draw—a random, computerized lottery. So it was more likely that they would be placed in different schools—especially now that Manu lived in another school district. If that was the case, they only had a week or so left together after the break.

Around them, students of all ages poured out through the school gate in small groups, chattering and laughing boisterously. Of course, the entrance was permanently brimming with life, with everyone flocking in and out of school. Today, it was even livelier than usual—which was not surprising given that, with a long winter break ahead full of new adventures and unknown possibilities, they had all become millionaires in the currency of time.

겨우 간신히 영호를 따라잡은 만우가 가쁜 숨을 몰아쉰다. 평소 같으면 어김없이 둘이 함께 교실을 나서곤 했지만, 차도리의 죽음 이후로 영호는 유령 같은 존재가 되어 버렸다. 그나마 학교에는 나타났으나 그저 말없이 조용히 왔다가 사라졌고, 단순한 인사말 이상은 그 어떤 말도 하지 않았다. 그 누구도 가까이하고 싶지 않았고, 특히나 이전처럼 웃고 농담을 주고받고 하는 것 따위는 도저히 견딜 수조차 없었던 것이다. 그래서인지 절친한 친구인 만우마저 외면해 온 것이다. 만우는 이런 영호의 갑작스런 돌변에 대해 상당히 섭섭해한 것은 사실이었지만, 차도리에 대한 일도 이미 알고 있었기에 그저 시간이 지나면 나아지겠거니 하고 별말 하지 않았다.

하지만 오늘은 달랐다. 오늘은 장장 40일간의 겨울방학이 시작되는 날. 몇 주 내내 못 보게 될 것이 분명했고, 더군다나 방학이 끝난 후에는 얼마 지나지 않아 학교가 바뀌고 중학교에 진학하게 될 텐데, 학교 배정 결과가 임의적인 컴퓨터 추첨에 의해 결정되기 때문에 서로 다른 학교에 배정될 확률이 높았다—특히나 만우가 다른 학군에 속하게 된 지금은 더더욱. 정말 그렇게 된다면 방학이 끝나고 함께할 날도 고작 일주일쯤밖에 남지 않은 셈이었다.

주위에는 크고 작은 아이들이 지지배배 웃고 떠들며 삼삼오오 교문을 나서고 있었다. 물론 교문 주위는 들어오고 나가는 아이들 무리로 항상 분위기가 들떠 있었지만, 오늘은 평소보다도 유난히 활기찼다. 그도 그럴 것이 긴긴 겨울방학을 앞두고 새로운 모험이 기다리는 미지의 가능성에, 모두가 시간의 백만장자가 된 듯한 마음에 부풀어 있었던 것이다.

평소였다면—특히나 오늘 같은 날은—그 누구보다도 먼저 나서서 그런 분위기를 만끽했을 영호였다. 하지만 오늘만은 그런 느낌이 너무나도 싫었다. 싫었을 뿐만 아니라 잠시도 견딜 수 없어 최대한 빨리 그 자리를 벗어나고 싶었다. 그래서 마지막 시간이 끝나자마자 서둘러서 교실을 나섰고, 그런 영호의 뒤를 만우가 허겁지겁 책가방을 챙겨 들고 따라나선 것이다.

"야, 구미호!" 영호의 뒤를 따라가던 만우가 다시 소리쳤다. "기다려 보라니까! 왜 그렇게 빨리 걷는 거냐!"

만우가 기어이 영호를 따라잡아 앞을 가로막았다. 영호가 그런 만우를 피해 가려 했지만 만우가 번번히 앞을 막아선다.

"뭐가 그렇게 급해? 어쨌든, 여기 이거!"

Youngho had always been one of the first to revel in such happy thoughts—especially on a day like this. But he simply couldn't take it today. He couldn't even bear the thought of it and had to get away as quickly as possible. As soon as the last class ended, Youngho headed straight for the exit. Manu packed his bag in a hurry and dashed after him.

"Hey, Foxy!" Manu called out again behind Youngho. "Wait for me! You're walking too fast!"

He eventually caught up with him and stood in front, blocking his way. Youngho tried to walk around him, only to be blocked again.

"What's the rush? Anyways, here!"

8-1 시간의 백만장자들·The Time Millionaires

Manu took something out of his satchel and thrust it toward Youngho's face. It was an envelope. Youngho stared at the pristine white paper without a word.

"Take it! Before I change my mind!"

They made Christmas cards in art class earlier today. Youngho didn't get to finish a single one, as he just sat there, cutting the colored paper into tiny bits and pieces. Needless to say, he didn't have a card for Manu.

"Well, you certainly don't act as if you deserve one," grumbled Manu. "But it's already got your name written on it. Just take it!"

Manu waved the envelope in his buddy's face, his patience clearly wearing thin. Without thanking him—or even meeting his eyes—Youngho snatched the card from Manu's hand, pulled down the side zipper of his backpack, and shoved it inside, still unopened. It was the final straw for Manu.

"How can you do this to me?" he protested, exploding in frustration. "We won't see each other for more than a month, and then we'll probably be put into different schools after that!"

At last, Youngho glared at Manu, his eyes burning like fire.

"And whose fault is that?" he snapped. "It's because *you* moved, knowing full well we were about to change schools. Don't you tell me *you* didn't know exactly what was going to happen!"

만우가 가방에서 무언가를 꺼내 영호 앞에 불쑥 내민다. 봉투였다. 영호의 눈이 멍하니 만우의 손에 들린 새하얀 봉투를 바라보았다.

"받어! 마음 바뀌기 전에!"

마침 오늘 있었던 미술시간에 크리스마스카드를 만들었다. 하지만 영호는 색종이만 조각조각 자르고 있다가 결국 한 장도 못 만들었다. 만우에게 줄 카드도 물론 없었다.

"그냥 하는 꼴 봐서는 콱! 카드구 뭐구, 으휴!" 만우가 궁시렁댄다. "어쨌든 이왕 너 이름 썼으니까 얼릉 받어!"

만우가 참을성의 한계에 다다른 듯, 손에 든 카드를 영호의 눈앞에 흔들었다. 영호는 고맙다는 말도 없이—만우의 얼굴 한 번 제대로 쳐다보지 않은 채—손에서 카드를 가로채듯 빼앗아 가방 옆 지퍼를 열고 밀어넣었다. 봉투조차 뜯어보지 않았다. 만우가 참다 못해 드디어 폭발했다.

"너 이래두 되는 거냐?" 하고 따진다. "인제 거의 한 달 넘게 못 보구, 또 보나마나 뻔히 서루 다른 학교 배정될 텐데!"

끝내 영호가 만우를 노려보았다. 두 눈이 불처럼 타오른다.

"그게 누구 때문인데?"하고 바로 쏘아붙였다. "바루 니가 학교 바뀌는 거 알면서 하필 그때 이사 가서! 그러면 어떻게 될 꺼라는 거 뻔히 다 알면서두!"

Manu seemed taken aback by Youngho's sudden outburst of resentment. After a moment's awkward silence, he replied in an exasperated, but soft voice.

"Youngho, that's not fair," he said. "You know very well I had absolutely no choice. My parents—"

"You had no choice!" barked Youngho, cutting him short. "Do I look like I have any choice in anything, then? Just go away and leave me alone, like everybody else!"

Manu looked down, a pained expression on his face.

"You're still upset about Chadori, I know, Youngho," he said quietly, putting a hand on Youngho's arm. "I know it's hard, but you just have to accept the fact that your dog is dead now and move on."

"What do you know about how I feel? Just leave me alone, I said!" Youngho bellowed. "Chadori is not just a dog!" Then, his voice cracking into a whimper, he added, "He is . . . He is . . ."

Tears ran down Youngho's face—tears he thought had dried up. Unfortunately for Manu, the grief that had been building inside Youngho erupted right at that moment. The excited chatter nearby came to an abrupt halt, and everybody stopped to gawk at them, looking from one to the other. Youngho stormed out of the gate and started running—away from there, far away from everything. He left Manu standing there, looking shocked and lost for words.

영호의 갑작스런 감정폭발에 만우는 순간 움찔한 듯했다. 잠시 거북한 정적이 흐르고, 만우가 울분을 억누르는 듯 조용한 목소리로 대답했다.

"김영호, 너두 알잖냐." 만우의 해명. "내가 무슨 힘이 있냐. 우리 부모님이—"

"힘이 없어서 그랬다구!" 영호가 만우의 말을 끊고 버럭 소리를 질렀다. "그래서! 난 어디 무슨 힘이 있어 보여? 그냥 나 혼자 있게 꺼져 버려! 전부 다!"

만우가 참담한 표정으로 우두커니 땅만 내려다보았다.

"영호 너 차도리 일 때메 많이 힘든 거 나두 알어." 만우가 영호의 팔에 손을 얹으며 조심스레 말을 꺼냈다. "힘들긴 하지만서두, 너네 집 개 그렇게 된 거는 인제 그냥 기정사실루 받아들이구 너두 살아야 하지 않겠냐."

"니가 알기는 뭘 알어! 참견하지 말구 나 혼자 있게 꺼지라니까!" 영호가 비명을 지르듯 큰 소리로 외쳤다. "차도리는 그냥 개가 아니란 말야!|" 그리고는 말을 채 잇지 못하고 목이 메어 울먹였다. "차도리는...... 차도리는......"

눈에서는 그동안 메말라 버렸다고 생각되었던 눈물이 주르륵 흘러내렸다. 그동안 말없이 쌓여 온 슬픔이 죄 없는 만우에게 한꺼번에 폭발해 버린 것이다. 신나게 떠들며 지나가던 아이들이 순식간에 쥐 죽은 듯 조용해지고, 놀란 표정으로 영호와 만우를 번갈아 바라보았다. 영호는 그대로 곧장 도망치듯 학교를 뛰쳐나왔다. 그리고는 무작정 달렸다. 그냥 이 자리에서, 모든 것에서 벗어나고 싶었다. 충격에 할 말을 잃은 듯 제자리에 얼어붙어 서 있는 만우를 뒤로한 채.

8-2 터져 버린 기대의 풍선·The Bubble Bursts

영호는 차도리의 안락사 이후로 매일 그래 왔듯이 학교를 나서자마자 곧장 차도리와 함께 산책하던 공원으로 가서 혼자 무작정 걸었다. 마음속 깊은 곳에 쌓이고 쌓이다 막혀 버렸다고 생각되었던 슬픔이 드디어 출구를 찾았는지 한꺼번에 거센 파도가 되어 밀려왔다. 조용히 눈물을 흘리다가는 또 큰 소리로 엉엉 울고, 그렇게 눈물도 점차 소리 없는 흐느낌으로 말라 갔다. 사람들이 쳐다보아도 개의치 않았고, 혹자 마음씨 좋은 행인들이 무슨 일이 있냐, 도움이 필요한 것은 아니냐 물어봐도 그냥 무시하고 도망치듯 피해 갔다. 한참을 걷고 또 걷던 영호는 차도리와 둘이 하던 것처럼 강둑 계단에 앉아 저녁노을을 바라보았다.

As he did after school every day since Chadori's death, Youngho headed straight to the park where they used to go for a walk together and wandered around alone. The sorrow that had been trapped deep within found an outlet at last and gushed out in torrents; quiet tears soon turned into bawling sobs and then gradually abated into a silent weep. People stared, but Youngho didn't care. Some good-hearted strangers asked if something was wrong and if they could do anything to help, but he just ignored them and walked away. Youngho plodded around the park for a while. Then he sat on the steps down by the riverbank and watched the sunset, like he used to with Chadori.

The setting sun colored everything red, gold, pink, purple, and orange, just like before—the sky, the clouds, the apartment blocks along the riverbank—the whole world around them. The same world Youngho and Chadori used to gaze at together. Everything seemed to be in auburn flames, which reminded him of Chadori's fur against the sunset.

They never even got to play soccer again.

After sitting there in the cold for hours, crying and watching the sunset, Youngho felt strangely calm. Sadness ran its course through his body, spreading from head to toe, all the way to his fingertips. It lingered there for a while, then gradually dissipated, leaving a slightly weary sensation. Before he knew it, the sun had already plunged behind the mountains, and it was beginning to get dark. Feeling a surge of fatigue followed by an irresistible hunger, he headed home.

The whole family was gathered for dinner that evening, even though it was a weekday—it had been a while since they last had dinner together. They sat around the coffee table as usual. They were having Korean barbecue, grilling slices of meat—beef brisket today—on a table grill, and made *ssam,* wraps with salad leaves, with the grilled meat, accompanied by boiled rice, sesame oil dip, and several side dishes. Since Chadori's death, Youngho had been keeping quiet even at home, except for the bare essentials. Mom broke the silence first.

지는 햇빛은 이전처럼 모든 것을 빨강, 노랑, 또 핑크, 보라색, 주황색 등으로 물들여 갔다—하늘. 구름. 강변에 늘어선 아파트 단지...... 주위의 모든 세상. 차도리와 늘 함께 바라보던 바로 그 세상. 붉게 타오르는 그 세상을 보고 있자니 마치 노을에 불타는 차도리의 털을 보고 있는 것만 같았다.

결국 차도리와 축구도 다시 해 보지 못했다.

그렇게 추운 강둑에 앉아 울고 또 울며 지는 노을을 바라보니, 마음이 어느 정도 진정되는 듯도 했다. 슬픔은 머리부터 발끝까지 몸 구석구석 퍼졌고, 손끝에서 한동안 머물다가 나른한 여운만 남긴 채 서서히 사라져 버렸다. 어느새 해도 산 너머로 넘어가 버리고 이제 서서히 어두워지기 시작했다. 영호는 갑자기 밀려오는 피로를 느끼고 배도 고프고 해서 곧장 집으로 향했다.

평일임에도 불구하고 오늘은 온 가족이 모여 저녁을 먹었다. 이렇게 함께 밥을 먹어 보는 것도 정말 오래간만이었다. 늘 그러듯 거실 탁자에 옹기종기 둘러앉았다. 오늘은 고기—차돌박이—를 구워 쌈을 싸 먹었다. 밥, 반찬, 참기름장 등 제법 갖출 것은 다 갖추었다. 차도리의 안락사 이후 영호는 집에서도 꼭 필요한 몇 마디 외에는 별말이 없었다. 엄마가 먼저 침묵을 깼다.

"Youngho, your winter break began today, didn't it?" she said, making a conscious effort to sound lighthearted. "And it will be Minji's turn in a few days!"

Youngho felt much better after crying his eyes out in the park. He decided to open his mouth for once.

"Yeah, it's about time! I can finally get some sleep. . . I'm gonna sleep all day, every day, for at least a week!" he said, ending with a long yawn and stretching his arms wide in an exaggerated breaststroke.

While what Youngho said was nothing special, the other three seemed pleasantly surprised to see him join the everyday conversation; they exchanged looks of relief with one another when he was not looking. The atmosphere around the dinner table brightened considerably. The evening news was on, and the weatherman predicted cold weather with clear skies in the days leading up to Christmas. On Christmas Day, though, it was likely to snow.

"A white Christmas . . . so romantic, isn't it?" said Mom, smiling dreamily and turning to Youngho and Minji. Then she seemed to remember something. "Minji, are you going to Christmas Mass at the cathedral downtown—like you and your friends did last year?"

"We are going to a Christmas service, yeah," Minji replied, "but at another place this year—a small church next to school. I think it's Protestant . . . All the good-looking boys in my grade go there, you know."

Dad jumped at the first chance to tease Minji.

"오늘부터 영호는 벌써 겨울방학이구나, 그치?" 하며 애써 명랑하게 들리려는 듯 말했다. "또 며칠 지나면 민지 차례네!"

공원에서 마음껏 울고 나서 어느 정도 마음이 풀린 영호. 이번에는 입을 열어 대답해 보기로 했다.

"어, 드디어! 잠두 실컷 자구…… 최소한 일주일은 하루 종일 잠만 자야지!" 영호가 큰 하품과 함께, 양팔을 한껏 뻗어 개구리헤엄을 치듯 기지개를 켜는 것으로 말을 맺었다.

별다른 말은 아니었지만, 영호가 다시 일상의 대화에 참여하기 시작했다는 것 자체에 다들 내심 놀라고 또 반가워했고, 영호가 안 보는 사이 서로 안도의 눈빛을 주고받았다. 그렇게 저녁상 분위기는 유난히도 화기애애해졌다. TV에서는 저녁뉴스가 흘러 나오고, 일기예보에서는 앞으로 크리스마스까지 며칠간은 춥지만 맑은 날씨라는 것, 하지만 크리스마스 당일은 눈이 내릴 확률이 높다는 것을 예고했다.

"화이트 크리스마스…… 정말 운치 있겠다, 그치?" 엄마가 낭만에 젖은 듯 미소 지었다. 그러다 문득 생각난 듯, "참, 민지 너 올해두 시내 성당에 크리스마스 미사 보러 갈 꺼니?" 한다. "왜 작년에 친구들이랑 가지 않았어?"

"어, 크리스마스 예배 보기는 볼 껀데……" 민지의 대답. "근데 올해는 다른 데 가기루 했어—학교 앞에 있는 작은 교회야. 개신교라는 것 같던데…… 우리 학년에 잘생긴 남자애들이 다 거기 다니거등."

누나를 놀릴 수 있는 절호의 기회를 포착한 아빠.

"Catholic one year, Protestant the next," he commented playfully. "You'll soon run out of churches to go to! How about trying the Buddhist temple next Christmas?"

"Dad!" Minji protested, pouting.

"Oh, no . . . they probably don't celebrate Christmas there!" he said dramatically. "Christmas is about the birth of baby Jesus, isn't it?"

With his index finger raised, he stopped suddenly as if a new idea struck him.

"Or . . . hang on a second ," he continued with theatrical relish. "Or . . . what if it's *fashionable* next year to celebrate Christmas in a Buddhist temple? Then you must follow where the trend leads, of course! They're a peaceful lot, the Buddhists—I don't think they'd mind!"

Minji crossed her arms and turned away with a snort.

Mom came to Minji's rescue. "Stop harassing her!" she said, trying hard to suppress a chuckle. "It's up to Minji what she does, isn't it!" She grinned at Minji and added, "Never mind—he's only teasing you!"

Minji dropped her head, shook it with a sigh, and then started giggling uncontrollably. Then she crumpled a paper napkin into a ball and threw it at Dad. The four of them laughed heartily together for the first time in ages. They chatted well past dinner, late into the night.

"야, 너는 교회 갔다가 성당 갔다가……" 하고 장난스럽게 말을 던진다. "내년에는 또 어디들 행차하실려구? 내년 크리스마스 때는 아예 절에 가서 공양드려 보지 그러냐!"

"아빠!" 민지의 입이 뾰로통해졌다.

"참…… 절에는 크리스마스 공양은 없을 수도 있겠네!" 아빠의 과장된 말투. "크리스마스는 아기 예수님 탄생을 기념하는 날이니까 말이야, 그치?"

아빠는 다시 무슨 새로운 아이디어가 떠올랐다는 듯 검지손가락을 치켜들고 갑자기 말을 멈췄다.

"아니면 잠깐……" 그리고는 아주 재미있다는 듯 극적으로, "아니면 혹시나 내년 크리스마스 때는 또 알어? 절에 가서 공양드리는 게 유행일지. 그럼 당연히 유행 따라서 절에 가야지 뭐, 안 그래? 불교에서는 평화를 사랑하잖냐—뭐라고 안 할 것 같은데?"

누나가 팔짱을 끼고는 *흥!* 하고 고개를 돌렸다.

옆에서 지켜보던 엄마가 끼어들었다. "아이, 참, 당신두!" 그리고는 터져 나오는 웃음을 참으며, "민지가 어떻게 하든 그건 당사자 마음이지, 안 그래?" 하고 민지를 보며 웃었다. "신경 쓰지 마—아빠가 그냥 너 놀리자구 그러는 거야!"

누나가 고개를 푹 숙이고 절레절레 흔들더니, 스스로도 참을 수 없다는 듯 깔깔 웃음을 터뜨렸다. 그러더니 밥상 위에 놓인 종이티슈를 구깃구깃해서는 아빠에게 던진다. 온 가족이 함께 오래간만에 큰 소리를 내어 웃음을 터뜨렸다. 네 가족은 저녁을 먹고 늦은 시각까지 담소를 나누었다.

8-3 올해는 크리스마스 어디서 쇨까요? · Where to Celebrate Christmas This Year?

9

하얀 크리스마스 양말

THE WHITE CHRISTMAS STOCKING

며칠이 한 걸음에 불쑥 지나가 버리고, 벌써 크리스마스이브. 겨울방학이 시작된 이후로 영호는 거의 하루 종일 잠만 자며, 특별히 하는 일 없이 보냈다. 그저 밥 먹을 때만 겨우—그나마 끼니를 거를 때는 빼고—일어나는 식이었다.

Days rolled by, and it was Christmas Eve already. Since the beginning of the winter break, Youngho had been leading a simple existence, mostly sleeping all day, everyday. He barely got up for meals—at least some of them.

Despite opening up to his family briefly on the day winter break began, Youngho was still struggling to come to terms with Chadori's death.

Lying in bed, Youngho woke to the sound of a gentle *knock knock* on his door.

"Young-ho—Kimmm—!" Mom's voice chirped from the other side of the door, in that weird singsong tone she used a lot these days. "It's al—*ready* eleven o'*claw*-hock! *Time* to eat your *break*-fast! Or are you planning to skip it a-*gain*—like you did *yes*-ter-day . . . and the day be-*fore* . . . and the day be-*fore* that?"

"Coming," Youngho grunted, still half asleep.

A little breakfast didn't sound so bad right now, actually. His stomach gave a low grumble in agreement.

Late-morning sunshine poured in through the window above the headboard, and the familiar sight of his bedroom came into view: a desk with an office chair, a chest of drawers, and a poster showing dog breeds and their temperaments. Toys now served as decorations—a plush boar hanging by the neck from the ceiling, a stuffed dinosaur baring its fangs atop the drawers, and a row of plastic fighters lining up next to it.

Another boring old day in my boring old room, Youngho thought. *No school, no more walks in the park with Chadori, no warm tongue tickling my cheek, telling me to get out of bed. No reason to get up.*

"*Youngho*—oh! I'm clear—ing the *tay*-ble in a- *min*ute
if yore not having *break*—fast!" Mom's voice sang again.

방학 첫날 저녁에는 가족들과 잠시 담소도 나누고 했었지만, 차도리의 죽음에 대해서도 아직 마음이 정리가 되지 않은 상태였다.

영호는 침대에 누운 채로 낮게 *똑똑똑* 방문 두드리는 소리에 잠이 깼다.

"김—영—호!" 방문 밖에서 엄마의 목소리가 들렸다. 요즘 엄마가 자주 쓰곤 하는, 노래하는 듯한 아주 어색한 소리. "인제 *벌*-써! 열한시가 되—었*네*— 나와서 아침 먹어*야*—지! 아님 또 굶—으—시—*게*—요— 어제*처*—럼 그제*처*—럼 엊그제*처*—럼!"

"알써……" 영호가 잠에서 덜 깨서 툴툴댔다.

지금 뭘 좀 먹어 두는 것도 그렇게 나쁘지는 않을 것 같았다. 배에서도 찬성하는 듯 낮게 *꼬르륵* 소리가 났다.

침대 머리맡 창문으로 늦은 아침 햇살이 쏟아져 들어오고, 방의 익숙한 사물들이 눈에 들어왔다. 책상과 그 앞에 놓인 의자, 서랍장, 반려견 품종별 특징을 다룬 포스터. 이제는 장식품이 되어 버린 장난감들—천장에 목메달아 놓은 멧돼지 인형과 서랍장 위에서 이빨을 드러내고 있는 공룡 인형, 그 옆에 줄지어 선 모형전사들.

지겨운 이 방에서 또 지겨운 하루가 시작되네, 하는 생각이 들었다. 학교도 쉬고, 차도리와 늘 가는 공원 산책도 없고…… 일어나라고 내 얼굴을 간지럽히는 따뜻한 혀의 촉감도 없지 않은가. 굳이 일어나야 할 이유가 없다.

"*영호*—야—! 지금 아침 안 먹을 *거*—면 상 치—*운*—다—!" 엄마의 노래하는 목소리가 다시 들린다.

With a sigh, Youngho pulled himself out of bed. It took a Herculean effort, almost as if he were forcing a magnet off an iron surface. He dragged himself out of his pajamas, put on the same clothes he had flung on the floor the night before, and went out to the kitchen. He found some toast and a half-eaten omelet at the table. Mom was sitting alone, drinking coffee and doing something on her laptop. Minji was probably out with friends already, and Dad . . . no idea. Mom looked up from the computer screen as Youngho emerged from his room.

"Why . . . good morning!" she said, with a surprised grin. "You're up for breakfast today!" Then she jumped up from her seat and added, "Hold on a sec . . . Let me warm the toast for you!" Stretching one arm toward the kitchen counter to grab the frying pan, she went on, "I'll make a new omelet for you too!"

"It's okay . . . I'll just eat these here," Youngho replied curtly and started munching on the cold and rubbery toast mechanically.

"Of course, if you want," Mom muttered, looking disappointed.

Her outstretched arm fell back down. She pulled out a chair opposite Youngho, sat down, and watched him eat for a while in silence. Then she said in a gentle but determined voice,

"You should start getting up and doing things now, Youngho. You promised me you would at least *try* to get back on your feet and live your life to the fullest—remember our conversation a few days ago?"

영호는 한숨을 푹 쉬며 침대에서 몸을 일으켰다. 마치 철판에서 자석을 떼어내듯 엄청난 노력을 요하는 일이었다. 느기적느기적 잠옷을 벗고는 전날 밤 방바닥에 내팽개쳐 놓았던 옷을 주섬주섬 주워 입고 부엌으로 나갔다. 식탁 위에는 구운 식빵 몇 조각과 반쯤 먹다 남은 오믈렛이 남아 있었다. 엄마는 혼자 식탁에 앉아 커피를 마시며 랩톱 컴퓨터로 무언가를 하고 있었다. 누나는 이미 친구 만나러 나갔을 테고, 아빠는...... 모르겠다. 영호가 방에서 나오자 엄마는 컴퓨터 화면에서 눈을 떼어 고개를 들었다.

"어...... 일어났네?" 엄마가 놀란 표정으로 웃으며 말했다. "오늘은 아침두 다 먹구!" 그리고는 후다닥 자리에서 일어나며, "잠깐만, 빵 데워 줄게!" 하더니, 또 싱크대에 놓인 후라이팬을 향해 팔을 뻗으며 "오믈렛두 새로 해 줄게!" 하고 덧붙였다.

"괜찮아...... 그냥 이거 먹으면 돼." 영호의 무뚝뚝한 대답. 그리고는 그냥 기계적으로 다 식고 눅진눅진해진 빵을 씹었다.

"그래...... 그러던지." 엄마가 실망한 듯 혼잣말처럼 중얼거렸다.

뻗었던 팔이 힘없이 떨어지고, 영호 맞은 편 의자를 빼고 앉아 먹는 모습을 잠시 묵묵히 바라보았다. 그리고는 부드럽지만 단호한 목소리로 한마디했다.

"이제 너두 일어나서 뭔가 해야지, 영호야. 다시 벌떡 일어서서 제대로 된 삶을 살려고 최소한 노력이라도 해 보기로 엄마랑 약속했잖아—나랑 며칠 전 했던 말 기억 나지?"

The day after the winter break had started, Youngho had a long conversation with Mom, concluding that he "just had to accept Chadori's death, though hard, as an inevitable fact of life." Mom had said more or less the same things when Grandpa passed away. "All living things die eventually"; "Chadori was lucky to lead a good life, live long, and die without much suffering"; and "as for the rest of us, it is our duty to honor the dead by living our lives to the fullest."

Easier said than done. Youngho grasped all this in his head, but his heart just refused to accept it. Nonetheless, Youngho promised Mom that he would at least give it a try.

It was true that Mom made a great deal of effort to make him feel better. Since Chadori's death, Mom had been making excuses to linger around Youngho as much as she could. For one thing, she had taken up baking and always hung around the kitchen, from where it was easy to keep an eye on Youngho's bedroom. Not that he minded. He enjoyed having access to all kinds of cakes and cookies—his new favorite was blueberry muffins. Even when he stayed up late at night, she didn't nag like she used to. Instead, she also found reasons to stay up until Youngho went to bed.

Still, she didn't set up the Christmas tree as she had promised—her excuse being that she couldn't find the old plastic tree and the box of ornaments.

"Youngho, you did say you would at least give it a try, didn't you?" repeated Mom. "Can you say something?"

"I said I would," Youngho grumbled through a full mouth.

겨울방학이 시작된 다음 날, 영호는 엄마와 긴 대화를 나눈 끝에 결론을 내렸었다. 즉 "차도리의 죽음은 어렵지만 어쩔 수 없는 자연의 순리이니 받아들일 수밖에 없다." 엄마는 할아버지가 돌아가셨을 때도 거의 같은 말을 했었다. "모든 살아있는 것들은 언젠가는 죽게 마련이다." "차도리처럼 행복한 삶을 살며 장수하고 큰 고통 없이 갈 수 있었던 것은 오히려 더할 수 없는 축복이다." 그리고 "이 세상에 남은 우리는 각자 주어진 삶을 충실하게 사는 것만이 먼저 세상을 뜬 자에 대한 도리이다."

말은 쉬웠다. 머리로는 이해가 갔지만, 정작 마음으로부터 받아들이기는 어려운 말이었다. 그러나 최소한 노력은 해 보겠다고 엄마와 약속했었다.

엄마가 영호의 마음을 달래기 위해 갖은 정성을 다한 것도 사실이다. 차도리의 안락사 이후로 엄마는 갖은 핑계를 대며 최대한 영호의 곁을 맴돌았다. 예를 들면 베이킹을 시작했다는 이유로, 영호의 방을 지켜보기 좋은 부엌에서 거의 살다시피 했다. 영호도 그런 엄마의 노력이 싫지는 않았다. 온갖 종류의 쿠키와 케이크는 언제나 환영이었고, 특히 최근 가장 맛있었던 것을 꼽자면 블루베리 머핀. 엄마는 영호가 늦게까지 안 자고 있어도 이전처럼 잔소리를 하지도 않았고, 오히려 엄마도 구실을 만들어서는 뭔가 하면서 영호가 잠이 들 때까지 깨어 있었다.

하지만 약속했던 대로 크리스마스트리를 하지는 않았다. 이유인즉슨 예전에 쓰던 모조 트리와 장식용품을 찾지 못했다는 것.

"영호야, 최소한 노력은 해 보겠다구 했었지?" 엄마가 반복했다. "뭐라고 말 좀 해 봐."

"그런다구 했잖아." 영호가 입에 음식을 가득 물고 불만에 찬 목소리로 우물댔다.

He gulped down his cold breakfast, not saying much despite Mom's best efforts to engage him in conversation, and hurried back to his room as soon as he had finished eating.

"I would start by sorting through your schoolbag if I were you!" Mom's voice said behind him. "And make sure you put everything in its place afterward!"

Once in his room, Youngho slammed the door behind him and sat on his unmade bed, staring into space. He repeated what Mom had said in his head. *You should start getting up and doing things now, Youngho. You promised. But do what? And as if I haven't tried! She just doesn't understand, does she? Nobody does!* Annoyed with Mom and mad at the world, Youngho took it out on the mattress he was sitting on—he punched it as hard as he could. His fist sank in with a muffled *thud!* The bouncy surface sprang back to life instantly.

Nothing mattered anymore. Youngho found it downright impossible to confront the reality that Chadori was gone. Everything was still in a haze, and he just wished that it had all been a terrible nightmare—that Chadori was playing hide-and-seek with him, lurking around the corner about to jump on him. At the same time, he knew only too well that it was just his wishful thinking.

I won't find Chadori anywhere, anymore—no matter what I try.

그리고는 애써 대화를 계속해 보려는 엄마의 노력에도 불구하고, 다 식은 아침을 말없이 단번에 씹어 삼키고는 다 먹자마자 서둘러서 방으로 돌아왔다.

"책가방 정리부터 시작해 보는 게 어떨까?" 뒤에서 엄마의 목소리가 들린다. "그리구 다 하구 나서 내용물 제자리에 넣는 거 잊지 말구!"

문지방을 넘어서자마자 영호는 방문을 *쾅* 닫고, 아직 개지 않은 이불을 뭉개고 침대 위에 앉아 허공을 응시했다. 그리고는 엄마가 한 말을 머릿속에 되뇌었다. *이제 너두 일어나서 뭔가 해야지, 영호야...... 엄마랑 약속했잖아. 하지만 뭐를 하란 말이야? 게다가 노력을 하지 않은 것도 아닌데. 엄마는 아무 것도 이해 못해...... 아니, 그 누구도 이해할 수 없어!* 엄마에 대한 불만과 세상에 대한 분노에 가득 찬 영호. 죄 없는 침대 바닥만 주먹으로 있는 힘을 다해 내리쳤다. 주먹 밑으로 매트리스가 둔하게 *퍽!* 소리를 내며 꺼지더니 금세 다시 탄력성을 회복하고 솟아올랐다.

더 이상 아무 것도 의미가 없었다. 차도리가 없는 현실을 받아들인다는 것 자체가 아예 불가능했고, 모든 것이 아직도 희미한 꿈처럼 느껴졌다. 그냥 모든 것이 끔찍한 악몽에 불과하기를 바랄 뿐이었다. 차도리가 영호와 숨바꼭질을 하며 모퉁이에 숨어있다가 언제라도 불쑥 튀어나올 것만 같았다. 하지만 그러면서도 모든 것이 그저 영호의 바람에 불과하다는 사실도 잘 알고 있었다.

이제는 그 어디서도, 어떻게 해서도 차도리를 볼 수 있는 방법이 없다.

Sometimes Youngho wished he could just have one more glimpse of him, even if it was merely a fleeting illusion out of the corner of his eye. It would be enough if he could somehow fool himself into feeling that Chadori was still there beside him. Not just look at a photo or watch a video clip, but really *feel* it, even if it lasted no more than one brief second—the brown-and-white head peeking at him from behind the door, the *tap tap tap* of his paws pattering across the floor, or perhaps a whiff of his fur in the air.

But the cold, hard truth was staring Youngho in the eye: He just couldn't deny the fact that Chadori was no longer there with him. Even his illusions had evaporated. A white vase on a brown table was nothing more than an inanimate object, stripped of the heart-warming possibility that it could be his white snout between the reddish-brown patches around his eyes. Deprived of the association with the little paws scuttling across the room, raindrops on the windowpane were just cold water dripping. Even the soothing scent of Chadori's fur had been exterminated by Mom's lemon wipes. Perched on his bed, Youngho furiously repeated Mom's words in his head for the second time.

You should start getting up and doing things now, Youngho.

In truth, he had no desire for anything anymore and just wanted to go back to sleep.

가끔 영호는 그저 눈가에 비친 환상이라도 좋으니, 아주 잠깐이라도 한 번만 더 차도리를 볼 수 있었으면 하는 생각을 하곤 했다. 설령 착각이라도 좋았다. 그저 차도리가 옆에 있는 느낌으로 충분했다. 그냥 사진이나 동영상으로 보는 것이 아니라, 단 1초에 지나지 않더라도 좋으니 정말 사실이라고 느껴보고 싶었다—밤색과 흰색 털이 섞인 머리가 문 뒤에서 빼꼼히 내다보고 있는 듯한 느낌. 그 발이 *타닥탁탁* 소리를 내며 마룻바닥을 지나가는 소리. 스쳐 지나가는 듯한 털 냄새.

그러나 영호에게 직면한 현실은 너무나도 차갑고 잔인했다. 더 이상 차도리가 옆에 없다는 사실을 부인할 수가 없었던 것이다. 심지어 차도리의 환상까지도 메말라 버렸다. 갈색 탁자 위에 놓인 하얀 꽃병은 차도리 눈 주위 붉은 갈색 털 사이 하얀 주둥이일 수도 있다는 마음 훈훈한 생각 없이는 그저 생명 없는 사물에 불과했다. 창문을 두드리는 빗소리는 그 작은 발이 마룻바닥을 재빨리 가로지르는 소리일지도 모른다는 가능성을 제외하고는 단순히 찬물 방울 떨어지는 소리일 뿐이었다. 그나마 영호의 마음을 달래주던 털 냄새마저도 엄마의 레몬향 청소포에 전멸되어 버렸다. 영호는 침대 위에 올라 앉아 엄마가 한 말을 머릿속에 다시 떠올리며 분개했다.

이제 너두 일어나서 뭔가 해야지, 영호야.

하지만 사실 이제 더 이상 아무것도 하고 싶지 않았고, 그저 다시 잠만 자고 싶을 뿐이었다.

Youngho contemplated not sorting through his schoolbag, simply to spite Mom, but then again, she would go on and on about it for the entire break and never leave him in peace. Come to think of it, the last time he organized anything was almost six months ago during the summer break. Mom had forced him to do it then too; she made him promise to do it regularly on his own next time.

With a deep sigh, Youngho grudgingly got up, snatched up his schoolbag from under the desk, and emptied its contents onto the floor. Then he put things in place as he had been told: textbooks on the bookshelves, the pencil case and stationery neatly stacked in the desk drawer, and trash on the side for further sorting. And there was a lot of trash—candy wrappers, clementine peels, empty chip bags, even a crushed chocolate milk carton. Mom sorted trash with almost religious zeal these days, and everybody else in the household had no choice but to follow suit. With a grunt, Youngho imagined his classmates asking back at school, "What did you do during winter break, Youngho?" and himself replying cheerfully with a big, toothy grin: "I sorted through the garbage in my schoolbag. Boy, it was so much fun!"

Then something else slid out of the schoolbag. It was the Christmas card from Manu—the one he had given Youngho on the day winter break started. Overwhelmed by his own feelings, Youngho had forgotten all about it until now. The crisp white envelope had "To Foxy" written on it.

영호는 그냥 반항심에서 책가방 정리를 하지 말까도 생각해 보았지만, 그럴 경우 편하게 쉬기는커녕 방학 내내 잔소리를 들을 것이 뻔했다. 생각해 보면 무언가 정리를 해 보는 것도 거의 6개월 전 여름방학 때 이후로 처음인 것 같다. 그때도 엄마가 시켜서 반강제로 했다. 엄마는 다음 번에는 영호가 스스로 알아서 정기적으로 하겠다는 약속을 받아 냈었다.

하는 수 없이 영호는 크게 한숨을 쉬고 일어나, 책상 밑에서 책가방을 휙 낚아채듯 집어 들고는 그 내용물을 방바닥에 쏟았다. 그리고는 엄마가 시킨 대로 하나둘씩 제자리에 정리했다. 책은 책장에, 필통과 기타 학용품은 책상 서랍에 차곡차곡 정리해 넣고, 쓰레기는 옆에 따로 모았다. 쓰레기도 엄청나게 많이 나왔다. 사탕 껍질에 귤 껍질, 빈 과자봉지, 또 찌그러진 초코우유 곽까지…… 엄마는 요즘 거의 광적으로 쓰레기 분리수거에 열중해서, 나머지 가족들도 따라 할 수밖에 없는 처지였다. 방학이 끝나고 반 친구들이 "영호 너는 겨울방학 때 뭐 했니?" 하고 물어볼 때, 이빨을 드러내고 활짝 웃으며 "응, 난 책가방 쓰레기 분류했어. 참 재미있었다!"라고 대답할 자신의 모습을 상상하니, *으윽!* 하는 신음소리가 절로 나지 않을 수 없었다.

그러던 중 무언가 가방에서 툭 떨어졌다. 겨울방학 하던 날 만우가 준 크리스마스카드였다. 스스로의 감정에 휩싸여서 지금까지 까맣게 잊고 있었던 것이다. 새하얀 봉투에는 '구미호'라고 써 있었다.

With horror, Youngho recalled what had happened after school that day; he couldn't remember every single detail, but he had definitely been very rude to Manu. He bitterly regretted it now and felt truly ashamed. Manu had gone out of his way to make the card, and Youngho just shoved it into his bag without even thanking him—or giving it so much as a glance, for that matter. To add insult to injury, he humiliated him by losing his temper and going berserk in front of the whole school. And Manu's only crime? Being a good friend. Sick to his stomach with guilt, Youngho assumed that Manu must be furious with him.

He had to make up with him before it was too late—or rather, he owed him an unconditional apology. But what if he only made it worse by getting in touch with him now? Youngho faced a terrible dilemma. After some thought, he concluded that he would give it some time and wait until Manu's anger subsided—and everything was forgotten.

Eager to see what Manu had made for him, Youngho opened the envelope and took out the card. Against a red background stood a dark-green paper cutout tree, wrapped in gold and silver ribbons and decorated with stickers shaped like baubles and Christmas ornaments. The space above the tree had "Merry Christmas" written on it in white Korean letters while, below, it read "My Best Friend" in navy in English. Everything was covered in glitter.

영호는 불현듯 그날 학교가 끝나고 있었던 일이 떠올랐다. 자세히 기억은 안 나지만, 분명한 것은 만우에게 상당히 심하게 대했다는 점이었다. 영호는 그런 자신의 행동이 매우 후회스럽고 부끄럽게 느껴졌다. 만우가 특별히 정성스럽게 만든 카드인데, 고맙다는 말 한마디 없이, 눈길 한 번 주지 않은 채 그냥 가방에 밀어 넣은 것이 아닌가. 그뿐 아니라 폭발하듯 화까지 내며 창피를 주었다. 그것도 전교생이 다 보는 앞에서. 만우에게 단 한 톨의 죄라도 있었을까? 그저 좋은 친구가 되어 준 것 하나 뿐이었다. 엄청난 죄책감에 시달리기 시작한 영호. 만우는 분명 대단히 화가 나 있을 것이다.

어쨌든 더 늦기 전에 화해를 하기는 해야 할 텐데...... 화해라기 보다는 영호 쪽에서 무조건 싹싹 빌어도 모자랄 일이었다. 그런데 지금 섣불리 연락했다가 공연히 화만 부추기는 것이 아닐까. 정말 망설여지는데...... 결국 생각 끝에 영호는 좀 더 시간을 두고 만우의 화가 풀릴 때까지—그래서 모든 것이 잊혀지기를—기다려 보기로 했다.

한시바삐 만우가 만들어 준 카드를 보고 싶어진 영호. 봉투를 뜯고 카드를 꺼내 보았다. 빨간색 바탕에 진초록색 색종이를 잘라 만든 크리스마스트리가 붙어 있고, 그 위는 금색·은색 리본으로 둘러서 크리스마스 장식 볼, 오너먼트 등 여러 가지 모양의 스티커로 장식되어 있었다. 또 트리 위 공간에는 하얀 글씨로 '메리 크리스마스'라고 한국말로, 밑에는 남색으로 MY BEST FRIEND, 즉 '나의 가장 친한 친구'라고 영어로 씌어 있었다. 그리고 카드에는 온통 반짝이가 뿌려져 있었다.

Manu's handmade Christmas card—he had clearly spent a considerable amount of time and energy putting it together, even though he wasn't really into arts and crafts. *Did he get help with it? No*—Youngho saw him make it himself at school, cutting and gluing the bits and pieces. *I didn't exactly watch him the whole time, but why would he need help with something so trivial? Plus, the handwriting is unmistakably Manu's.*

It even smelled as if it had some perfume on it. Chuckling to himself, Youngho shook his head. *You must be kidding, Dumpling! You're such a weirdo, you know that . . . a weirdo like me!* The fragrance was unmistakable—it was gingerbread.

The glitter, together with the gingerbread aroma, somehow reminded him of the extraordinary home decor store, Paradise on Earth, and its magnificent Christmas decorations: the tall Christmas tree welcoming the boys as soon as they walked through the door, the countless twinkling lights on the ceiling, the objects from all around the world, the mesmerizing music, and the smell . . . Not to mention the exquisite taste of the gingerbread cookies, of course.

Lost in the memory of that day, Youngho lifted the card closer to his nose for a proper sniff. Instantly, he sneezed—*Achoo!*—and realized that he had inhaled the glitter. Now with glitter sparkling all over, he shook his head again with a grin.

Then he remembered how he had once sneezed like that, scattering glitter all over himself one Christmas Day many years ago. He sorely missed how it was then; he desperately wished to go back—restore the happy family he had once known, and see Grandpa and Chadori again.

만우가 손수 만든 크리스마스카드—미술과는 거리가 먼 만우였지만, 대단한 시간과 노력을 투자한 흔적이 역력했다. *설마 누가 만들어 준 건 아니겠지? 아냐*—분명 학교에서 오리고 붙이고 직접 만드는 걸 봤다. *뭐 계속 지켜본 건 아니지만, 이런 쓰잘데없는 것 도움은 받아서 뭐해? 글씨도 분명 만우의 글씨다.*

뿐만 아니라 향수 뿌린 냄새까지 났다. 영호는 키득키득 웃으며 고개를 설레설레 저었다. *너 지금 장난하니, 군만두, 넌 정말 괴짜야...... 나같은 괴짜!* 향기는 의심의 여지도 없이 생강 과자 향이었다.

반짝이와 생강 과자의 향기는 왠지 모르게 만우와 함께 들렀던 인테리어 상점 '지상천국'과 그 멋진 크리스마스 장식을 연상시켰다. 문을 들어서자마자 두 소년을 환영해 주던 대형 크리스마스트리, 천장에서 수없이 반짝이던 전구들, 세계 곳곳에서 들여온 듯한 각종 물품들, 신비한 분위기를 자아내던 음악, 또 그 향기...... 물론 너무나 감미롭던 생강 과자의 맛을 빼놓을 수 없었다.

그날 생각에 사로잡힌 영호. 향기를 제대로 음미해 보려고 카드를 들어 코에 더 바짝 가까이 대었다. 그리고는 순식간에 *에취!* 하고 재채기를 해 버렸다. 반짝이를 들이마신 것이다. 온몸이 반짝이로 뒤덮여 빛나게 된 영호. 다시 고개를 저으며 웃어 버렸다.

그리고는 수년 전 크리스마스, 지금처럼 반짝이 때문에 재채기를 했던 것, 그래서 반짝이가 날려 온 몸에 뒤덮였던 일이 새삼 기억났다. 정말 너무도 그때가 그리웠고, 그 옛날로 돌아갈 수만 있다면...... 하는 마음이 간절했다. 행복했던 그때 그 가족을 다시 되찾을 수만 있다면. 또 할아버지와 차도리를 다시 볼 수만 있다면.

9-1 에취!·Achoo!

어느새 소리 없이 눈물이 핑 돌았다.

갑자기 육중한 아파트 문이 열렸다가 *쿵!* 하고 닫히는 소리가 났다. 놀란 영호는 마치 못할 짓을 하다 들킨 사람처럼 얼른 손등으로 눈물을 훔치고는 다시 책가방을 주워 들었다.

"엄마, 나 왔어! 아...... 집에 오니까 너무 따뜻하고 좋다!" 누나의 목소리가 들리고, 발자국 소리가 총총 영호의 방문 앞을 지나간다. "밖은 너무 추워! 근데 다들 어디 갔어?"

"엄마가 문 *쾅* 닫지 말라구 했지?" 엄마는 엄했지만 화난 목소리는 아니었고, "아빠는 밖에 볼일 보러 나가시구, 영호는—" 하면서 속닥속닥 목소리가 낮아졌다.

Before he knew it, Youngho was sniffling silently.

Suddenly, he heard the apartment's heavy front door open and slam shut with a loud *bang*! As if he had been caught in the act of doing something wrong, Youngho quickly wiped away the tears with the back of his hand and picked up the schoolbag again.

"Mom, I'm home! Oh . . . it's so nice and warm in here," Minji's voice announced as footsteps scurried past Youngho's door. "It's freezing outside! Where's everybody?"

"What did I say about not slamming the door, hmm?" Mom's voice sounded firm, but she didn't seem mad. "Dad's out running errands, and your little brother is—" Then her voice dropped to a whisper.

Minji seemed to whisper something back. Youngho's ears pricked up. *Are they talking about me?* He tiptoed to his door, stooped with one ear glued to it, and tried to decipher the inaudibly low voices. He couldn't make out anything they were saying, though.

"Youngho! How are you doing with that schoolbag of yours? Let me know if you need any help!" Mom's voice sounded as if she knew exactly what he had been doing.

Youngho jumped. Tiptoeing away from the door, he answered quickly, trying to sound as nonchalant as possible.

"Yes—I'm on it right now, Mom!"

Eyes still glistening with tears but shaken out of his melancholy mood by the surprise, Youngho continued sorting through the schoolbag. After he had put most of the things in order, he also found the card-making set Mom had bought him for his art class before winter break started.

Everything was still brand-new and untouched, apart from the colored paper he had cut into bits and pieces—to look as though he was doing something in class. Youngho opened the set to take a look inside. The enclosed instruction sheet listed the following contents exactly: blank paper cards in red, green, gold, and silver; blank sheets of colored paper, also in red, green, gold, and silver; felt embellishments shaped like baubles in pink, blue, yellow, white, and mauve; stickers of Santa Claus, Rudolph, gingerbread men, candy canes, holly bushes, and baby angels blowing trumpets; ribbons shredded to look like tinsel in gold, silver, turquoise, and rose gold; and gold and silver glitter in little plastic jars the size of Youngho's thumbnail.

누나도 역시 속삭이며 뭐라고 대답하는 것 같았다. 귀가 쫑긋해진 영호. *내 얘기 하는 건가?* 살그머니 다가가 구부정한 자세로 문짝에 머리를 대고 속삭이는 목소리에 귀를 기울였다. 하지만 소리가 너무 낮아 무슨 말을 하는지 전혀 알아들을 수가 없다.

"영호야! 가방 정리 잘 하구 있는 거지? 필요하면 엄마한테 도와 달라구 해!" 마치 영호의 일거수일투족을 보고 있는 듯 엄마의 목소리가 들렸다.

화들짝 놀란 영호. 살금살금 문에서 멀어지고, 최대한 멀쩡하게 들리려고 노력하며 재빨리 대답했다.

"네—지금 하고 있어요, 엄마!"

눈은 아직도 눈물에 젖어 있었지만 갑자기 놀란 바람에 울적한 맘이 쏙 달아난 영호. 책가방 정리를 계속했다. 그렇게 대충 다 정리하고 보니 겨울방학 하기 전 엄마가 미술 준비물로 가져가라고 사 준 크리스마스카드 만들기 세트도 나왔다.

조각조각 잘라 버린 색종이—수업 시간에 그저 뭔가 하는 척 하느라고—를 제외하고는 모두 다 전혀 손도 대지 않은 새것 그대로 남아 있었다. 영호는 카드 만들기 세트 안에 뭐가 들었을까 뜯어서 열어 보았다. 첨부된 설명서에 의하면 정확히 다음과 같은 내용물이 들어 있었다—카드지 빨간색, 초록색, 금색, 은색. 색종이 역시 빨간색, 초록색, 금색, 은색. 방울 모양 펠트 장식 핑크, 파랑, 노랑, 흰색, 연보라색. 갖가지 모양의 스티커—산타 할아버지, 루돌프 사슴, 생강 과자 인형, 지팡이 사탕, 홀리베리, 나팔 부는 아기 천사 등 종류도 다양했다. 리본을 잘라 만든 틴셀 모루 금색, 은색, 청록색, 로즈 골드. 영호의 엄지손톱만 한 플라스틱 통에 담긴 반짝이 금색•은색.

Will I be needing these again? Youngho thought to himself. *Maybe I could put up a miniature Christmas tree on the desk?*

It would serve the double purpose of celebrating Christmas on the one hand and making a silent protest to Mom and Dad on the other. But it didn't really matter what Mom and Dad thought, or how they reacted in the end. He knew only too well celebrating Christmas wouldn't turn back the clock— perhaps he just wanted to relive even a sliver of the happiness it once brought him. Whatever he did, he was doing it for himself, not because he expected something from his parents.

That's it! Let's do it!

Youngho started looking through the card-making set again. He had more than enough decorations but no tree. *What am I supposed to do now?* He could always make a paper tree, but he wasn't particularly good at that sort of thing. He could also go out and *buy* one, but he didn't want to venture outside either. He felt way too lazy to take a shower too. Plus, he had recently spent the last bit of his pocket money on a new armor for his character in a computer game! Shaking his head dismally, Youngho sat back down on the edge of the bed. *Typical! A great idea, but no money to make it happen . . .* Sitting hunched over, Youngho dropped his head. His eyes caught sight of his awkwardly big feet.

언제 쓰게 될 때가 있을까? 하는 생각이 들었다. *책상 위에 미니 크리스마스트리나 만들어 세워 볼까?*

한편으로는 크리스마스를 쇠기도 하면서 또 다른 면에서는 엄마 아빠에게 침묵의 시위를 하는 두 가지 목적을 달성할 수 있을 것이다. 하지만 결국 엄마 아빠가 어떻게 생각하고 무슨 반응을 보일지는 그다지 중요하지 않았다. 굳이 크리스마스를 쇤다고 해서 지나간 시간을 돌이킬 수 있는 것은 아니라는 사실을 누구보다도 잘 알고 있었다—그렇다면 크리스마스가 연상시키는 행복을 조금이라도 다시 한번 맛보고 싶어서였을까. 어쨌건 부모님으로부터 무언가를 바란다기보다는 무엇보다도 스스로를 위해서 하는 일이었다.

그래! 해 보는 거야!

카드 만들기 세트를 다시 훑어 보기 시작했다. 그런데 장식품은 많은데 정작 트리가 없다. *이젠 어떻게 해야 하나?* 종이로 트리를 만들 수도 있었지만, 영호는 그런 것에는 특별한 재주가 없었다. 또 나가서 사올 수도 있기는 했다. 하지만 특별히 밖에 발을 디디기도 싫었을 뿐더러, 지금 샤워를 하고 하는 것도 귀찮았다. 게다가 마지막 남은 용돈까지 얼마전 PC게임 캐릭터 갑옷 바꾸느라고 다 써 버렸다! 영호는 비참하게 고개를 저으며 다시 침대 모서리에 앉았다. *또 이 모양 이 꼴이군! 아이디어는 좋은데 자금이 부족하네......* 영호는 구부정하게 앉아 고개를 떨구었다. 볼품없이 크기만 한 발이 눈에 들어왔다.

Clumsy and out of proportion to the rest of his body, they looked as if they had grown even more lately.

Even my feet are so ugly—they're just monstrously big! he sneered to himself.

If they kept growing at this rate much longer, he might not be able to find socks that fit him when he grew up. *I'll have to start wearing stockings like women!* Youngho pictured himself dressed like an old lady, pulling on long stockings, and then scoffed at his own thought. *Am I finally going out of my mind, or what? Wearing stockings!*

He then sat bolt upright with the idea that had come to mind. *That's it! A stocking!* He had everything else but the tree. *Who even needs the tree when I could hang a Christmas stocking?*

Youngho set his mind to making a Christmas stocking, and putting the decorations from the card-making pack on it, to hang over his bed instead of setting up a miniature Christmas tree. *A weird kind of Christmas stocking, perhaps—but who cares?* Happy with the thought, he started hunting for a suitable stocking. As he had no money, it had to be something he could find at home. *A red sock, perhaps?* He looked in his drawers.

He remembered the home decor store and the miniature Christmas stockings hanging on its door. They were red, lined with white. Unfortunately, Youngho didn't have any red socks lined with white—or even simple red ones for that matter. Mom loved buying all kinds of colorful socks for Youngho, a bit too much for his taste sometimes, but he couldn't find red ones when he needed them.

최근 들어 더 커 버린 듯, 어색하고 신체의 다른 부위에 비해 아주 불균형적으로 보였다.

발까지 정말 못생겼다—괴물처럼 자라 버렸네! 혼자 비아냥거리듯 웃었다.

이대로 계속 가다가는 어른이 되면 맞는 양말이 없을 것이다. *여자들처럼 스타킹을 신고 다녀야 할지도 모르겠네!* 영호는 할머니처럼 옷을 차려입고 긴 스타킹을 신는 자신의 모습을 상상하고는, 스스로의 터무니없는 생각에 코웃음을 쳤다. *드디어 미쳐 버린 거야, 뭐야? 스타킹을 신다니!*

그리고는 갑자기 떠오른 생각에 영호가 벌떡 일어나 앉았다. *그래, 그거야! 바로 양말이야, 양말! 다른 건 다 있는데 크리스마스트리가 없다...... 그럼 크리스마스 양말을 걸면 되지, 굳이 크리스마스트리가 왜 필요해?*

미니 크리스마스트리가 아닌 크리스마스 양말에다 카드 만들기 세트에 든 장식을 달고 침대맡에 걸기로 결심한 영호. *좀 괴상한 크리스마스 양말이 되겠지만, 그것이 무슨 상관일까?* 이 생각에 만족한 영호는 얼른 적합한 양말 찾기에 나섰다. 돈이 한 푼도 없었으므로 집에서 찾을 수 있는 것이어야 했다. *빨간 양말이면 좋겠지?* 서랍장을 뒤져 보았다.

인테리어 상점 문에 달려 있던 미니 양말이 생각났다. 그 양말은 빨간 바탕에 흰색으로 둘러져 있었다. 하지만 영호는 빨간색에 흰 둘레가 진 양말은 없었고, 그냥 단색 빨간 양말조차 없었다. 엄마는 갖가지 색 양말을 잘 사 줘서 어쩔 때는 너무 알록달록 좀 지나치다 싶을 정도였지만, 정작 필요할 때는 하필 또 빨간 색은 없었다.

Without sound, Youngho opened the door a sliver for a quick reconnaissance of the kitchen. It sounded as if Mom was still talking to Minji about something, but he couldn't see them. He scuttled across the corridor and sneaked into Mom and Dad's bedroom to peer into their wardrobe. No red socks. Dad's socks, in particular, were all either black or white, maybe some gray—incredibly boring.

Youngho remembered seeing Minji wear red socks once before, nice and long ones that came up to the knees—which would be perfect for the purpose. But if he got caught, it was certain death. Youngho decided he wasn't prepared to risk his life yet, even for the finest Christmas stocking. *I am far too young to perish already!* Mom's socks were even smaller than his own, and the roomiest ones were Dad's. Yet black was a bit too gloomy for Christmas, and it left no other choice.

Youngho grabbed several pairs of the cleanest-looking white socks from Dad's drawers. He tried his best to maintain a high standard: first prioritizing the fresh white color and then sniffing them to make sure they didn't smell of Dad's feet. He had to make it back to his room fairly quickly before Dad came back home and Mom and Minji had finished talking.

Clutching the socks, he tiptoed back to his room. Then, he picked a suitable one, laid it out on the desk, and started putting the embellishments from the card-making set on it. After some time, he used up almost everything and the sock itself was completely buried underneath the decorations. As the finishing touch, he made a loop with the last remaining piece of the golden ribbon and hung it over the bed.

영호는 소리 없이 방문을 빼꼼히 열고 부엌 쪽의 동정을 살펴보았다. 엄마는 아직도 누나와 무언가 얘기를 나누고 있는 것처럼 들렸지만, 보이지는 않았다. 재빨리 살살 복도를 건너 안방으로 몰래 들어가 엄마 아빠의 옷장을 들여다보았다. 그러나 빨간 양말은 없고, 특히 아빠 양말은 죄다 검정색 아니면 흰색밖에 없었다. 고작 해 봐야 회색—엄청나게 김이 샜다.

문득 이전에 누나가 무릎까지 올라오는 빨간 양말—지금 이럴 때 딱 좋을 만한—을 신었던 것이 생각나긴 했지만, 만에 하나 들키기라도 하면 그야말로 죽음이었다. 아무리 근사한 크리스마스 양말을 준다고 해도 인생을 포기하기는 아직 너무 이르다는 결론을 내렸다. *벌써 스러지기엔 내 나이가 너무 젊지 않은가!* 그런데 엄마 양말은 오히려 영호 것보다도 작고, 그나마 크기가 가장 넉넉한 것은 아빠 양말인데...... 그래도 크리스마스인데 검은 색은 좀 너무 우울한 것 같고...... 선택의 여지가 없었다.

영호는 아빠의 서랍에서 가장 깨끗해 보이는 흰 양말 몇 켤레를 골라서 빼 보았다. 먼저 새하얀 색상을 우선으로 했고, 혹시나 아빠의 발냄새가 남아 있지는 않나 킁킁 냄새도 맡아 보는 등 최선을 다해서 철저한 엄선 과정을 거쳤다. 하지만 아빠가 집에 들어오기 전, 또 엄마와 누나가 대화를 마치기 전에 그래도 빨리 방으로 돌아가야 했다.

영호는 양말을 손에 움켜쥐고 살금살금 방으로 향했다. 그리고는 가져온 양말 중 적합한 것 한 짝을 골라 책상 위에 올려놓고 크리스마스카드 세트에 들어 있는 장식을 꺼내어 달았다. 잠시 후 카드 세트에 들어 있던 장식품을 거의 다 쓰고 나니, 정작 양말은 장식에 묻혀 전혀 보이지 않았다. 마무리 겸, 마지막 남은 금색 리본 조각으로 고리를 만들어 침대맡에 걸어 보았다.

It wasn't exactly a work of art, but it wasn't too bad either. *Not too bad at all. With my own Christmas stocking in place, maybe even Santa Claus himself will answer my call! Hang on a sec—isn't Santa Claus just a fantasy figure created by grown-ups to keep their children happy?* But now that he had made and hung a Christmas stocking over his bed, it felt like Santa Claus really existed and would visit him tonight. Of course, he hadn't made a Christmas stocking expecting to get a present in return. Whether he got a present or not was beside the point. *Of course, it doesn't matter if I receive something or not! No way!* He blushed at his own overreaction, which seemed ridiculous. Nonetheless, Youngho couldn't help but sense a strange expectation rising within him.

뭐 특별하게 예술 작품까지는 아니었지만, 그래도 그다지 나쁘지는 않아 보였다. 아니, 그런대로 제법 괜찮았다. *이렇게 직접 크리스마스 양말까지 만들어 건 지금, 과연 산타 할아버지가 내 정성에 응할 것인가? 잠깐—그나저나 산타는 어른들이 애들 좋으라고 꾸며 낸 상상 속의 존재 아닌가?* 그런데 크리스마스 양말을 일단 만들어 침대맡에 달고 나니, 왠지 산타가 정말 있어서 오늘 밤 영호를 찾아올 것만 같았다. 물론 뭐 꼭 선물을 받아 내려는 마음으로 크리스마스 양말을 만든 것은 아니었다. 선물을 받고 안 받고 하는 것 자체는 그다지 중요하지 않았다. *뭐 받느냐 안 받느냐 하는 것 따위는 당연히 중요하지 않아! 절대 상관없어!* 영호는 스스로의 과민반응이 터무니없이 느껴져서 얼굴을 붉혔다. 그런데 자신도 모르게 은근한 기대감에 부풀어 오르는 것은 왜일까.

10

양들의 합창, 스포츠카, 아기 오리, 그리고 한 권의 사진첩

SINGING SHEEP, FAST CARS, DUCKLINGS, AND A PHOTO ALBUM

이제 잠자리에 들 시간. 이빨을 닦고 잠옷으로 갈아입은 후, 불을 끄고 이불 속에 들어갔다. 결코 이르지 않은 시각임에도 불구하고 잠은 오지 않았다.

It was bedtime. Youngho brushed his teeth, changed into his pajamas, turned the light out, and crept into bed. It was getting late, but he found it impossible to fall asleep.

He tried everything he could think of—he lay down, tucked himself in, kicked his blanket away, pulled it back again, closed his eyes, opened his eyes, closed them again, kept still for a while, turned on his side, lay on his stomach, turned back to face the ceiling, and so on. But nothing seemed to work.

Then he tried counting imaginary sheep. It was something he had read in one of Minji's magazines—an age-old technique supposed to work wonders for sleepless nights. One sheep jumped off the cliff . . . two sheep jumped off the cliff . . . three sheep . . . He counted up to ninety-nine sheep that leapt off the precipice, but it was not helping. The more sheep he counted, the louder the chorus of imaginary bleating became. *Baaaaaa! Baaaaaa! Baaaaaa!* Eventually, Youngho was left with a choir of ninety-nine sheep bleating in his head. *All right, I'll try something other than sheep.* One-hundred flashy racing cars crashed over the singing sheep; one-hundred-and-one ducklings quacked on top of the bleating of the sheep and the revving of the car engines. Youngho's eyes were still wide open, staring at the ceiling. The more he tried, the more awake he felt.

It soon became unbearably boring and pointless to lie motionless in the dark, doing nothing. Youngho just felt as if he had to get up and do *something*. *But what?* There was nothing he could do in the room at this time of night. He bitterly recalled the time Mom had confiscated everything that might cause the slightest distraction from sleeping.

영호는 누워서 이불 속에 폭 들어갔다가, 다시 이불을 벗어 내쳤다가, 다시 덮고 눈을 감았다 떴다 다시 감았다가...... 잠시 가만히 누워 있다가, 옆으로 돌아 누웠다가, 엎드려서 누웠다가, 다시 돌아 천장을 보고 누웠다가 등등...... 온갖 것을 시도해 보았지만 결과는 마찬가지였다.

그다음에는 상상 속의 양 떼를 세어 보았다. 언젠가 누나가 보던 잡지에서 읽었는데, 잠이 오지 않을 때 쓰이는 오래된 비법이라고 했다. 양 한 마리가 벼랑을 뛰어내린다...... 양 두 마리가 벼랑을 뛰어내린다...... 양 세 마리가...... 아흔아홉 마리의 양이 절벽 아래로 곤두박질칠 때까지 세었지만 전혀 도움이 되지 않았다. 오히려 양을 세면 셀수록 상상 속의 양 떼의 합창 소리만 커져 갔다. *메에에에에! 메에에에에! 메에에에에!* 결국 영호의 머릿속에는 아흔 아홉 마리 양들의 합창단이 시끄럽게 노래를 해댔다. 그럼 양 말고 다른 것을 세 볼까. 백 대의 호화 스포츠카가 노래하는 양들 위로 떨어져 박살 나고, 아기 오리 백 한 마리가 양 떼들이 떠드는 소리와 자동차 엔진 소리 위로 꽥꽥댄 후. 영호는 그래도 눈이 말똥말똥해서 천장만 바라보았다. 노력을 하면 할수록 오히려 잠이 더 깨는 것 같았다.

곧 그렇게 어둠 속에서 아무 것도 하지 않고 가만히 누워만 있는 것이 견딜 수 없이 지루하고 헛되게 느껴졌다. 일어나서 꼭 무언가 해야 할 것만 같았다. *그런데 무엇을 한단 말이야?* 방에는 이런 밤중에 할 만한 일이 아무 것도 없었다. 잠 자는데 조금이라도 훼방이 될 만한 것은 깡그리 다 엄마에게 압수당한 일을 생각하면 아직도 치가 떨렸다.

그뿐만 아니라, 영호는 몇 달 전인가 어릴 적부터 모아 온 장난감까지 거의 모조리 자선단체에 기부해 버렸다. 그것도 누가 시키지도 않았는데 스스로 자진해서. 어느 날 TV에 나온 자선단체의 광고를 보고 한 일이었다. 그날 영호는 좋은 일을 했다는 훈훈한 느낌에, 또 자신이 너그러운 사람이라는 생각에 들떴었고, 아직도 그 일을 뿌듯하게 생각했다. 그렇지만 이럴 때를 대비해서 최소한도 몇 개만 남겨 두었으면 좋았을 것을. 물론 장식용으로 장난감 몇 개—엄마의 제의였다—남겨 둔 것이 있기는 했다. 하지만 그저 솜인형 동물과 모형 캐릭터 등뿐이었고, 지금 혼자 이것들을 가지고 소꿉장난을 하고 싶은 생각은 없었다. 그뿐인가. 휴대폰조차도 엄마가 깔아 놓은 *나이트타임 몬스터* 때문에 밤에는 무용지물이고......

On top of that, several months earlier, Youngho had given away most of his toys to charity—almost everything he had ever owned since he was a little boy. Nobody had made him do it. He had volunteered to do it himself one day after seeing a call for charity on TV. Giddy with warm feelings about his good deed, he felt like a truly generous person that day, and he was still proud of what he had done. But he could have saved at least a few things for times like this. He kept a small selection of toys for decorative purposes—Mom's idea—but they were just stuffed animals and plastic figures; it didn't interest him to play house with them right now. Plus, even his phone was useless at night because of Mom's *Nighttime Monster* app.

10-1 노래하는 양 떼, 스포츠카, 그리고 춤추는 오리들·Singing Sheep, Fast Cars, and Dancing Ducklings

Oh, the tragedy of my life! All this because I'm a kid! The only thing left that he could do at this hour was read schoolbooks, which seemed an absurd idea. *And it's winter break, for goodness' sake!*

Lying in his bed, tossing and turning, Youngho kept trying to think of something he could do without venturing out into the living room. Not that he wasn't tempted, but he couldn't risk it—Mom would surely take away what little daytime access he had left to the outside world if he got caught—a virtual prison, in other words. Eventually, he thought of the photo album in the night table. The day Mom had taken Youngho's computer and books away, she printed out some pictures from his phone and made a photo album for him. Since then, every so often, she would print more recent photographs and add them to the collection. Mom was good at that kind of thing—making scrapbooks and such. Youngho remembered Mom gently putting the album down on his nightstand. She had said,

"Here you go! We managed just fine without computers when I was your age—or cellphones, for that matter. You can flip through these if you're awake at night again!"

Youngho had never opened the album. Not even once. At first, he was mad at Mom and, not wanting to have anything to do with it out of rebellion, shut it away inside his night table drawers. Then, he simply forgot about it.

He switched the bedside lamp on and sat up. He reached into the top drawer. The photo album wasn't there. He couldn't remember exactly where he had put it. He pulled out the middle drawer and peered in—not there either.

아, 내 인생의 비극이여! 어리다는 이유 하나만으로! 영호가 지금 이 시간에 할 수 있는 것은 단 한가지, 교과서 읽는 일밖에는 없었다. 터무니없는 생각이었다. *그것도 지금은 겨울방학인데!*

그렇게 침대에 누운 채 몸을 뒤척이며 거실까지 나가지 않고도 할 수 있는 것이 뭐가 있을까 궁리해 보았다. 뭐 나가 보고 싶은 생각이 없었던 것은 아니지만 혹 그러다 들키기라도 했다가는 그나마 지금 낮에 할 수 있는 것들마저 금지당할 것이 불 보듯 뻔한 일이었기 때문이다—그야말로 *가상의 감옥*이었다. 그러다 결국 침대 옆 서랍에 들어 있는 사진 앨범이 생각났다. 컴퓨터와 책 등을 압수당하던 그날, 엄마는 영호의 휴대폰에 들어있는 사진들을 뽑아 사진첩을 만들어 주었었다. 또 그 이후로도 가끔씩 최근에 찍은 사진들을 뽑아 앨범에 넣어 주곤 했다. 엄마는 스크랩북 꾸미기 같은 것을 잘 했다. 사진첩을 침대맡 서랍 위에 살포시 올려놓으며 엄마가 하던 말.

"자, 여기 있어! 내가 네 나이쯤 됐을 땐 컴퓨터 없이두 다들 잘만 살았어. 또 휴대폰이 어딨어...... 다시 밤에 잠 안 오면 이거나 한 번씩 봐!"

아직까지 열어 본 적도 없었다. 단 한 번도. 처음에는 엄마한테 화가 나서 반항심에서 그랬고, 침대 맡 서랍 속에 넣어 둔 채 손도 대지 않았다. 그 후로는 그냥 잊어버리고 있었던 것이다.

영호는 침대맡 램프를 켜고 일어나 앉아 가장 윗서랍을 열어 보았다. 사진첩은 그 안에 없었다. 서랍장 어디에 넣어 두었는지 정확히 기억이 나지 않는다. 중간 서랍을 열어 그 안을 들여다보았다—역시 없기는 마찬가지였다.

Could Mom have taken it away because I've never opened it? Now he wanted it even more. Finally, he opened the bottom drawer. *Ta-da—it was there!* Now he remembered. Angry with Mom, he had shut it away in the lowest drawer and, since then, had never given it so much as a second glance.

Youngho carefully lifted the light-blue photo album from the drawer. He tried to shut the drawer without a sound, but it still made a loud grinding noise in the dead of night. Then, he rested the photo album on his lap and looked down at the cover. The hardback front read "Youngho's Photo Book." Each letter was a felt cutout in a different pastel color: pink, green, orange, yellow, purple, and blue. Mom had decorated the cover with cutout balloons in red, navy, and orange, not forgetting the sun peeking from behind a white cloud in the background. Everything was made of felt. Youngho vaguely remembered this too—*this is so Mom!*

More inclined to appreciate Mom's photo book now, Youngho lifted the cover and opened the first page. He saw a picture from a family holiday they went on when he was little. It was the same picture as the one on the wall above the sofa in the living room. Grandpa and Chadori were in it too; they were all smiling and looking happy. With a grin, Youngho leafed through the pages. His eyes glinted as he found the recent additions, including the ones he had taken with his friends at school throughout the year. For example, he saw a photo from the class picnic, where everybody was trying to make a funny face—the weirder, the better!

내가 한 번도 보지 않았다는 이유로 엄마가 다시 가져갔나? 점점 사진첩이 더 보고 싶어졌다. 마지막으로 가장 밑 서랍을 열어 보았다. *짜잔—그 안에 들어 있었다!* 그제야 기억이 났다. 엄마에게 화가 난 영호는 서랍장 가장 밑에 넣어 두고 그 이후로는 눈길조차 한 번 주지 않은 것이다.

서랍 안에 놓여 있는 연파란색 앨범을 조심스레 꺼내 들었다. 소리 없이 서랍문을 닫으려고 해 보았지만 한밤중의 정적 속에 서랍은 크게 *드르륵* 소리를 내며 닫혔다. 그리고는 앨범을 무릎 위에 올려놓고 표지를 내려다보았다. 하드커버 표지에는 핑크, 초록, 주황, 노랑, 보라색, 파란색 등 글자마다 다른 파스텔색 펠트지로 오려 붙여서 '영호의 사진첩'이라고 씌어 있었다. 빨간색, 남색, 주황색의 풍선도 달려 있었다. 하얀 구름 뒤에서 해가 빼꼼히 얼굴을 내밀고 있는 배경까지 모든 것이 펠트지로 만든 것이었다. 어슴프레 기억이 나는 것도 같다. *딱 엄마 스타일이다!*

엄마의 사진첩에 점점 더 관심이 끌린 영호는 표지를 열고 첫 페이지를 펴 보았다. 어렸을 때 온 가족이 휴가를 갔던 사진이 붙어 있었다. 거실 소파 위 벽에 달려 있는 것과 같은 사진이다. 할아버지와 차도리도 있었고, 모두가 웃으며 행복해 보였다. 빙그레 미소 지으며 몇 페이지를 계속 넘겨보다가, 올해 한 해 학교 친구들과 찍은 것을 포함해서 새로 추가된 사진들을 발견한 영호의 눈이 빛났다. 소풍 가서 반 친구들과 같이 웃긴 표정을 지으며 찍은 사진 등. 괴상하면 괴상할수록 최고!

Youngho also spotted the pictures taken after the dress rehearsal for the end-of-the-year classroom play, where everybody was posing as something completely opposite of their roles. They had performed a simplified version of *A Christmas Carol*. Youngho played Scrooge and Manu was given the role of one of the passersby. Manu was dressed up as an English gentleman—the suit, the cane, the wig, the mustache, and all. In the picture, though, he looked as if he were trying to pick his nose with the cane, which was impossible in reality. But Manu created a kind of clever optical illusion: He placed the tip of the cane on one cheek, while the camera captured the opposite side; Then he turned his head slightly toward the cane and away from the camera. Since the cane tip was hidden behind his nose, the final picture ended up looking as though Manu was picking his nose with the cane! Done poorly, it could have been quite a lame joke, but Manu carried it out skillfully—it was hilarious then and even more so looking at the picture now.

Youngho couldn't help but chuckle to himself as he remembered every single detail—Manu's fluttering nostrils, eyes half-closed squinting at the camera, and his lips pouting as if trying to look seductive. Everybody doubled up, nearly collapsing with laughter. With a hand covering his mouth, Youngho now felt more awake than ever as he tried to muffle the sound of his own laughter. He laid the photo album down on the night table—taking care to leave it open on the page he had been looking at—got up and sat on the side of the bed.

또 반에서 했던 연말 연극의 마지막 무대 연습이 끝나고, 각자 맡게 된 인물의 분장과는 정반대되는 엉뚱한 포즈를 취하고 찍은 사진이 나왔다. 그때 "구두쇠 스크루지" 연극을 하면서 영호가 스크루지 영감 역을, 만우가 지나가는 사람 역을 맡았었다. 만우는 점잖은 영국 신사 복장으로 양복을 차려입고 지팡이, 가발에다 콧수염까지 달고 있었다. 그런데 사진에는 마치 지팡이로 콧구멍을 쑤시고 있는 것처럼 보였다. 지팡이로 코를 쑤시는 것은 사실상 불가능한 일이었으나, 만우는 일종의 기발한 착시 효과를 사용했었다. 즉 지팡이 끝을 한 쪽 뺨에 대고 카메라가 반대쪽 얼굴을 포착하게 한 뒤, 얼굴이 카메라에서 조금 멀어지게끔 지팡이 방향으로 고개를 반쯤 돌리니까, 사진에는 지팡이 끝이 코 뒤로 가려져서 마치 지팡이로 콧구멍을 쑤시고 있는 것처럼 보였다. 사실 까딱했으면 상당히 썰렁했을 수도 있는 상황에서 만우가 너무나도 능숙하게 해내는 바람에, 당시에도 대폭소였지만 사진으로 보는 지금 오히려 더 웃겼다.

아직도 세세한 것까지 다 떠올라서 혼자 생각만 해도 *키득키득* 나오는 웃음을 참을 수가 없었다. 코구멍을 벌렁거리면서 눈을 게슴츠레 뜬 채로 카메라를 응시하며 매혹적인 양 입술을 내민 그 모습. 다들 배꼽을 잡고 나동그라질 수밖에 없었다. 손으로 입을 막고 터져 나오는 웃음을 참다가 이제 아예 잠이 쏙 달아나 버렸다. 영호는 서랍장 위에 사진첩을 내려놓고—물론 보던 페이지를 펴 놓는 것을 잊지 않았다—아예 다시 일어나서 침대에 걸터앉았다.

His stomach complained, demanding something to eat, but he didn't want to go all the way out to the kitchen and risk getting told off for not being in bed at this hour. His eyes scanned the room and located a small basket full of clementines Mom had put on the desk earlier. But Youngho had brushed his teeth already and wasn't about to repeat the same mistake he made once before when he was little; he already had his share of that nasty bitter taste when he tried to eat a clementine straight after brushing his teeth.

Then his Christmas stocking came into view, hung on one side of the headboard over the night table, suspended over the open photo book. It was still very much empty, of course. Youngho suddenly wished for nothing else but a slice of pizza as a Christmas present—piping hot pizza. His mouth began to water at the mere thought of it. Raising an eyebrow, he dismissed the idea as utter nonsense. *Who gets a pizza slice as a Christmas present?*

Come morning, will I find anything in the Christmas stocking? Will Mom and Dad recognize my desperate wish? Or maybe even Santa Claus? A part of him refused to believe in such thoughts as anything more than a mere fantasy. On the other hand, he was not entirely denying the possibility of finding something, anything, in the stocking tomorrow morning, whether it was from his parents or Santa Claus. He honestly didn't care what it was. *It might just as well be a piece of leftover pizza crust!* Youngho shook his head at his own crazy thoughts and crept back into bed.

배에서 밥 달라고 투정을 부려 댔지만, 달리 부엌까지 나가기도 귀찮았고 또 이 시각에 안자고 일어났다고 야단맞을 위험도 있었다. 방을 둘러보니 책상 위에는 엄마가 낮에 가져다 놓은 귤이 작은 소쿠리 가득 놓여 있었다. 하지만 이빨을 닦은 후라 손대기가 꺼려졌다. 어렸을 적에 한 번 이빨 닦은 직후 귤을 먹었다가, 그 엄청나게 쓴맛에 호되게 당한 적이 있기 때문이다.

그때 탁자 위에 펴진 사진 앨범 위로 침대 머리맡 귀퉁이에 달려 있는 크리스마스 양말이 시야에 들어왔다. 물론 아직도 텅 비어 있었다. 영호는 문득 크리스마스 선물로 그 무엇보다도 피자나 한 조각 생겼으면 정말 좋겠다는 생각이 들었다. 김이 모락모락 나도록 따끈따끈한 피자...... 생각만 해도 군침이 돌았다. 그리고는 다시 한 쪽 눈썹을 치켜뜨고 스스로의 엉뚱한 생각을 일축했다. *피자를 크리스마스 선물로 받는 사람이 어디 있어?*

그런데 과연 아침이 오면 양말 속에 무엇인가 들어 있기는 있을까? 엄마 아빠가 내 간절한 소망을 알아줄 것인가? 아니면 산타 할아버지가 응해 줄까? 한편으로는 허황된 꿈일 뿐이라고 일축하면서도, 또 어떤 면에서는 내일 아침 양말 속에 무언가 들어 있을 가능성을—그 무엇이라도 좋았다—완전히 배제하지는 못했다. 부모님이건 산타 할아버지건 간에. 솔직한 마음으로 그것이 무엇이냐는 그다지 중요하지 않았다. *하다못해 먹다 남은 피자빵 부스러기라도 좋아!* 영호는 스스로의 엉뚱한 생각에 고개를 저으며 다시 이불 속에 들어갔다.

Still wide awake, Youngho picked up the open photo album again and resumed where he had left off. Turning the pages and laughing silently, his gaze fell on the picture of Chadori against the sunset. He was bathed in light, the colors of his coat drenched in the golden hues of the setting sun. His rusty-brown back glowed bright orange; his chest and tummy shimmered in sparkling pearly white, almost like the color of new snow. Suddenly reminded of just how much he missed him, Youngho began to flip through the pages, looking for other pictures of Chadori. There they were! To his delight, he found lots of them: the two of them together in the park playing soccer; with another dog they met in the park; learning new tricks in a training session with Grandpa, and more.

Many of the pictures had Grandpa in them too. Youngho wistfully reminisced—how much it meant for him to have Grandpa around, although he didn't know it at the time. It was Grandpa Lee, Grandpa's close friend who also used to frequent the park, who took most of the pictures. Youngho hadn't seen him in a while, come to think of it. The photos showed an aging but spirited Grandpa with a twinkle in his eye and always a joke or two up his sleeve. Youngho was reminded of how sorely he missed Grandpa too. He could almost hear Grandpa's animated voice, cracking an old joke and laughing heartily only days before he passed away. As Youngho looked at pictures of the happy trio, his lips spread into a smile at the fond memories. *I would choose a chance to see Grandpa and Chadori once more over any Christmas present!*

아직도 잠은 오지 않고, 펼쳐져 있는 사진첩을 다시 들고 마지막 보던 부분부터 계속해서 보기 시작했다. 한참 사진을 보며 소리 없이 웃다가, 저녁노을을 배경으로 찍은 차도리의 사진을 보게 되었다. 차도리의 털은 금빛으로 저물어 가는 태양에 흠뻑 젖어서, 등에 있는 붉은 밤색 털은 불타는 주홍색으로, 가슴과 배에 있는 흰 털은 진주처럼 빛나면서도 금방 내린 눈처럼 더없이 희게 보였다. 새삼 차도리가 너무나도 보고 싶어진 영호는 차도리의 사진을 찾아서 사진첩을 뒤져 보게 되었다. *찾았다!* 천만다행으로 차도리의 사진은 많았다. 차도리와 공원에서 축구공을 차며 노는 사진...... 공원에서 다른 개를 만나서 같이 찍은 사진...... 할아버지한테 새로운 재주를 배우며 훈련받다가 찍은 사진 등.

할아버지와 함께 찍은 사진도 많았다. 그 당시에는 알지 못했지만, 곁에 할아버지가 계셨던 것이 얼마나 큰 힘이 되어 주었던지—밀려오는 추억에 가슴이 뭉클해졌다. 같은 공원에 종종 오시곤 하던 친구분 이 씨 할아버지가 찍어 주신 사진들이 대부분이다. 지금 생각해 보니 못 뵌 지 꽤 된 것 같았다. 사진 속의 할아버지는 비록 나이가 드셨어도 정정해 보이셨고, 항상 장난기로 눈이 빛나며 농담을 잘하시곤 했다. 할아버지도 너무 보고 싶었다. 돌아가시기 불과 며칠 전까지도 한물간 농담을 던지고는 자지러지게 웃으시던 목소리가 아직 귀에 생생하게 들려오는 듯 했다. 영호는 할아버지와 차도리와 셋이 찍은 사진을 들여다보며 떠오르는 소중한 추억에 씩 미소 지었다. *크리스마스 선물은 안 받아도 좋으니, 할아버지와 차도리를 단 한 번만이라도 더 볼 수 있었으면 좋겠다!*

10-2 파란 사진첩·The Blue Photo Album

계속해서 사진첩의 페이지를 넘기다가 마지막 사진까지 다 본 영호는 사진첩을 다시 서랍에 넣어 두고—이번에는 가장 윗서랍에 보관했다—불을 끄고 그제서야 잠이 들었다. 그리고 얼마나 잤을까. 영호가 다시 눈을 떴을 때는 아직도 칠흑 같은 밤이었다.

어둠 속을 더듬어 휴대폰 화면에 손을 대니 바로 화면이 켜졌다. 시간은 12월 25일 새벽 5시. *벌써? 크리스마스 새벽이다!* 상상 속의 자명종이 밝은 무지개처럼 색색 가지 빛을 내며 번쩍이고, 알록달록 색종이 조각들이 천장에서 떨어져 휘날리는 듯했다.

Youngho continued to flip through the photo book for a while. Having reached the last photo, he put the album back —this time in the top drawer—turned out the light, and fell asleep at last. How long was he asleep? It was still pitch-dark when Youngho opened his eyes.

He fumbled for his phone. The locked screen lit up instantly to show 05:00 A.M., December 25. *Already? Christmas morning!* Youngho's mental alarm clock blared, flashing in bright rainbow colors, and imaginary confetti fell from the ceiling.

The Christmas stocking! But then again—*Nah,* he thought. *Mom and Dad wouldn't get up this early just to put something in my Christmas stocking! And I was up quite late last night, too, which makes the chance even slimmer.*

But wait! What if Santa Claus stopped by while I was asleep? Could there be a miracle, after all?

He scrambled through the dark to look for the Christmas stocking. Smothered in decorations, it wasn't that hard to find, even without the light on. His fingers brushed against the inside of the sock but didn't find anything. *Maybe there was something in it, but my fingers just couldn't locate it?* Youngho switched the light on and peered inside. It was empty, all right. And nothing by the bed or elsewhere in the room either.

Have I done it all wrong? Maybe I haven't made the Christmas stocking properly and failed to send the right signals to Santa Claus? Is it because it was only an ordinary white sock? Or . . . Then again, of course, there's no such thing as Santa Claus!

Youngho felt let down—mostly by himself for being so naive. Regretting that he had wasted his precious morning sleep, he heaved a sigh, hit the pillow again, and instantly fell back asleep.

참, 크리스마스 양말! 하다가 금세 다시 *아냐,* 하고 생각을 달리 했다. *엄마 아빠가 내 크리스마스 양말에 선물 하나 넣으려고 이 새벽에 일어날 리가 없지. 게다가 지난 밤 새벽 이른 시간까지 안 자고 있었으므로 그럴 확률은 더더욱 낮다.*

아니 잠깐! 잠 든 사이에 산타 할아버지가 왔다 가셨으면? 과연 기적이 일어날 수 있을 것인가?

영호는 얼른 어둠 속을 더듬었다. 크리스마스 양말은 장식품이 잔뜩 달려 있어서 불을 켜지 않고도 찾는 것이 그리 어렵지 않았다. 그러나 양말 안을 아무리 더듬어 보아도 손가락에는 아무것도 만져지지 않았다. *혹시 무엇인가 들어 있는데 내 손가락이 못 찾는 것은 아닐까?* 불을 켜고 아무리 들여다보아도 양말 속은 텅 비어 있었다. 침대맡에도, 방을 훑어보아도, 역시 아무것도 없기는 마찬가지였다.

내가 무언가 제대로 못 한 걸까? 양말을 어설프게 만들어서 산타 할아버지에게 제대로 신호가 안 갔나? 보통 하얀 양말로 만들어서 그런가? 아니면...... 그러면 그렇지, 산타가 있기는 어디 있어!

영호는 스스로의 터무니없는 순진함을 나무람과 동시에, 소중한 아침잠만 놓친 것이 아깝게 생각되었다. 그리고는 한숨을 내쉬며 다시 베개를 베고 순식간에 잠이 들었다.

11

눈부신 빛의 문

THE PORTAL OF BLINDING LIGHT

영호는 깊은 잠에 빠져 있었다. 바깥은 아직도 어두웠지만, 맑게 개인 하늘에 높이 뜬 초승달이 눈이 부시도록 밝았고, 창문을 통해 비친 은색 달빛은 자는 소년의 평화로운 얼굴 위를 비추었다.

Youngho was in a deep slumber. It was still dark outside, but the sky was clear and the crescent moon was high and dazzling. Its silver beams reached through the window and shone on the peaceful face of the sleeping boy.

Then, something peculiar happened. When Youngho turned over in his bed and half opened his eyes, he caught sight of something unusual. Though half asleep, he could still discern the silhouette of somebody stooping over his bed doing something.

It was certainly not normal! If it had happened at another time—half asleep or not—he would have jumped out of bed at once, running and screaming for help. Strangely, however, he was not afraid—not in the slightest. It felt as if something perfectly natural was taking place. The mysterious guest was standing over his Christmas stocking. *Could it be Santa Claus? Or is it just a thief? If it is a thief, why is be looking in the Christmas stocking? Is he hoping to find and steal a kid's Christmas present? It has to be a very bored thief . . .*

Now wide awake, Youngho sat up in his bed to take a proper look at the unexpected guest, who was wearing a Santa suit. The face met his gaze. It looked so familiar—that part was certain, even in the dark. *I knew it!* The eyes that were staring back at Youngho's were . . . *Dad's, of course!* Youngho looked up at Dad with a playful smile on his face. *I'm touched that Dad has gone out of his way to stage all this just for me!* The Christmas stocking had been a success, undoubtedly.

At the same time, his disguise was so elaborate. *Dad is doing all this just to put a present in my Christmas stocking*? Plus, Youngho was supposed to be asleep and wouldn't have been able to see him. *Anyways, Dad really nailed his Santa makeover—he looks at least twenty years older!*

순간 참으로 기이한 일이 벌어졌다. 막 이불 속에서 돌아눕던 영호. 무심결에 눈을 반쯤 떴다가, 눈에 익지 않은 무언가를 보게 된 것이다. 잠결에도 어둠 속에서 누군가가 침대 맡에 어정쩡하게 서서 무언가를 하고 있는 윤곽이 눈에 들어왔다.

평소에 있는 일이 절대 아니었다! 다른 때에 비슷한 일이 생겼더라면—잠결이든 아니든—당장 나 살려라 비명을 지르며 자리에서 뛰쳐나갔을 것이다. 그런데 이상하게도 전혀 무섭지 않았다. 마치 당연히 있을 일이 아주 자연스럽게 전개되는 것처럼 느껴졌다. 이름 모를 방문객은 영호의 크리스마스 양말 너머로 서 있는 것처럼 보였다. *산타 할아버지인가? 아니면 그냥 도둑일까...... 그런데 도둑이라면 왜 하필 크리스마스 양말 속을 들여다보고 있는 것일까? 어린애 크리스마스 선물이 있나 보고 훔쳐가려는 도둑인가? 참 할 일 없는 도둑인가 보다......*

영호는 이제 잠이 다 깨서, 더 자세히 보려고 자리에서 일어나 앉았다. 예기치 않은 방문객은 산타 할아버지 옷을 입고 있었고, 영호를 돌아보는 얼굴이 아주 낯이 익었다. 어둠 속에서도 그 점만은 분명했다. *그러면 그렇지!* 고개를 돌려 영호를 바라보는 그 두 눈은...... *당연히 아빠였다!* 영호는 장난스런 미소를 지으며 아빠를 올려다보았다. *아빠가 나 하나를 위해서 이렇게까지 공을 들이다니, 감격인데!* 크리스마스 양말이 성공적인 효과를 거둔 것은 의심의 여지가 없었다.

이와 동시에 아빠는 변장도 참 철저하게 잘 한 것 같았다. *내 크리스마스 양말에 선물 하나 넣으려고 이렇게도 공을 들였나?* 게다가 영호가 자고 있었으면 보지도 못했을 것이다. *어쨌건 간에 산타 분장 정말 잘 했네—최소한 20년은 더 늙어 보이는데!*

But hang on a sec, could he lose this much weight overnight as well? Youngho had seen him last night and he hadn't been this thin. Youngho blinked, trying to shake off the sleep from his eyes. Then he gasped. Those kind eyes looking into his with a gentle expression were . . . not Dad's! In the dark and still half asleep, Youngho had seen what he thought he was supposed to see. Standing tall over him, the shadowy figure clearly outlined in the moonlight was none other than—

"Grandpa?"

But he has passed away a year ago!

Oh, my Lord, Jesus, Buddha, Allah, and the holy muffin! Who's this? Youngho was speechless. Throwing the blanket aside, he sprang out of bed immediately. Tears of joy welled in his eyes.

Chadori peeped out from behind Grandpa and hurried toward Youngho, cheerfully wagging his tail. Falling to his knees at once, Youngho wrapped his arms around him. After a moment, he managed to free one arm to pet him on the head, the other arm holding on to him as if he never wanted to let go of him again. Then he murmured, his voice cracking,

"Chadori, you troublemaker . . . I've missed you so much! Where have you been all this time?"

그런데 잠깐, 하룻밤 사이에 이렇게 살도 빠질 수가 있나? 영호가 지난 밤 아빠를 보았을 때까지만 해도 이 정도로 날씬하진 않았다. 영호는 최대한 잠을 떨쳐보고자 눈을 깜박거렸다. 순간 *헉!* 숨이 멎어 버리는 듯했다. 자상한 표정으로 영호를 바라보는 순한 그 눈은…… 아빠가 아니었던 것이다! 그냥 어둠 속에서, 또 아직 잠에 취해서, 스스로가 당연히 보아야 한다고 생각했던 것을 본 것일 뿐이었다. 영호의 눈앞에 훤칠하게 서 있는, 달빛에 선명하게 비친 그림자의 주인공은 다름아닌—

"하……할아버지……?"

벌써 1년 전에 돌아가셨는데 어떻게……!

하나님 맙소사, 예수님, 부처님, 알라님, 성스런 머핀이여! 이건 또 누구야! 영호는 말문이 막혀 버렸다. 당장 이불을 걷어 제치고 침대 밖으로 뛰쳐나가고, 감격의 눈물이 눈에 고였다.

할아버지 뒤에서 차도리가 고개를 쏙 내밀고 꼬리를 흔들며 나오는 것이 아닌가! 영호는 그대로 털썩 무릎을 꿇고 차도리를 부둥켜안았다. 잠시 후 한 손을 들어 그 머리를 쓰다듬어 보면서도 다시는 놓치기 싫은 듯 차도리를 끌어안은 팔을 풀지 않았다. 그리고는 목이 메여서,

"차도리 임마…… 얼마나 보구 싶었는지 알어, 너! 도대체 어디 갔다가 이제 나타난 거야……"

With tears in his eyes, Youngho rubbed his cheek against the crown of Chadori's head. He could feel the soft, down-like fur he knew so well. In turn, Chadori joyfully wagged his duster tail and licked his face. Sure enough, the gentle brush of Chadori's tongue was blissfully warm and endearingly rough as always! Youngho chortled with delight and looked up at Grandpa, keeping his arms around Chadori's shoulders.

"Grandpa! What's going on? I missed you so much!"

His face radiant with joy, Grandpa replied,

"We missed you, too, Youngho! Very, very much—more than you can ever imagine!"

Youngho felt something warm rise in his chest and form a lump in his throat. He looked from Grandpa to Chadori and then back again. He simply kept looking at them like that for a while, back and forth. He just couldn't believe his own eyes. He finally sat back down on the side of the bed and opened his mouth, with Chadori snugly between his knees, stroking him as he spoke.

"What happened? I thought you had . . . p-p-passed away a while ago!"

Grandpa pulled out the chair from under the desk and sat down. The moonlight shone over his face, clearly outlining his features.

"Yes, we both did, Chadori and I," he replied with a grin. "But we've been granted a short visit back to this world—thanks to you, Youngho!"

Youngho was overjoyed to hear this, but he had no idea what he could possibly have done to deserve all this.

두 눈에 눈물이 그렁그렁한 채로 차도리의 머리 위에 뺨을 부벼 보았다. 영호가 너무나도 잘 알고 있는, 부드럽고 폭신한 털의 느낌이었다. 차도리도 반가운지 그 먼지털이 꼬리를 흔들며 영호의 얼굴을 핥았다. 아니나 다를까, 차도리의 혓바닥은 여느 때처럼 더없이 따뜻하고 다정한, 그러나 살짝 깔끄러운, 그런 감촉이었다! 영호는 너무나 기뻐서 *키득키득* 웃으며, 두 손으로 차도리의 어깨를 끌어안은 채 할아버지를 올려다보았다.

"할아버지! 어떻게 된 거예요? 얼마나 보구 싶었다구요!"

할아버지가 기쁨에 넘치는 표정으로 대답하셨다.

"우리도 너 너무 보고 싶었다, 영호야. 상상도 할 수 없이 많이……"

영호는 가슴에서 무언가 뜨거운 것이 올라와 목에 차는 것을 느꼈다. 그리고는 할아버지를 보다가 차도리를 돌아보고, 또 다시 할아버지를 바라보고. 그렇게 번갈아가며 보기를 몇 번을 했을까. 그저 눈을 의심하지 않을 수 없었다. 그리고는 끝내 침대에 걸터앉아서 입을 열어 말했다. 아직도 차도리를 다리 사이에 쏙 끼고 계속해서 쓰다듬는 것은 물론.

"할아버지! 근데 어떻게…… 도, 도, 돌아가신 지 꽤 된 줄 알았는데?"

할아버지가 책상 앞에 놓인 의자를 빼 앉으셨다. 달빛에 할아버지의 이목구비가 뚜렷하게 비쳤다.

"그랬지…… 차도리랑 나랑 둘이 다." 할아버지가 빙긋 웃으며 대답하신다. "하지만 이 세상에 잠깐 다녀갈 수 있게 허락을 받았다고나 할까—다 우리 영호 덕분이지!"

영호는 이 말을 듣고 너무도 기쁜 것은 사실이었지만, 자신이 했다는 일이 무엇인지는 전혀 이해가 가지 않았다.

"What did I do, Grandpa? Whatever it was, I'm so glad!" he said brightly. "Did I do something right—for once?"

"You called upon us in your heart, you see. Your wish built a bridge of sorts."

Chadori started wagging his tail enthusiastically as if to say thank you. It was all very well, but Youngho still found it hard to grasp. *Heart? Wish? Bridge? It sounds a bit like the horoscope Minji's obsessed with these days.* Grandpa nodded knowingly, pulling the chair closer to Youngho and placing a hand on his shoulder.

"Even after departing from this world, spirits can travel back sometimes," he said, "Briefly, and only when living souls remember them. Like you did, Youngho. Over time, when there is no longer a single living soul to remember them, spirits also fade away."

Grandpa's gaze drifted toward the moon outside the window, his eyes twinkling as they reflected its brilliant light. Looking back to Youngho, he continued,

"From time to time, truly exceptional individuals are born who are remembered generation after generation. These spirits live on, immortal throughout time—'immortal souls,' so to speak."

"Can you also turn into an immortal spirit, then, Grandpa?" Youngho's eyes stared at Grandpa in disbelief.

"Well, it remains possible," Grandpa said, smiling apologetically. "But not thanks to anything I did in my lifetime . . ."

"내가 뭘 어떻게 했는데요, 할아버지? 그게 뭐든 간에, 너무 잘됐네요!" 하고 밝게 말했다. "내가 뭘 잘 한 게 있나? 태어나서 처음인 것 같은데요!"

"영호가 마음속으로부터 우리를 불러 줘서, 그 바람이 일종의 다리를 세워 주었지."

차도리가 고맙다는 말을 하려는 듯 열심히 꼬리를 흔들었다. 다 좋기는 했지만 솔직이 이해는 잘 가지 않았다. *마음? 바람? 다리? 누나가 요즘 광적으로 보는 별자리점에 나오는 말 같은데......* 할아버지는 이해한다는 듯 고개를 끄덕이며, 의자를 가까이 끌어 영호의 어깨에 손을 얹으셨다.

"한 번 떠난 영혼도 세상에 다시 다녀갈 때가 있단다. 아주 잠깐, 살아 있는 사람이 생각해 주는 경우에만. 영호 네가 한 것처럼 말이다. 세월이 지나가고 결국 아무도 생각해 주는 사람이 없게 되면, 영혼도 사라져 버리게 된단다."

창밖으로 눈을 돌려 달빛을 응시하는 할아버지의 눈이 그 밝은 빛을 반사하며 반짝였다. 그리고는 다시 영호를 돌아보고 말을 계속하신다.

"그러다가 가끔씩 후세 사람들이 두고두고 생각하고 기려 주는 훌륭한 위인들이 나오지. 그런 영혼들은 시간이 지나도 사라지지 않게 된단다—말하자면 '불멸의 영혼'으로 남는 것이지."

"그럼 할아버지도 불멸의 영혼이 되실 수 있는 거예요?" 영호의 두 눈이 믿기지 않는다는 듯 할아버지를 바라보았다.

"글쎄, 아주 불가능한 얘기는 아니지." 그렇게 대답하시고 할아버지는 다시, "뭐 내가 생전에 이룩해 놓은 것이 있어서 그런 건 아니겠지만 말이다" 하며 머쓱한 미소를 지으셨다.

As he spoke, Grandpa took a clementine from the basket on the desk, peeled it nonchalantly—as if it were just another mundane thing to do—and put a piece in his mouth, apparently enjoying it a great deal.

"Oh, I've missed clementines so much!"

Can spirits eat and taste food? Youngho wondered immediately. *True, clementines were Grandpa's favorite fruit before he passed* . . . Grandpa finished the first one in no time and started on another, making sure to round up the peels neatly and toss them into the trash can. Youngho silently observed Grandpa and thought for a while. Gingerly, then, he plucked up the courage to mention something that had been on his mind since Grandpa passed away.

"By the way, Grandpa, there's something I've been wondering."

"What is it, Youngho?" said Grandpa, looking up from the third clementine in his hand. "Of course—you can ask me anything!"

"Did you go to heaven after you . . . well . . . died?" Youngho ventured timidly. "And if you did," he added, his voice dropping to a whisper without meaning to, "are you allowed to play computer games every day there?"

Grandpa nearly choked on the clementine in his mouth and folded in half with a guffaw.

"Haha! Computer games!"

After laughing heartily for a while, he said at last,

"You are as imaginative as ever, Youngho! Yes, you could say that it's a kind of heaven. But they don't have computers, no. Lucky for me!"

그리고는 말을 하시면서 책상 위에 있는 바구니에서 귤을 한 개 꺼내시더니, 아무렇지도 않게—마치 늘 있는 일인 양—껍질을 까서 한 쪽 떼어 입에 넣으셨다. 아주 맛있게 드시는 것처럼 보였다.

"아, 귤이 얼마나 먹고 싶었는지!"

영혼도 음식을 먹고 맛을 볼 수 있나? 영호가 즉시 생각에 사로잡혔다. *귤이 할아버지 살아 계실 때 제일 좋아하시던 과일인 건 사실인데……* 할아버지는 재빨리 하나를 다 드시고 또 하나를 까시면서, 깔끔하게 껍질을 모아 휴지통에 버리는 것까지 잊지 않으셨다. 영호는 잠시 묵묵히 할아버지를 바라보며 생각에 잠겨 있다가, 조심스레 용기를 내어 말을 꺼내 보았다. 할아버지가 돌아가신 이후 내내 궁금하게 생각하던 것이 있었던 것이다.

"할아버지…… 궁금한 게 하나 있는데요."

"뭔데?" 할아버지가 세 번째 귤을 손에 든 채 고개를 들어 물으신다. "물론이지, 뭐든지 다 물어봐!"

"할아버지, 그럼…… 돌아…… 가시고 나서…… 천국에 가신 건가요?" 영호가 수줍게 말을 꺼내 보았다. "그리고 천국에 가면……" 자신도 모르게 목소리가 낮다 못해 기어들어 간다. "천국 가면 매일 PC 게임 할 수 있어요?"

할아버지가 드시던 귤이 목에 걸린 듯 기침을 하셨다. 그리고는 배꼽을 잡고 웃음을 터뜨리신다.

"허허허…… PC 게임……!"

그렇게 한참을 실컷 웃다가 끝내 대답하셨다.

"우리 영호는 여전히 상상력이 풍부하구나! 뭐 일종의 천국이지, 그래…… 그런데 컴퓨터는 없어요. 천만다행이지 뭐냐!"

Grandpa roared with a new fit of laughter, almost gasping for breath. Then he staggered across the room toward the chest of drawers, clutching his stomach and still unable to stop laughing. Nonplussed and slightly offended by Grandpa's laughing at a perfectly valid question, Youngho looked away from him and murmured,

"You must get really bored. What kinda heaven is that!"

Chadori looked from Grandpa to Youngho and tilted his head.

Grandpa was now standing, leaning against the chest of drawers. *Am I not quite awake yet? Or is it the darkness?* Grandpa looked as if he was in better shape than Youngho remembered. *And what is that aura surrounding him?*

At first, he believed it was the moonbeam coming in through the window. *I'm not so sure anymore, now that Grandpa walked away from it.*

"Grandpa, you look grcat, I must say!" Youngho said, impressed. "And you almost glow. Have you turned into an angel after you died?"

"No, I'm no angel," Grandpa replied with a chuckle. "But I am flattered that you think so!"

"Then how come you look much younger than before?"

"It's not so easy to explain," said Grandpa, but then he seemed to think again after taking one glimpse at the bright eyes of his grandson, looking expectantly up at him.

"But you're an intelligent boy, Youngho. I will do my best!"

할아버지는 다시 한 번 대폭소를 터뜨리더니, 숨이 찬 듯 침대 맞은편에 있는 서랍장까지 휘청거리며 걸어가셨다. 그러면서도 배꼽을 잡고 웃음을 멈추지 못하셨다. 아주 정당한 질문에 대폭소를 터뜨리는 할아버지의 반응에 당황스럽기도 하고 화도 난 영호가 고개를 돌리며 중얼거렸다.

"에이, 재미없어...... 그게 무슨 천국이야!"

차도리가 영호와 할아버지를 번갈아 보며 고개를 갸우뚱거렸다.

할아버지는 이제 서랍장을 기대고 서 계셨다. *그런데 내가 아직도 잠이 덜 깬 건가? 아니면 어두워서 그런 것일까?* 할아버지는 영호가 기억하는 것보다도 더 건강해 보이셨다. *게다가 할아버지를 둘러싼 저 빛은 무엇일까?*

처음에는 창문을 통해 들어오는 달빛인 줄 알았다. *할아버지가 달빛에서 멀어지신 지금은 잘 모르겠다.*

"근데 할아버지, 몸이 너무 좋아 보이세요!" 영호가 감탄하며 말했다. "그리고 몸에서 광이 나요. 돌아가신 다음에 천사가 되신 건가요?"

"아니, 내가 무슨 천사냐......" 할아버지가 키득키득 웃으며 대답하셨다. "그런데 영호가 그렇게 생각해 주니 기분은 좋구나!"

"그럼 어떻게 옛날보다 훨씬 더 젊어지셨어요?"

"설명하기가 그리 쉽지가 않은데 말이다......" 하시다가는, 기대에 찬 표정으로 할아버지를 올려다보는 손자의 초롱초롱한 눈망울을 보고는 생각을 달리하시는 듯했다. .

"그래도 우리 영호는 참 똑똑한 애지. 이 할애비가 최대한 노력해 보마!"

He paused as if to collect his thoughts, then started his explanation, articulating each word carefully.

"The boundaries of time and space exist only when you're alive, you see. Things like the body or age are meaningless in the spirit world. That's why a spirit has no particular age. You're far too young to grasp all this, of course . . ."

Quite frankly, Youngho didn't think he was too young for anything anymore, but he had to admit that Grandpa's answer was somewhat more complicated than expected.

"Spirits can only appear the way a living person thinks of them. They lack the power to create their own images, if you know what I mean," Grandpa continued. "Only living souls have that power. A spirit can turn up as a baby or an old man, depending on your remembrance—an angel or a monster."

Grandpa could turn into a monster? How cool!

Youngho pictured Grandpa as a monster in his head—a hideous sea monster with razor-sharp teeth the size of huge machetes, threatening the southern shores and attacking local fishing boats. Excited, he gaped slightly as he smiled in expectation, waiting for Grandpa to make a frightful transformation into a sea monster. But Grandpa didn't change into anything despite Youngho's best efforts.

"How come you're not turning into a monster, Grandpa?" Youngho wondered after a while, disappointed. "I'm trying very hard to conjure you as a sea monster, instead of Grandpa—but I'm not very successful!"

할아버지는 생각을 정리하려는 듯 잠시 말을 멈추었다가, 한마디 한마디 또렷이 설명을 시작하셨다.

"그러니까 말이다...... 시간과 공간에 얽매이는 건 이 세상 살아가는 동안의 얘기지. 영혼의 세계에서는 육체나 나이 따위는 의미가 없어요. 그래서 영혼은 특별한 나이가 없는 것이란다. 네가 물론 너무 어려서 이해하기 힘들겠지만......"

영호는 솔직히 스스로 더 이상 너무 어리다고는 생각하지 않았으나, 할아버지의 말씀이 생각했던 것보다 좀 복잡한 것은 사실이었다.

"영혼은 살아있는 사람이 생각해 주는 대로만 나타날 수 있는 것이란다. 스스로의 형체를 만드는 능력이 영혼에게는 없어요. 무슨 말인지 알겠니......" 할아버지가 설명하신다. "살아 있는 생혼만이 그럴 수 있는 힘이 있단다. 영혼은 생혼이 어떻게 기억해 주느냐에 따라서 아이로 나타날 수도 있고 노인이 될 수도 있고, 또 천사가 될 수도 괴물로 나타날 수도 있는 거예요."

할아버지가 괴물로 나타나신다? 오...... 쿨!

영호는 머릿속에 할아버지가 괴물로 나타나시는 모습을 그려 보았다—할아버지가 흉측한 바다 괴물로 변해서, 식칼보다 크고 면도날보다 날카로운 이빨을 드러내고 남해 바다에 나타나 어선을 위협한다...... 기대감에 들뜬 영호가 입을 헤 벌리고 웃으며 할아버지가 무시무시한 바다 괴물로 변신하기만을 기다렸다. 하지만 영호의 갖은 노력에도 불구하고 할아버지는 그 어떤 변신도 하지 않으셨다.

"할아버지, 왜 괴물로 변신 안 해요?" 잠시 후 실망한 영호가 묻는다. "할아버지 대신 바다 괴물로 나타나게 해 볼려구 엄청 노력했는데—잘 안 되네요!"

"Once you call upon an image of a spirit, it's much harder to change it again," said Grandpa. "I'm more than happy with the way you've remembered me in the first place. You don't need to change that now!" he added, laughing. "And the sea is miles away from here in any case! What would a sea monster do without the sea?"

Confused, Youngho just blinked, staring at Grandpa.

"If you're not an angel, are you Santa Claus now, or what?"

He meant it as a joke, of course, since Grandpa was wearing a Santa suit. There was nothing strange about that—it was Christmas, after all.

"Yes, in a way," whispered Grandpa as if revealing a secret. "I'm not Santa Claus himself, but—"

"Really? Why not?" said Youngho. He was beginning to feel comfortable enough to be a little cheeky now.

"I've been given a chance to work as his helper, you see," he explained. "For tonight and tonight only."

His what? thought Youngho incredulously. It was not quite the answer he had expected. Chadori's tail set off in a new flurry of motion.

"And it has everything to do with your Christmas wishes," continued Grandpa. "Not to mention your good deed, of course."

Good deed? Youngho thought to himself. *Is he talking about the toys I donated to charity? It hasn't been for nothing then! Hang on a sec! How could Grandpa know about that? It was after he passed away! If he knows about that, it's maybe true that he is Santa Claus's helper, after all.*

"영혼은 일단 형체를 불러내면 다시 모습을 바꾸기가 어렵단다." 할아버지의 대답. 그리고는, "나는 영호가 처음 기억해 준 모습이 아주 마음에 드는데? 지금 또 바꿀 필요는 없지!" 하면서 웃으셨다. "게다가 바다는 여기서 거리가 한참 될 텐데, 바다 괴물이 바다 없이 뭘 어떻게 하라고?"

혼동스러워진 영호가 할아버지를 바라보며 눈만 깜박거린다.

"그럼 천사가 아니면 이제 산타 할아버지라도 되신 건가요?"

물론 농담이었다. 할아버지는 산타 복장을 하고 계셨고, 그것 자체도 이상할 것이 없었다. 더군다나 오늘은 크리스마스 아닌가.

"그렇다고 할 수 있지" 하시며 할아버지는 무슨 비밀이라도 드러내듯 속삭이셨다. "내가 산타 할아버지는 아니지만—"

"정말요? 왜 아니예요?" 영호가 할아버지를 떠본다. 벌써 농담을 할 만큼 편하게 느껴졌나 보다.

"산타 할아버지 조수로 일할 수 있는 기회가 주어졌다고 할 수 있지." 할아버지의 설명. "오늘 단 하룻밤에 한해서."

산타 할아버지 뭐? 도저히 믿겨지지가 않았다. 이런 대답이 나올 줄은 정말 몰랐다. 차도리가 다시 힘차게 꼬리를 흔들었다.

"다 우리 영호의 크리스마스 기원 덕분이지." 할아버지가 계속하신다. "물론 좋은 일도 했고 말이야."

좋은 일? 무슨 좋은 일? 자선단체에 기부한 장난감 얘기하시는 건가? 이런 성과가 있을 줄이야! 영호가 생각했다. *잠깐만! 할아버지가 그걸 어떻게 아시지? 돌아가신 다음이었는데! 그 일을 아신다면 산타 할아버지 조수라는 것도 사실일 수도 있지 않나?*

"Are you in charge of bringing presents to all the children in the world, then?" Youngho asked, his mouth agape, his initial disbelief melting away.

"No," answered Grandpa, "The role of helping Santa Claus is a duty shared by many—it's more like an opportunity for spirits to pay a short visit to this world and see the loved ones they've left behind. Occasionally, a privileged few get to play such roles during their lifetime. The world population has practically exploded in recent decades, hasn't it! It has become quite a job for Santa Claus to visit all the children in the world in one night—even with his magical abilities."

"But what about Chadori?" Youngho said. "Is he Rudolph's helper, or what?" He had to suppress his laughter, remembering the times when he had played soccer with him. Chadori would always run off with the ball after a while.

If he ran off with the present they were delivering, Grandpa might have to chase him all night!

"In a way, yes," replied Grandpa. "He's helping with the sleigh."

"Ah . . . he'll be great at that!" said Youngho proudly as he pictured Chadori pulling Santa Claus's—or his assistant's—sleigh. "You've got a sleigh too? Wow!"

Doing his best to put everything together—Grandpa the assistant Santa Claus, Chadori the reindeer substitute, and their Christmas sleigh—Youngho stood up from where he had been sitting and took a few steps closer to Grandpa to get a better look.

"그럼 할아버지가 세계 어린이들 전부 다 선물 가져다주는 거예요?" 영호의 입이 저절로 벌어졌다. 초기에 반신반의하던 마음이 녹아내리기 시작했다.

"아니란다." 할아버지가 대답하신다. "산타 조수는 본디 한 명만 있는 것이 아니라, 영혼들이 생전 아끼고 사랑하던 사람들을 잠깐이라도 찾아볼 수 있는 기회가 주어지는 것이라고 보면 돼. 또 살아 있는 동안 산타 조수 역할을 맡게 되는 경우도 더러 있지. 최근에 세계 인구가 거의 폭발하다시피 했는데, 세상 그 많은 어린이들을 산타 혼자서 하룻밤 사이에 어떻게 다 일일이 찾아가겠니—아무리 마법의 힘을 동원하더라도 말이다!"

"그럼 차도리는요?" 영호가 말했다. "차도리는 그럼 루돌프 사슴 조수인가요?" 하고 물으면서도 함께 축구공을 차고 공놀이를 하던 기억에 막 터져 나오려고 하는 웃음을 참을 수가 없었다. 항상 차도리가 잘 나가다가 공을 물고 달아나곤 하던 생각이 났기 때문이다.

만약 크리스마스 선물을 나르다가 차도리가 물고 달아나면, 할아버지는 차도리 뒤를 밤새도록 쫓아다녀야 할 수도 있겠다!

"그렇다고 볼 수 있지." 할아버지가 대답하신다. "차도리는 썰매를 끄는 일을 돕지."

"와...... 아주 잘 할 것 같은데요!" 차도리가 산타—아니, 산타 조수—의 썰매를 끄는 모습을 상상해 보니 더할 나위 없이 뿌듯했다. "할아버지 썰매도 있어요? 와......"

모든 것을 종합해 보려 애쓰던 영호—산타 조수가 되신 할아버지, 루돌프 사슴 대타 차도리, 할아버지와 차도리의 크리스마스 썰매—앉은 자리에서 일어나 할아버지를 더 자세히 관찰하기 위해 몇 발짝 다가섰다.

From up close, Grandpa's Santa suit wasn't quite what Youngho had imagined at first. It was red and white, all right, yet something was different about it. *But what?* Youngho began to examine Grandpa from head to toe. Ironically, he could see him even better now that Grandpa had stepped out of the light; the glowing aura around him made it easier to see him in the dark.

Am I dreaming? Youngho could hardly believe his eyes. He tilted his head sideways like Chadori—the result was the same. Youngho could swear that Grandpa's Santa suit looked as if it were modeled after a *hanbok,* the traditional Korean dress. *A Santa Claus helper in a hanbok?* Was this a practical joke? *Grandpa hasn't changed a bit, even after his time in heaven!*

"Grandpa, are you sure you're Santa's helper? Isn't that a *hanbok* you're wearing? I mean, I thought Santa Claus—or his helpers—had a special suit of their own!"

"Yes, you're right, and we do, but these are times of globalization, aren't they? I thought you would know better than anyone, Youngho!"

Globalization. I've heard that word before . . .

"Yeah, but . . ."

"No 'buts!'" Grandpa declared. "Santa Claus and his helpers also enjoy greater freedom in this modern age."

How many helpers does Santa Claus have? It was starting to sound as if he had quite a team. Grandpa had already mentioned there was more than one.

그런데 가까이서 보니 할아버지의 산타 복장은 처음에 생각했던 것과는 좀 달랐다. *빨갛고 하얀 것은 같지만, 그래도 무언가가 다르다. 뭐가 틀릴까?* 영호는 할아버지를 머리부터 발끝까지 뜯어보기 시작했다. 신기한 것은 할아버지가 빛에서 멀어지고 나서 오히려 더 잘 보인다는 점이었다. 할아버지는 몸에서 일종의 광이 났고 또 그 빛은 어둠 속에서 더 보기가 쉬웠다.

꿈인가 생시인가? 영호는 스스로의 눈을 의심하지 않을 수 없었다. 차도리처럼 고개를 갸우뚱하고 옆으로 보아도 결과는 마찬가지였다. 할아버지의 산타 복장이 꼭 우리나라 전통 한복처럼 보였던 것이다. *산타 조수가 한복을 입어? 장난하시는 건가? 천국에 가신 뒤에도 하나도 안 변하셨네!*

"할아버지, 진짜 산타 조수 맞으세요? 입고 계시는 게 한복 아닌가요? 산타 할아버지, 아니 산타 조수는 특별한 복장이 따로 있을 줄 알았는데요!"

"응, 그렇지, 따로 있지. 그런데 요즘은 세계화 시대 아니냐. 우리 영호가 누구보다도 더 잘 알 텐데 말이다."

세계화—어디서 들어본 말인데……

"그래두 그렇지……"

"그래도 그런 거야!" 할아버지가 웃음으로 단정 지으셨다. "요즘 같은 현대 사회에서는 산타 할아버지와 그 조수들도 훨씬 더 자유로워졌어요."

도대체 산타 할아버지 조수가 몇 명이길래? 그 수가 꽤 되는 것처럼 들렸나. 할아버지가 이미 여러 명이라고 말씀하셨다.

"Santa Claus continues to keep his image according to tradition, of course, given the symbolic importance of his presence," said Grandpa. "But his helpers are no longer bound to the Santa uniform, no!"

It was all beginning to sound a little too complicated for Youngho. Thoroughly engaged with his own explanation, though, Grandpa continued and announced triumphantly, raising a fist in the air:

"*He* and *she* can wear whatever they please!"

"*She*! You mean . . . women can also become Santa's helpers?"

"Of course, they can!" Grandpa looked at Youngho as if it was self-evident. "You can call such a helper 'santa mama' or 'santa grandma,' depending on the case."

"'Santa mama' or 'santa grandma' . . ." Youngho mumbled after Grandpa.

"Yes, there are not only mothers and grandmothers but also brothers, sisters, and everyone in between!"

"S-Santa b-brothers and sisters?" Youngho stammered in disbelief.

His head was spinning as if his brain had just turned a cartwheel on its own inside his skull. Or should he say *his or her own*—now that these "santa brothers and sisters" had opened up a whole world of new possibilities?

"Yes, you can also refer to them as 'santas' or 'Christmas spirits' collectively!"

"산타 할아버지는 당연히 전통에 따라 이미지 관리를 하시지. 그 상징적인 중요성이 있으니까 말이다." 할아버지가 설명하셨다. "하지만 그 조수들은 이제 더 이상 산타 제복은 입지 않아도 돼요!"

이 모든 것들이 점점 너무 복잡하게 들리기 시작했다. 하지만 설명에 몰두하신 할아버지는 말을 계속하시면서 주먹 쥔 팔을 번쩍 들고 위풍당당하게 외쳤다.

"남자건 여자건, 원하는 복장을 할 수가 있지!"

"*여자!* 그럼…… 여자도 산타 조수가 될 수 있다는 말씀이세요?"

"물론 되지!" 할아버지가 당연한 것을 묻는다는 듯 영호를 보셨다. "여자 조수는 각 경우에 따라서 '산타 엄마,' '산타 할머니,' 이렇게 부르지."

"'산타 엄마,' '산타 할머니'…… " 영호가 할아버지를 따라 낮은 목소리로 되뇌인다.

"그렇지! 그리고 엄마, 할머니뿐 아니라 형, 누나, 그리고 그 사이사이 모두가 다 있지!"

"사, 산타…… 형, 산타 누나요?" 도저히 믿기지 않은 영호가 말을 더듬기 시작했다.

마치 머릿속에서 뇌가 혼자 한 바퀴 재주를 넘은 것처럼 머리가 핑핑 돌았다. 산타 형과 산타 누나들이 전혀 새로운 가능성의 장을 연 지금, 영호의 뇌는 남자일까 여자일까?

"그렇지, 그냥 일반적으로는 '산타,' 또는 '크리스마스 영혼'이라고 하면 돼!"

11-1 영호의 뇌가 재주를 넘어요·Youngho's Brain Turns a Cartwheel

"산타 또는 크리스마스 영혼……" 아직도 알 듯 모를 듯, 긴가민가한 영호. 천천히 고개를 끄덕이며 할아버지의 자율 산타 조수 한복을 좀 더 자세히 뜯어보았다. 할아버지의 빨간 벨벳 산타 한복의 단을 두른 보송보송한 흰 물질이 달빛에 비추어 진주처럼 오묘하게 어른거렸다. *무엇으로 만들어진 걸까? 내가 잘 알고 있는 친숙한 물질인 것만은 분명했지만, 딱 무엇이라고 꼬집어 말하기가 어렵다.*

상당히 어리둥절해하는 영호를 본 할아버지. 어깨동무를 하며 말하셨다.

"우리 영호가 궁금한 것이 참 많은가 보구나!"

"네." 영호가 기어들어 가는 목소리로 대답한다. *'궁금한 것이 많다'는 좀 과소평가 같다. 이런 경우에 비슷한 반응을 보이지 않는 사람이 있을까?*

Santas or Christmas spirits . . . half-convinced and still quite confused, Youngho nodded slowly and took another good look at Grandpa's independent santa grandpa *hanbok*. The fluffy white material lining the velvety red fabric at the hems shimmered with a mysterious pearly sheen in the moonlight. *What is it made of? It's definitely something familiar, but I can't quite put my finger on it.*

Grandpa seemed to notice that Youngho was feeling overwhelmed. He wrapped an arm around his grandson's shoulders.

"You must have so many questions," he said.

"Yeah," muttered Youngho, barely audible. *Inquisitive is an understatement. Who wouldn't be at a time like this?*

Looking delighted by Youngho's keen interest, Grandpa proffered his hand, a twinkle in his eye.

"In that case, how would you like to come along with me and pay a short visit to the feast of Christmas spirits all over the world?" he said. "After all, it happens only once a year and doesn't last that long, you know. You can also catch a glimpse of the spirit realm at the same time!"

Youngho's ears pricked up. *Is this for real?*

"I would love to!" he shouted excitedly.

As if he understood every word, Chadori started wagging his tail eagerly.

Then, as soon as the words left Youngho's lips, something truly wondrous happened. In an instant, all the light in the world seemed to pour in through Youngho's bedroom window in a *whoosh*—starlight, moonlight, streetlight, and whatnot—and an enormous portal of blinding light formed where the door had been. It was larger than the wall itself—if such a thing were even possible. As if gently beckoning him to enter, it opened wide with a clear, bell-like chime before Youngho.

Youngho placed his hand in Grandpa's. With a boldness that even surprised him, he left his empty bed behind and stepped into the resplendence of pouring light toward the unknown. Chadori followed the pair close behind, his feathery duster tail waving in the air like a flag.

할아버지는 영호의 비상한 관심에 흐뭇해하시는 것 같았고, 두 눈을 빛내며 손을 내미셨다.

"그럼 이번 기회에 잠깐 할아버지랑 온 세상 산타들 크리스마스 잔치 구경 가 보지 않을래? 어차피 일 년에 한 번밖에 없는 행사일뿐더러 또 그다지 오래 가지도 않거든. 영혼의 세계 구경도 할 겸 말이다!"

영호의 귀가 솔깃했다. *진짜?*

"갈래요!" 영호가 좋아서 외쳤다.

차도리가 마치 영호와 할아버지의 대화를 다 알아들었다는 듯 반갑게 꼬리를 흔들었다.

영호가 입을 떼자마자 참으로 기이한 일이 벌어졌다. 순간 세상 모든 빛—달빛, 별빛, 가로등빛, 다른 모든 빛—이 *쏴악!* 하며 창을 통해 쏟아져 들어오는 듯하더니, 영호의 방문이 있던 자리에 눈부신 빛의 대문이 생겨난 것이다. 문은 벽 한 면보다 클 정도로 웅장했고—이것이 과연 있을 수 있는 일이라면—마치 들어오라고 살며시 손짓하듯 낮게 청아한 종소리를 울리며 활짝 열렸다.

영호는 할아버지의 손을 잡았다. 그리고 이제까지 경험해 보지 못한 대담함에 스스로 놀라며, 텅 빈 침대를 뒤로한 채 쏟아지는 빛의 찬연함 속으로 발을 들이고 미지의 세계로 향했다. 그 뒤를 그림자처럼 따라가는 차도리의 복슬복슬한 먼지털이 꼬리가 깃발처럼 휘날렸다.

– 2권에서 계속 –

– TO BE CONTINUED IN BOOK II –

11-2 미지의 세계로 들어서다·Stepping into the Unknown

토론 주제

DISCUSSION TOPICS

1. 내가 가장 좋아하는 등장인물은 누구이며, 그 이유는 무엇인가?
2. 이 소설에서 인테리어 상점 '지상천국'이 가지는 의미는 무엇일까?
3. 이 책에서 쓰이는 언어사용 기법 또는 수사법의 예를 찾아보자. (예: 직유법, 은유법, 동음이의어, 두운법, 모순법 등)
4. '프롤로그'란 무엇인가? 책 내용에 어떻게 기여할까? (또는 기여하지 않을까?) 그 이유는 무엇일까?
5. 작가가 오감을 사용한 예를 들어 보자. 장면 묘사에 어떤 영향을 끼치는가?
6. 『영호와 차도리 제1권: 영혼의 세계로 가는 문』의 결말은 무엇인가? 적절한 결말이라고 생각하는가?
7. 기존의 고정관념에 따른—혹은 그와 상반되는—내용을 찾아보자. 상반되는 이유는 무엇일까?

8. 가장 마음에 드는 삽화는 무엇이며, 그 이유는? 소설 전개에 도움이 된다고 생각하는가?
9. 다음에서 음식이 가지는 의미와 역할은 무엇일까? A) 이 소설 내에서 B) 나의 문화권에서 C) 일반적인 우리 모두의 삶에서.
10. 책 내용 중 다음 테마를 논해 보자. 우리가 평소 익숙한 관점과 어떤 차이가 있는가? A) 크리스마스 B) 문화와 종교의 다양성 C) 남녀평등.

---

1. Who is your favorite character and why?
2. What is the significance of the home decor store Paradise on Earth in the story?
3. Discuss the stylistic devices or figures of speech found in the book (e.g. simile, metaphor, pun, alliteration, oxymoron, etc.).
4. What is a prologue? Does it—or doesn't it—add to the story? Why?
5. How does the author exploit the five senses, and what do they add to the story?
6. How does *Youngho and Chadori, Book I: The Door to the Spirit World* end? What do you think about it?
7. Do you find stereotypes or counterstereotypes in the book? Where and why?
8. Which illustration is your favorite and why? How does it contribute to the story?
9. What role does food play (*a*) in the story, (*b*) in your culture, and (*c*) in our lives in general?

10. Explore the following themes in the book. Are they different than what you're used to? How? (*a*) Celebrating Christmas, (*b*) Cultural and religious diversity, and (*c*) Gender equality.

영호와 차도리 퀴즈

YOUNGHO AND CHADORI QUIZ

(해답은 bkchu.com에서 확인하실 수 있습니다.)

1. (초보–중견) 프롤로그의 두 번째 삽화 '0-2 하늘을 나르는 개들'에 등장하는 캐릭터는 총 몇 명일까요?
2. (중견) 1장에서 수업에 집중하지 않고 딴짓하는 사람은 누구일까요? 대신 무엇을 하고 있나요? (힌트: 책을 읽고 또 그림도 함께 보세요!)
3. (중견) 1장에서 영호는 만우 어머니가 만들어 주신 음식 중 하나로 '북경오리 타코'를 꼽지요. 보통 북경오리는 어떻게 먹을까요? (힌트: 요리사가 손님에게 어떻게 대접할까요?)
4. (중견) 2장에서 영호가 전에 한 번도 들어 보지 못한 것들은 무엇인가요? 설명해 보세요.(힌트: 책을 읽어 보세요)
5. (상급) 삽화 중 하나에 망치와 톱, 두 가지 물체가 숨겨져 있습니다. 찾을 수 있나요? (힌트: 책을 보세요)

6. (귀재) 4장의 삽화 '4-1 먼 옛날의 크리스마스'에서 현실과 동떨어진 내용이 하나 있어요. 무엇일까요? (천문학자라면 금세 알 수 있을 거예요!)
7. (신동) 8장의 첫 번째 삽화 '8-1 시간의 백만장자들'에서 특별한 의미를 가진 숫자가 있습니다. 그 숫자는 무엇이며, 왜 사용되었을까요?
8. (중견) 작가가 8장 세 번째 삽화 '8-3 올해는 크리스마스 어디서 쉴까요?'를 그리면서 빠뜨린 것이 하나 있습니다. 무엇일까요? (힌트: 책을 읽고 그림도 함께 보세요)
9. (자유 의견) 10장 첫 번째 삽화 '10-1 노래하는 양떼, 스포츠카, 그리고 춤추는 오리들'에서 누가 가장 멋지게 노래하고 춤추나요? 모든 대답이 정답입니다!
10. (중견) 11장 첫 번째 삽화 '11-1 영호의 뇌가 재주를 넘어요'에서 영호를 방문한 손님은 몇 명인가요? 그들이 누구인지 꼽아 보세요.

(Answers can be found at bkchu.com)

1. (Easy–Intermediate) How many characters do you see in the second illustration in the Prologue (0-2 *Dogs in the Sky*)?
2. (Intermediate) In Chapter 1, who is not paying attention to the class? What are they doing instead?

(Hint: You have to read the book *and* look in the illustrations!)

3. (Intermediate) In Chapter 1, Youngho names Peking Duck tacos as one of his favorite dishes that Manu's mother made for him. How is Peking Duck usually served? (Hint: How would a chef serve it?)
4. (Intermediate) In Chapter 2, what are the things that Youngho has never heard of before? Can you explain what they are? (Hint: You have to read the story!)
5. (Advanced) There are two objects—a hammer and a saw—hidden in one of the illustrations. Can you find them? (Hint: It's in the book!)
6. (Completely geeky) In the illustration in Chapter 4 (4-1 *Once upon a Time on Christmas Day*), one tiny detail does not correspond to reality. What is it? (Hint: An astronomer may find this easy!)
7. (For the culturally savvy) In the first illustration in Chapter 8 (8-1 *The Time Millionaires*), what is the significant number? Why is it used in this context?
8. (Intermediate) In the third illustration in Chapter 8 (8-3 *Where to Celebrate Christmas This Year?*), I forgot to add something to the picture. What can it be? (Hint: You have to read the book *and* look in the illustration!)
9. (An open question) In the first illustration in Chapter 10 (10-1 *Singing Sheep, Fast Cars, and Dancing Ducklings*), who's the diva in your opinion? Remember—there are no right or wrong answers!

10. (Intermediate) In the first illustration in Chapter 11 (11-1 *Youngho's Brain Turns a Cartwheel*), how many visitors does Youngho have? Who are they?

작가 소개

ABOUT THE AUTHOR

주보경 周輔京

1974년 서울에서 출생했다. 1남 1녀 중 차녀로 만 17세가 되기 불과 몇 주 전 도영하여 영국 브리스톨 대학에서 영문학과 철학을 복수전공 했다. 이후 프랑스, 멕시코, 온두라스, 미국 캘리포니아 등지에서 수학하거나 근무했고, 2002 FIFA월드컵 한국/일본™ 대회에서는 FIFA월드컵 공식 홈페이지의 한국어 담당 편집자 2인 중 1인으로 활약하기도 했다. 언어습득 및 그에 잇따른 문화체험은 '자아 발견'의 척도가 되어 준 소중한 경험으로 남았고, 이 시기의 정열은 『영호와 차도리』 시리즈의 초석이 되었다.

캘리포니아 재학 중 지금의 남편을 만나 노르웨이에 정착했으나, 결혼 6개월 만에 뇌종양 진단을 받았고 수술을 불과 며칠 앞두고 뇌출혈로 반신마비와 시각·청각장애를 입게 되었다. 이후 6년간 재활에 전념하며 숨쉬기부터 밥 먹기까지 생활 전반의 모든 것을 다시 배워야 했다. 입 근육까지 마비되어 노르웨이 언어재활사들에게 발음을 교정받는 과정에서 초기에는 노르웨이 억양이 강했다.

하지만 포기하지 않았다. 끝내 인생의 '전성기'를 재활로만 보낼 수는 없다고 느꼈고, 어린 시절의 꿈이던 작가 겸 삽화가의 길을 걷기 시작했다. 마비되지 않은 오른팔로 글을 쓰고 그림을 그렸으며, 불행 중 다행으로 발음 이외 언어 능력도 잃지 않았다. 주보경 작가는 한국어, 영어, 프랑스어, 노르웨이어, 스페인어 등 5개 국어에 능통하며, 작품 집필 언어는 한국어와 영어이다. 『영호와 차도리』 시리즈는 첫 시리즈물이자 데뷔작이다. 현재는 노르웨이 스타방에르(Stavanger)에서 남편, 반려견 오스카—2025년 당시 7살—와 함께 살고 있다. '차도리'는 오스카를 비롯해 에밀, 빅토르 등 가족이 함께해 온 반려견들을 바탕으로 한 캐릭터이다.

B.K. Chu was born in Seoul, South Korea, in 1974. The youngest of two children, she moved to England to continue her education weeks before she turned 17. She graduated with a degree in English literature and philosophy from the University of Bristol before going off to work, travel, and study further in France, Mexico, Honduras, and California, USA. She also worked as one of the two Korean editors for FIFA's official website for the 2002 FIFA World Cup

Korea/Japan™. She found much happiness in learning languages and meeting people from all cultures. The fun and joy she experienced during this period formed the cornerstone of the *Youngho and Chadori* series.

While studying in California, she met her future husband and later settled in Norway. Only six months after the wedding, however, she was diagnosed with a brain tumor. A brain hemorrhage days before the operation meant she ended up with half her body paralyzed. She also lost most of her hearing in one ear, and her vision became impaired.

She spent six years in rehabilitation, having to relearn everything from scratch—from breathing to eating. Her partially paralyzed lips meant that she also had to relearn to speak—at the beginning with a strong Norwegian accent acquired from her speech therapists.

Nevertheless, she never gave up. Determined not to spend her life solely in rehabilitation, she decided to work on her childhood dream of writing and illustrating books. With her right arm largely unaffected, she could still type and draw. Her language skills also remain intact, and she still speaks five languages fluently—Korean (her mother tongue), English, French, Norwegian, and Spanish. She writes in English and Korean. *Youngho and Chadori* is her first book.

B.K. Chu lives with her husband and their four-legged son, Oscar—who turned seven in 2025—in Stavanger, Norway. Chadori is modelled after Oscar, Emil, and Victor. The latter two are family dogs that have passed on.

감사의 글

ACKNOWLEDGMENTS

다음의 사람들과 동물들에게 깊은 감사의 마음을 전하고자 한다. 무엇보다도 먼저, 전쟁의 폐허 속에서 삶을 일으켜 세우고 나와 오빠를 길러 주신 어머니와 아버지. 아버지는 끝내 한국어판 출간을 보지 못한 채 너무나도 일찍 영혼의 세계의 문턱을 넘어서셨다. 불굴의 의지와 노력 끝에 결국 인공위성공학자의 꿈을 이루어 낸 오빠 주환종. 어린 시절 오빠는 주인공 영호의 모델이 되기도 했다. 하지만 영호의 모든 문제아적 반항 기질은 절대적으로 작가 스스로의 것임을 미리 자수한다. 나에게 언제나 끝없는 사랑과 영감을 주는 남편 셰틸. 첫 자품 출판이라는 엄청난 무게에 허덕이던 나에게 때로는 해방, 때로는 방해(?)의 신선함을 선사했고, 내가 원할 때마다 솔직한 의견과 건설적인 조언을 아끼지 않았다. 기쁨과 행복의 원천, 네 발 달린 우리 아들 오스카. 춥고 어두운 노르웨이의 겨울을 컴퓨터 앞에서 보낼 때 내 차가운 발을 따뜻하게 감싸 주던 고마운 존재. 종종 삽화의 실제 모델이 되어 주기도 했다. 참으로 훌륭하신 시부모님 랑힐드와 투르. 언제나 우리의 정신적 기둥이 되어 주시고, 우리가 바쁠 때면 맛있는 저녁을 해 주시기도 오스카 산책을 대신 맡아 주시기도 했다. 지금은 영혼의 세계로 들어서셨지만 시어머니는 불구의 몸이 된 외국인 며느리가 재활원에서 돌아오면 맛있는 샌드위치를 만들어 주시던 따뜻한 분이셨다. 이 책을 구상하며 꿈꾸던 시절 어린이였던 조카들 마티아스, 알렉산더, 마틴, 신드레, 마리우스, 잉빌드, 안드레아스. 이제는 어른이 된 그들의 끝없는 열정과 에너지가 이 책의 근본이 되는 영감을 주었다. 사실은 육촌이지만 사촌이라고 부르며 어릴 적부터 따르던 수전과 남편 토니, 그 예쁜 딸들 브리아나와 크리스텐, 시누이 크리스틴과 남편 토르스타인, 형님부부 루네와 모니카, 그레타, 라써, 우니 하릴스타. 언제나 많은 힘과 끝없는 용기를 주었다. 많은 조언과 격려를 주신 노르웨이 아동작가 스베레 헨무. 그 차분한 존재로 언제나 나에게 도움을 주고 마음을 달래 주며 일상의 영감을 선사하는, 좋은 친구이자 도우미 언니 안나 달하임. 수정이 필요한 부분은 세심하게 짚어 주시고 원고의 오류나 오탈자를 하나하나 꼼꼼히 살펴 주신 영문판 편집자 조애나 부쓰와 Book Helpline 편집 서비스의 모든 분들. 미국 영어판 편집과 교열을 담당해 주시고 원고 전반을 샅샅이 뒤져가며 쉼표 하나도 놓치지 않고 엄청난 도움을 주신 리자 데이비스와 켈리 램. 켈리씨는 한영 대역판의 영문 검토를 맡아주시기도 했다. 한영 대역판 출판이 가능하도록 도움과 지원을 아끼지 않으신 좋은땅 출판사 여러분들. 미국 구어 사용에 대한 많은 질문을 참을성 있게 대답해 준 고마운 친구들 최선숙, 권은수, 이브라힘 부나파와 에드 큘레자. 항상 나의 노력과 작은 성과에도 함께 기뻐해 주고 격려를 아끼지 않은 에디트 비하리, 최수영, 앙쿠르 코타리. 한국어 원고 초본을 읽고 조언과 격려를 아끼지 않은 고마운 벗들 도연자, 황정선, 장희정, 정민아, 김미정. 희정아, 너는 지금 너무나도 일찍 천국의 사람이 되어 버렸구나. 너무 보고 싶지만, 언젠가 다시 만날 날을 기약해 보자. 영어판 초벌을 가장 먼저 읽은 당시 11세 소녀 디아나 도시(인도), 12세 소년 앤드루 노아 나, 엘리엇 김, 딜런 둘리스 (미국). 대학원 시절 스터디 파트너였으며, 한영 대역판 출판과 관련 아낌없는 조언과 격려를 해주었고 주인공이 사모하는 여학생의 영감이 되어 준 신지선 이화여대 교수. 모든 것이 어둡고 힘들게만 느껴질 때 나에게 희망의 불씨를 심어 준 대학원 시절 친구이자 지금은 부부로 맺어진 이재순과 에디 박종혁. 건강하고 총명하던 에디마저 너무도 일찍 영혼의 세계로 먼저 떠났다는 충격적인 소식을 들었다. 하늘나라에서 편히 쉬면서 우리를 기다려 줘. 아주 어릴 때부터 언제나 나를 믿고 격려해 준, 친형제처럼 함께 자란 사촌 오빠 주신일. 제2의 주인공 차도리의 이름 설정에 영감을 준 사촌—그러나 역시 사실은 육촌—주화령. 이모 임은숙. 살고 계신 필리핀을 방문하고 돌아온 어느 날 이 모든 이야기의 씨앗을 내 머릿속에 심어 주셨다. 그리고 아주 중요한, 빠뜨릴 수 없는 사실 하나. 영어판을 선불리 출판한 후에야 생각난 것인데, 이 책에 등장하는 무서운 박 선생님은 오로지 상상 속의 인물이며, 내가 아는 예쁘고 자상하신 박 교수님과는 전혀 유사한 점도, 관계도 없다는 것을 강조한다. 혹시 만에 하나 이 책을 보고 놀라셨다면, 진심으로 사죄드립니다!

I would like to express my deepest appreciation to the following people—and a dog: first and foremost, my mother and father, for giving my brother and me everything when life granted them very little to start with after the Korean war—Father, you passed away too soon, before seeing the Korean edition published; my brother, Hwanjong, who has finally fulfilled his dream of becoming a satellite engineer after years of unwavering will and efforts—his image as a boy even served as the model for the protagonist, Youngho, but I must confess that all of Youngho's rebellious and troublemaking tendencies are entirely the author's own; my beloved husband, Kjetil, for being the source of endless love, inspiration, and much-needed distraction, as well as for providing me with candid views and constructive feedback whenever I needed them; my four-legged son, Oscar, for being a fountain of joy, warming my feet through cold, dark winter days when I sat alone at the computer, and for being a real-life model for my illustrations; my incomparable parents-in-law, Ragnhild and Tor, for your constant support, delicious dinners for the family, and walks with Oscar. Ragnhild, we lost you shortly after the COVID–19 swept across the world, but we try to stay as strong as we can, so that you will be proud of us; Mathias, Aleksander, Martin, Sindre, Marius, Ingvild, and Andreas, the family children that are no longer children, for their endless energy and inspiring enthusiasm for life; my wonderful nieces Breana and Kristen as well as their mother—my cousin and lifelong role model—Susan, for motivating and encouraging me; Kristin, Torstein, Monica, Rune, Grete, Lasse, and Unni Harildstad for giving me strength and lifting my mood at different times; Norwegian writer Sverre Henmo for his kind, patient, and most helpful advice; my helper and dear friend, Anna Dalheim, who shares my love of dogs and books, for her calming and reassuring presence; the editor, Joanna Booth, for meticulously pointing out where improvement was due and combing through the manuscript for errors and typos; everybody at Book Helpline editing services for facilitating the arduous editing process; Lisa Davis and Kelly Lamb, the US edition copyeditor and proofreader respectively, for their colossal contribution to this volume, scrutinizing the manuscript for inconsistencies and redundancies, and not missing a single comma. Kelly also took charge of proofreading the English text in this bilingual edition; everyone at G-World, who offered infinite help and support in making the publication of this bilingual Korean–English edition possible; my dear friends Sunny Choi, Eunice Kwon, Ibrahim Bounafaa, and Ed Kulesza for answering my tedious questions about American English usage; my precious friend and former colleagues, Edit Bihari, for always applauding my efforts and achievements, however small; my old school friends Soo Young Choi and Ankur Kothari, for offering their kind help and advice whenever and wherever needed; my dear friends, Yeonja Do, Sue Hwang, Heejung Jang, Mina Jung, and Mi Kim, for reading the original Korean manuscript and providing me with genuine support and invaluable feedback—Heejung, you are now in heaven and I will miss you dearly until I see you again; Andrew Noah Na, Dhyana Doshi, Elliot Kim, and Dylan D'Ulisse for being the first young readers of the English edition and bravely agreeing to feature in the reader testimonials on the back cover when I was—and still am—but an unknown debut writer; Professor Jisun Shin of Ewha University and my study partner at the Monterey Institute of International Studies back in California—who generously offered invaluable advice and encouragement regarding the publication of this bilingual edition, and who also served as the inspiration for the girl the protagonist admires; my cherished friends and married couple Jae Soon Lee and Eddie Park, for giving me hope when everything seemed bleak and gloomy—Eddie, who was always bright and strong, I just learned the shocking news of your premature passing. Rest in peace in heaven and wait for us; my cousin slash brother, Shinil Oppa, for believing in me since I was a toddler; another cousin of mine—really a second cousin—Hwaryeong, who inspired me to decide on the Korean name of Chadori, the second protagonist; and my dear aunt Grace Im, who started this whole story by planting the seed of inspiration in my head one day after visiting her in the Philippines, although neither of us knew it at the time. And something very important—it only occurred to me *after* publishing the first English edition in haste: The scary "Mrs. Park" in this book is a fictional character and bears absolutely no resemblance to the kind and graceful Professor Park from my graduate program. If I startled you somehow, please do know that it was purely coincidental. My sincere apologies!

저작권 ⓒ 주보경, 2025
초판 1쇄 발행 2025년 12월 12일
지은이 주보경
펴낸이 이기봉
표지 디자인 주보경
도서 디자인 주보경
펴낸곳 도서출판 좋은땅
주소 서울특별시 마포구 양화로12길 26 지월드빌딩 (서교동 395-7)
전화 02)374-8616~7
팩스 02)374-8614
이메일 gworldbook@naver.com
홈페이지 www.g-world.co.kr

ISBN 979-11-388-5137-4 (43810)